E, M

ROBERTA
and the
RENEGADE

***Also by Stephen and Janet Bly
in Large Print:***

Columbia Falls
Copper Hill
Fox Island

***Also by Stephen Bly
in Large Print:***

The General's Notorious Widow
The Outlaw's Twin Sister
The Senator's Other Daughter
Hidden Treasure

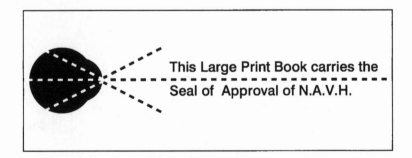

This Large Print Book carries the
Seal of Approval of N.A.V.H.

THE
CARSON CITY
CHRONICLES

BOOK THREE

ROBERTA
and the
RENEGADE

Stephen & Janet Bly

Thorndike Press • Waterville, Maine

Published in 2004 by arrangement with Stephen Bly.

Thorndike Press® Large Print Christian Fiction

The tree indicium is a trademark of Thorndike Press.

The text of this Large Print edition is unabridged.
Other aspects of the book may vary from the original edition.

Set in 16 pt. Plantin by Liana M. Walker.

Printed in the United States on permanent paper.

Library of Congress Cataloging-in-Publication Data

Bly, Stephen A., 1944–
       Roberta and the renegade / Stephen & Janet Bly.
       p. cm. — (The Carson City chronicles ; bk. 3)
    (Thorndike Press large print Christian fiction series)
       ISBN 0-7862-5829-2 (lg. print : hc : alk. paper)
       1. Carson City (Nev.) — Fiction. 2. Women pioneers —
    Fiction. 3. Outlaws — Fiction. 4. Large type books.
    I. Bly, Janet. II. Title. III. Series.
    PS3552.L93 R64 2003
       813'.54—dc22   2003014266

And I will give them an heart to know me,
that I am the Lord:
and they shall be my people,
and I will be their God:
for they shall return unto me
with their whole heart.

JEREMIAH 24:7, KJV

National Association for Visually Handicapped
——————————— serving the partially seeing

As the Founder/CEO of NAVH, the only national health agency solely devoted to those who, although not totally blind, have an eye disease which could lead to serious visual impairment, I am pleased to recognize Thorndike Press* as one of the leading publishers in the large print field.

Founded in 1954 in San Francisco to prepare large print textbooks for partially seeing children, NAVH became the pioneer and standard setting agency in the preparation of large type.

Today, those publishers who meet our standards carry the prestigious "Seal of Approval" indicating high quality large print. We are delighted that Thorndike Press is one of the publishers whose titles meet these standards. We are also pleased to recognize the significant contribution Thorndike Press is making in this important and growing field.

Lorraine H. Marchi, L.H.D.
Founder/CEO
NAVH

* Thorndike Press encompasses the following imprints: Thorndike, Wheeler, Walker and Large Pr int Press.

For
William H. Walston, retired

Chapter One

Carson City, Nevada . . . Sunday May 1, 1881

The scent of mint and clover sprang fresh and green from the manicured yard where two little boys played. Trees and bushes were trimmed and budding out. All was serene and pleasant under clear skies in the afternoon sunshine until . . .

"I shot you, Manitoba Joe! You're supposed to be dead."

"You missed me."

"I did not."

"Did too! The bullet went right over my head and hit the tree limb. That gave me time to drop to the ground, roll behind the tree, and send you off to kingdom come."

"Your gun jammed."

"Did not."

"Did too!"

"A Winchester '73 never jams."

"I thought you had a Henry rifle."

"I changed my mind."

This front-yard drama was monitored by a five-foot-four-inch, middle-aged lady with curly dark brown hair, delicate but sharply defined features, and a penetrating brown-eyed gaze.

"Timothy!" she called out from the Nevada Street porch of her two-story Carson City house.

At the sound of his grandmother's voice, he called back, "Grandma Judith, Douglas won't play fair!"

Judith Kingston wiped her hands on her white apron and slammed the screen door behind her. "Just what kind of game were you playing?"

"Douglas is the murdering captured bank robber, and I shot him dead — fair and square — and he wouldn't die."

"I always have to be Manitoba Joe," Douglas Day complained.

"And just who are *you?*" Judith asked her grandson.

"I'm Stuart Brannon!" he said and darted around the yard, blazing away with his gun stick.

"This is the Lord's Day, Timothy. I think you should find a more appropriate game to play."

"Do we have to, Grandma Judith?"

"I believe your father would agree."

"OK." Timothy jumped around in a circle. "I'll be the rajah and Douglas can be the thug who has stolen the princess's ruby. Come on, Douglas, I'll chase you with a spear while riding on my white Bengal tiger!"

Douglas looked up at Judith. "When my daddy was alive and we lived in Alaska, he helped me fight polar bears."

"Aw, you never lived there," Timothy chided.

"Did too!"

"Did not!"

"I'm glad you were able to come to church today, Douglas," Judith told the younger boy. "Can you stay for lunch?"

"Yep, and Mamma said she could stay too."

"That's nice. Where is your mother?"

"In a tree," the boy said, keeping his eye on Timothy.

Judith grabbed the sticks from both boys' hands. "Why is she in a tree?"

"My mom's an artist," Douglas said, a glint of pride in his eyes. "She wanted to paint a picture of a bird up real close. So she climbed a tree in the city park and is sketchin' it."

"Oh, I see. Well, why don't you two hike up to the park and tell your mamma lunch is about ready."

"Yes!" Timothy hollered. "And on the way, I'll be Snowshoe Thompson and Douglas can be the grizzly bear."

"I was the grizzly bear yesterday."

"No, you weren't."

"Was too."

"Nope, you were the mountain lion yesterday."

Judith watched as Timothy Kingston and Douglas Day trotted up the sidewalk to the west. Across the street, a girl wearing a ground-length, yellow cotton dress waved her arms. "Hi, Grandma Judith!"

"Hello, Alicia, darling. Are you hungry?"

"I could eat a whole pie," she said. "I'll go get Daddy and Grandpa Judge."

The six-year-old disappeared into the small white parsonage and Judith stepped back inside her kitchen.

Marthellen Farnsworth wore a white apron identical to Judith's while stirring a huge pot of beef stew at the stove. "How many are we serving?"

"Let's see . . . you, me, the judge, David, Timothy, Alicia, Douglas, his mother . . ."

Marthellen took a quick taste of the boiling stew and poured in some salt.

"Barbara Day is eating with us?"

"That's what Douglas said."

"I didn't see her at church."

"She sat in the back. She came in late and left early, before the benediction."

"Is Duffy coming, too?"

"I don't know if he's around town or not. If he does, you know he won't use a chair at the table. Where's Roberta?"

"She took a lunch out to Turner. She's going to eat with him at the mill," Marthellen said as she eased the heavy lid back onto the stew pot.

Judith sighed. "I'm glad to see Turner so hardworking. But seven days a week? The Lord gave us a day of rest, to remember Him, to be with His people, to —"

"I know," Marthellen said. "It's worried me, too. I hope he's not backsliding in his faith. I thought of Turner when David was preaching about giving our whole heart to the Lord."

"I'm hoping it's temporary. Surely he'll get back to church when the mill is in operation." Judith pulled out the Sunday silver and china, and Marthellen helped her spread the cream-colored damask cloth over the mahogany table.

"It will be nice to have the judge with us for a meal," Marthellen commented. "He's been eating downtown a lot more since David and the children moved back. The older he gets, the more he seems fond of quietness."

Judith placed a crystal vase filled with purple larkspurs and daisies in the center of the table. "I don't think that's entirely it. He dearly loves the children. However, he's had several cases that have troubled him. He keeps poring over the transcripts. That's when he needs a sanctuary that provides privacy, a place where he's not jostled about."

Marthellen tucked double-satin damask napkins by each plate, then they both gazed at the dining room window where two lizards crawled. From the underside, the lizards seemed like twins. But Judith noticed the feet. On one, the appendages had rounded, balloon-shaped endings. On the other, the toes were elongated, with one reaching longer — like a child making turkey shadows on a wall.

"When did you say Daisie Belle Emory would return home?" Marthellen asked.

"Not until tomorrow."

"Well, time must be flying, because it certainly looks like Daisie Belle driving up in Chug Conly's hack."

Judith ran into the living room. When she

14

peered through the gauze curtain on the glass and oak door, she saw the matron of Carson City society being escorted out of the black leather carriage.

"How did she manage to take a whole day off her trip?" Judith said aloud. She yanked off her apron and scurried out the door. "Daisie Belle! I was planning to meet you at the depot tomorrow."

Daisie Belle Emory released Chug Conly's hand. "Oh, I know, Judith, dear, but the nicest thing happened in Omaha. Mr. Leland Stanford was sending his empty private car back to San Francisco on the express and insisted that I take it. He is such a darling man."

I've never heard anyone call Leland Stanford a 'darling' man. Not even Mrs. Stanford. As Judith hugged Daisie Belle, she smelled the scent of strong lilac perfume. "How was New York?" she inquired.

Daisie Belle drew back and waved her arm in a dismissive gesture. "Everything moves so quickly back there. The fashions shift every week. You don't know how nice it is to be home in Nevada where nothing changes. In fact, that's the exact same dress you were wearing the day I left. And I don't think you've changed a bit in ten years!"

As Judith assimilated Daisie Belle's comments, they strolled over to the concrete step crouching streetside, awaiting its next short-legged carriage passenger's departure. *Well, I have washed and ironed this dress a few times while you were gone. You've been away six weeks.* She turned to the hack driver with the thick black mustache. "Chug, how is Mrs. Conly?"

He tipped his wide-brimmed felt hat. "Much better, Judith. Thank ya for askin'. She's been chewin' that ginger like you suggested, but she surely does pitch a fit to have to drink that prune vinegar."

Judith smiled. "It may not taste good, but it will sure help what's ailing her."

"Yes, ma'am." Conly looked at Daisie Belle. "Are you gonna stay a spell, Mrs. Emory?"

"Why don't you come join us for lunch, Daisie Belle?" Judith offered. "Marthellen has lots of beef stew and biscuits and peach cobbler."

"That depends. Is the judge going to be here?" Daisie Belle cooed.

Judith stared at the woman's flashing blue eyes and magnificent long eyelashes.

Daisie Belle chuckled and touched her friend's arm. "My, my, how easy you are to tease, dear Judith! Thank you for inviting me. I would love to stay but must get the house aired out and unpack my trunks. I'll have to get to Chan's Cleaners early in the morning. I came home with both trunks filled with soiled garments. It rained half the time I was in New York."

"I heard Colonel Jacobs took sick," Judith said.

"Yes, and he wasn't able to attend a single party until the last week I was there. I hardly saw him the entire time. And now he's gone home to Pennsylvania. It's just as well. We aren't that suited. But I did find some wonderful new fashions." She clapped her gloved hands together. "I bought you the most delightful little gift, but that crate was misplaced by the railroad. You would think that after ten years of transcontinental rails that they would know how to keep the luggage with the passengers."

"You didn't have to buy me anything," Judith said.

"Of course I did. It's a peace offering. I know you're still quite miffed at me for casting you as a talking squirrel in the Christmas pageant."

"I am not 'quite miffed,'" Judith replied. *Perhaps a slight bit miffed, but definitely not 'quite' miffed.*

"But the real reason I stopped by — and it has nothing to do with our dear, dear

Judge . . ." She waved at Alicia and Judge Kingston crossing the street to the Kingstons' backyard. "I simply couldn't pass your house without knowing if you heard the news."

Judith looked down Musser Street to see if the boys and Barbara Day were coming yet. "What news?"

"About our dear Peachy!"

"Did you see Peachy Denair in New York?"

"Not more than four days ago. Did she write to Roberta about the turn of events?"

"I haven't heard anything."

"Send Roberta out here; I want to tell you both at the same time," Daisie Belle said.

"Roberta's not here. She's out at the mill with Turner."

"Oh-h-h . . ."

"There's no announcement from that quarter," Judith quickly added. "Although Roberta did find herself a cute little house over on Fourth Street. She took off a few days from her clerk's duties to paint it. She'll be moving over there in a week or so."

Daisie Belle clapped her hands again. "Moving out on her own? How marvelous! How modern of her. Her own place . . . and still unmarried. That is, she and Turner didn't . . . they haven't . . . ?"

"Oh, no."

"Well, I would die if that had happened while I was away. And I do mean *die*." Daisie Belle Emory cleared her throat and pursed her red full lips. "Now, Judith dear, I can't stand it another minute. I have to tell you. Peachy Denair is engaged!"

Judith's hand flew to her mouth. "No!"

"Oh, yes. I saw the ring myself. Quite appropriate for the circumstance, I might add. And guess who the groom will be?"

"Wilton Longbake?" Judith said, almost choking on a gasp.

"Yes! Isn't that something? She really did it. She said she was going to New York to snag Mr. Longbake, and she did it."

"I am sure Roberta doesn't know about this."

"That's why I just couldn't wait to tell you. Now, I simply must get going."

The carriage lurched east on Musser toward Carson Street. Cinderella's charmed coach never looked any more regal than Chug Conly's old hack with Daisie Belle Emory in the back.

"Grandma! Grandma! Grandma!" a high-pitched voice cried out. Alicia sprinted toward Judith, arms outstretched. Judith squatted and grabbed up the girl with the big brown eyes.

"Do you like the way Daddy pinned my hair?" Alicia asked. "My best friend, Marjorie Walters, likes it. She's going to get her mamma to fix hers the same."

"Yes, I do. You look just like your mother, young lady."

"Mamma was real pretty, wasn't she, Grandma Judith?"

"She was one of the prettiest women in Nevada."

"Daddy says she was the prettiest woman in all of India, too. Am I pretty, Grandma?"

"Honey, it's a wonder the flowers just don't wilt with envy when you walk by. You put them all to shame."

"Grandma! Now you sound silly like Grandpa Judge."

Judith took the warm, soft little hand in hers. *Alicia Kingston, you are the only person on the face of this earth who can get Judge Hollis A. Kingston to act silly.* "Is your daddy coming over to eat?"

"He said he was too tuckered out after giving his long sherman. He's taking a nap."

"Then we'll bring him something for later."

"Can I sit by Grandpa Judge?"

"Grandpa will sit at the end of the table. You can be on one side of him and I'll be on

20

the other. How's that?"

"Just as long as I don't have to sit next to Douglas or Timothy."

A buckboard rumbled up behind them at the curbless streetside. Judith smiled up at the couple sitting in the buckboard. "Mr. and Mrs. Boyer! How are you two?"

"Jist as healthy as hogs, Judith," Levi called out.

"That's not exactly the metaphor I would use," Marcy said.

Levi tipped his hat to the shy little girl partially hidden behind Judith's skirt. "Hello, Miss Kingston."

"What do you say, Alicia?" Judith prompted.

"Hello, Mr. and Mrs. Boyer."

"And?" Judith prodded.

"It certainly is a beautiful day, isn't it?"

"You're right about that, little darlin'," Levi replied. "Is the judge home?"

"Yes, but he's just sitting down to lunch."

"Well, tell him the good news. I got that quarry supervisor's job out at the state prison."

"That's wonderful, Levi."

"It was the judge's recommendation that did it."

"I'm sure they hired the most qualified applicant."

"All I know is that the other candidate had half-a-dozen references and I just had one, and the warden told the board that one letter from Judge Kingston is worth twelve ordinary ones."

"Would you like to join us for lunch?" Judith offered.

Levi glanced at Marcy, who nodded approval, then sighed. "It's the only meal I won't have to hear, 'It's good, Marcy, darlin', but it ain't quite like eatin' at Judith's.'"

Judith narrowed her eyes and scowled. "Levi Boyer, you don't say that, do you?"

"Maybe once or twice."

"Marcy's a fine cook. You're just fortunate you didn't have to eat my cooking that first year after I was married."

"Really?" Marcy said as she climbed down from the buckboard.

"Was it bad?" Levi asked.

"Oh, yes. I cried most every night. But I promised the judge I'd get better. And he promised me as soon as we could afford it, we'd hire a cook! We both kept our promise."

"I have to admit, I was mostly thinkin' of Marthellen's cookin'," Levi amended.

Judith grinned. "I figured you were. Come on, we've got room. David is too pooped to join us."

"My daddy's a preacher and works on shermans," Alicia announced.

"And he's a very good one," Marcy said.

"Yeah," Levi said. "He sure put the fear into me today. I reckon I won't have to go to church again for a long time."

When they entered the dining room, Marthellen said, "Who can put the silver napkin rings on for me?"

"I can!" Alicia shouted. "Marjorie Walters showed me how. How many do we need?"

"Honey, that's something only the Lord and your Grandma know for sure." Marthellen turned to Judith. "Did Duffy talk to you?"

"I haven't seen him."

"He came to the side door and I sent him around front."

Judith scooted through the back porch to the west entrance. A young man, about thirty, with large ears and slightly stooped shoulders, sat on the porch staring across the street at the Presbyterian Church and softly playing a mouth organ tune that Judith didn't recognize.

"Duffy, how is it going for you?"

He leaped up, yanked off his cap, and tucked the mouth organ in his pocket. "Howdy, Judith. I was wonderin' if Douglas was here."

"He and Timothy went to the park to fetch his mother. They're going to join us for lunch. You're welcome too."

"No, ma'am. My mamma said I should respect other folks' privacy."

"But this isn't a private meal. It's more like a party. We're having a whole room full."

His eyes lit up. "In that case, Mamma said I should be polite and accept party invites with a cheerful attitude." His wide smile revealed white, crooked teeth.

"Shall I have Marthellen set a plate for you at the table?"

Duffy slumped down on the wooden porch. "I reckon I should eat out here on the step. I've been feedin' them hogs this mornin' and I'm too dirty to trounce through the house."

"Have you got started on building that other room to your house?"

"Ain't no reason to, now that the weather's turned pleasin'. The tent's good enough for me. Always has been. Drake's wife and boy need them two rooms in the cabin." Judith caught an aroma of hog manure and sage. "After all," he said, lowering his voice, "a man needs a little privacy of his own."

"I imagine you're right. But you really need to build a room by fall. No more winters in that tent for you, Duffy Day."

"I aim to do that, providin' I have the funds. It costs money to support a family, even if it is your brother's family."

"Barbara doesn't have a job yet?" Judith asked.

"I don't rightly think she's lookin', Judith. Ain't much call in Carson City for a poet and artist. But it ain't no bother. I promised Drake on the day he died that I'd look after his things."

"You're a very loyal brother." *I wonder if poor Drake really meant for you to support his wife too?* "Look, here they come."

Duffy stared to the south. "Nah, that's Tray and Willie Jane."

"No, I meant down that way." Judith pointed to the north, but Duffy paid no notice.

He hurried off, his face beaming as he said, "I reckon I should go help Douglas cross the street. I'm his favorite uncle, you know."

Judith turned to greet the approaching couple, strolling arm in arm. "Tray, Willie Jane, I haven't seen you in days."

Tray Weston tipped his hat. "We've had extra guard duty at the jail. There's a rumor that some of Manitoba Joe's pals will try to bust him out."

"I didn't think he had cohorts."

"No, ma'am, I don't believe he's sick."

"She meant Manitoba Joe's *friends*," Willie Jane said.

Tray looked blank. "Say, is that Levi Boyer in your house?"

"Yes, he and Marcy are staying for lunch."

"Well, I reckon we will too."

"Tray Weston, Judith hasn't asked us yet!" Willie Jane reprimanded.

"Please do stay," Judith said, with a slight grimace. *Maybe we should have done buffet style and forgotten about the table.*

"We would be delighted," Willie Jane said.

Tray pulled slightly ahead. "If you ladies will excuse me, I need to talk to Levi."

Willie Jane nodded at Duffy, Barbara, and kids as they crowded through the door after Levi and then she said in a low voice to Judith, "I've spent every evening this week with Fidora."

"How is she?"

"Doc Jacobs says the baby's in the wrong position. He's hoping it will move before she comes due."

"She still has a month," Judith said.

"That's what the doc says, but Fidora claims she counted the days. It should be tomorrow or the next day."

"That's a rather exact prediction."

"She ought to know."

How could a woman in that profession know when . . . or who? Judith leaned closer to Willie Jane. "She didn't happen to tell you —"

"The name of the father? She says she won't ever tell."

The young lady in long denim skirt and white lace collar blouse had her mother's brown eyes, curly hair, narrow face, and small, up-turned nose. But she had her father's thick, full eyebrows. She had been taller than her mother at thirteen, and taller than most women in Carson City by the time she left for college.

"Hi, Daddy," Roberta said. "How come you're working through your lunch hour on a Saturday?"

Judge Kingston slipped his gold wire-frame spectacles off and rubbed the bridge of his hawkish nose. With the light behind him, his thin gray-black hair and high forehead previewed baldness a few years away.

"I just need to catch up on a few things. Crime and litigation never seem to take a day off."

"Are you sure you don't come down here just to get some peace and quiet?" she chided.

"Of course not."

"Good, because ever since David and the kids came back from India, it seems like your house is a zoo."

"Is that why you wanted a place of your own?"

"Daddy! We've been all through this. I just felt that dropping out of college and returning home made me look like a failure."

"That's absurd. No one thinks that."

"Well, I do. But with a place of my own it seems as though I have a plan for my life, that I'm doing what I want to do, not what I have to do."

"Are you saying you're not expecting a certain young milling company speculator to ask you to marry him?"

"I'm expecting, all right. But this way I don't look nearly so desperate. Turner just wants to get the mill up and rolling before we make any more plans. In the meantime, I think my little house will make a very nice newlywed cottage later on, don't you?"

"What does Turner Bowman think about it?"

"I think he's worried he won't get invited over to your house for supper as much after we're married."

"Nonsense. Everyone in town eats there," the judge replied.

"Aha! You *are* overwhelmed by the crowd."

A tight grin broke across his mustached mouth. "Perhaps, at times."

"I think after I get my place all settled, you should come over to my house and have lunch with me every Saturday. Turner always works on Saturdays. Just you and me, nice and quiet."

"Sweetheart, your cooking is atrocious."

"You're quite right, Daddy. So, I think that you and I should have a quiet lunch every Saturday at the St. Charles Hotel, compliments of the judge."

"Now that could be more easily arranged," he said. "Would you like to begin today?"

"Oh, Daddy, I can't. I'm on my way out to the mill."

"They have the cook shack open?"

"No, I'm bringing box lunches . . . Marthellen fixed them. Turner and his crew have been putting in sixteen-hour days to get everything completed in time. He's determined to have the mill running by the May 16 deadline. He says it will be the most modern, efficient mill in the state."

"You know, darling, some people say it will be one mill too many."

"That's the gibberish of a jealous and

fearful competition," Roberta said.

"Maybe you're right about that. I hope, for Turner's sake, you are. Mills have to modernize to keep up."

"I think it was divine providence that the Consolidated Mill blew up last December. That provided the impetus for Turner and his sponsors to upgrade the equipment."

The judge frowned as he pondered her comment. "I'm not sure the premeditated placing of sticks of dynamite for the purpose of harm were in God's agenda, but the Lord can certainly use any circumstance to accomplish something good."

"That's what I meant." She paused. "What do you think about Peachy and Wilt?"

"I'm concerned, frankly," the judge said. "I've always liked Peachy, and you have been best friends for a lot of years. I don't know what to make of it."

"I think she'd be good for his children," Roberta said slowly, "but it scares me. I'm not sure where this will lead. She'll be living out the life that was almost mine. I can't believe she'd still fall for him after all she knew through me."

"The heart does strange things," the judge said.

"So does money. And so does a man who

feels betrayed and wants to get even." Roberta stomped her foot as she turned to the door. "I refuse to allow that man to come between me and my friend. Besides, I have a feeling she will need me again someday. But standing up for her at the wedding is out of the question. I've got to go, Daddy. Don't work all day."

"I won't. Are you taking a horse or a carriage?"

"Need you ask?"

"Be careful. Mr. Stanton has some half-wild beasts in that barn of his."

"Of course he does! Why do you think I always go to his livery?" She spun on the heel of her black lace-up boot and strutted out of the judge's office. The door swung partially closed behind her.

The judge overheard her conversation with someone in the outer office.

"Is the judge in?"

"Yes, but he's quite busy."

"This is important."

"I'm trying to keep the judge from needless interruptions."

"This ain't needless. Believe me, it's an emergency."

"Sheriff, you can't barge into my father's office just any time."

"I've been doin' it since you were no

higher than that desktop. I don't intend to stop now, Roberta Louise Kingston. Step aside."

"Do you have a warrant?"

"A warrant? How can I have a warrant? The judge is in there!"

"Roberta!" Judge Kingston called out. "When I complained about lack of privacy, I didn't mean Sheriff Hill!"

Her sheepish face popped into the doorway. "Sheriff Hill is here to see you, Judge Kingston."

The red-faced Ormsby County Sheriff blustered into the judge's office. "I've never in my life met a woman as stubborn as that daughter of yours!"

The judge leaned back in the oak captain's chair and loosened his black tie. "Oh, I have," he replied. "Now, what is this great emergency?"

"Manitoba Joe is pitchin' a fit."

"You haven't transferred him out to the state prison yet?"

"Not until next Friday. You know how Governor Kinkead is a stickler for protocol."

"What do you mean, he's pitching a fit?"

"He's been yellin', cursin', and bangin' on the wall ever since 7:30 this morning."

"My word, that seems excessive."

"You're tellin' me. He's about to drive the other prisoners and the guards plum distracted with his screaming demands."

"What is he demanding?"

"That Judge Hollis A. Kingston come to the jail and visit with him."

"Why didn't you come get me at 7:30 a.m.?"

"Because I didn't want him or the other prisoners to think they could get their way just by screamin'."

"And now?"

"Now, I just want that racket to stop."

"What does he want from me?"

The sheriff yanked the judge's hat off the peg near the door and tossed it to him. "I have no idea, but if we don't go find out, he's goin' to be hung right there in his cell . . . today."

Manitoba Joe Clark stood five feet tall. Some said he was five feet wide, but that wasn't quite true. He was not round. His full black beard was neatly trimmed and his round head was usually covered by a beat-up black felt hat with a Montana crease. Now his head was bare.

Real bare.

Manitoba Joe was completely bald down to his ears.

His brown eyes looked tiny in the large head and squinted above his full beard. Rumor claimed he could stop a cannon ball with his stomach. No one could remember seeing him actually do it, but few doubted he had the strength and nerve to try.

Stories followed him like tumbleweed trailing a dust devil. Some said he killed three mounties up in the British Possessions. Some said he picked up Big Johnny-One-Shot and threw him from Bridal Veil Falls. Some said he held up the Kansas Denver Railroad by pulling the rails out with his bare hands.

Few denied that the world in general would be a better place if Manitoba Joe were hung. And many debated whether a rope could actually break his neck.

"Joe!" the judge shouted from the end of the hallway.

"I need to talk to you, Judge."

"So I'm told."

"Come down here. It's private."

"Not until I get your word that you'll quit hollering after I leave, or I'll never speak with you again. You know I mean it. I always keep my word." The judge waited. "Did you hear me, Joe?"

There was a curse and a "Yep."

"Do you agree not to yell and scream after I'm gone?"

"Yep."

"Do you keep your word?"

There was a pause, then a firm "Yep."

Judge Kingston marched down the row of jail cells until he reached the last one. It was a ten-by-ten-foot cell with brick walls, brick ceiling, iron bars across a one-by-two-foot window, and an iron bar door. The judge carried an oak chair from the deputy's desk in one hand and a note paper in the other.

"Thanks for comin', Judge," Manitoba Joe growled.

"The sheriff was ready to shoot you if I didn't."

"Have you got any tobacco, Judge?"

"No, I don't."

"Other prisoners get tobacco privileges, Judge. Why is it they don't let me have any?"

Judge Kingston pulled a long wooden pencil out of his suit coat and jotted down a note. "I'll check on that, Joe. Is that why you asked to see me?"

The outlaw's raspy voice grew urgent. "I'm innocent, Judge. I did not kill Sam Tjader."

Judge Kingston scooted his chair closer to the bars.

"Don't get too close, Judge," a deputy warned from the other end of the hallway.

"Maybe you'd feel more comfortable if you didn't stand there watching, Deputy," the judge suggested.

"It's a rule, Judge. We've got to have an observer any time someone visits the prisoners."

Sheriff Hill yelled from behind the deputy. "For Pete's sake, that doesn't apply to Judge Kingston. Go get some coffee or something." The sheriff glanced down the hall. "Holler if you need anything, Judge."

Manitoba Joe gripped the steel bars. His eyes bored into the judge's. "I'm goin' to hang for somethin' I didn't do, and I cain't get no one to believe me."

The judge stayed steady, unmoved. "Nearly every man I ever sentenced to death has claimed the same thing."

Manitoba Joe turned his head and spat. "But it's the truth in my case."

"You had your time in court."

"My lawyer was incompetent and you know it."

"Atley Musterman was not incompetent, but he wasn't very thorough," the judge acknowledged. "He made no mistakes that would cause a mistrial, although I'm not sure why you chose him."

36

"I didn't hire Musterman."

"What do you mean?"

"He said some of my friends in Montana wanted to make sure I got legal representation and they paid his salary."

"What friends in Montana?"

"That's just it, Judge, he wouldn't tell me. He said they didn't want their names mentioned or the law would come lookin' for them."

"The truth is, a jury of honest, law-abiding citizens convicted you, Joe. The sentence for aggravated murder in pursuit of a crime is death by hanging. My only role was to make sure that the trial, and the sentencing, was carried out in a legal manner, which it was." The judge leaned back in the chair and rubbed his goatee. "What is it you expect of me?"

"Can you get them to postpone this hangin' until I sort this through?"

"Sort what through? You're in the county jail. In a few days you'll be contained in the state prison. You can hardly 'sort through' a crime while in jail."

"Judge, I ain't the fastest at thinkin'. And with that gallows starin' at me, my mind's confused most of the time. But I know I didn't shoot Sam Tjader."

The judge crossed his arms across his

chest, then crossed his legs. "OK, let's review the case and you tell me if we are both looking at the same facts. First of all, you have a notorious reputation across the western United States and Canada as being a ruthless and violent gunman and outlaw. Would you say that's an accurate description of how people view you?"

Manitoba Joe's eyes gleamed with pride. "I reckon that sums it up."

"And four witnesses testified they saw you go into the bank moments after Sam Tjader opened it on Tuesday, February 11th. Several minutes later they heard one gunshot, followed by shouting. A second gunshot blasted just as you opened the door. Then you ran out of the bank carrying about $25,000 in greenbacks and banknotes in a bank bag in one hand and a Colt .45 in the other. Is that correct?"

"I admit I robbed the bank, although I still can't figure out how he crammed that much money in that bag. I surely would have liked to have had the time to count it up and finger it a while."

"The reason you didn't is because you were captured on Carson Street after you ran in front of a six-horse stagecoach and were knocked flat while trying to steal one of the horses as it trotted through town."

Manitoba Joe clenched his stubby, powerful fingers around the bars. "It's worked before."

"But when the bag got trampled it burst, and the bank notes got caught in the stiff winds of that Chinook. Some suspect it blew those bills all the way to Mexico."

Manitoba Joe snorted. "I got half the town tryin' to chase the wind," he said. "Ever' word of what you said is true, Judge, but I didn't shoot Sam Tjader."

Judge Kingston leaned forward, his hands on his knees. "Sometimes, Joe, we get emotionally charged and we can do things that later on we don't remember doing. Could it be possible that you shot Sam in the heat of the moment and didn't realize it?"

"Nope, that theory don't hold. I've been holdin' up banks since I was fourteen. I don't get any more emotional doin' that than most folks do playin' croquet in a big old grassy yard."

"Well, then, give me some evidence that wasn't at the trial to prove you didn't do it. Any kind of delay that I would instigate has to be based on new evidence."

Manitoba Joe pressed his clenched fist on top his bald head. "How many empty casings were in my Colt when they yanked me out from under that six-up team?"

"Two, Joe . . . there were two fired brass casings."

"See, that proves it!" The prisoner slammed the bars.

"Proves what? The jury was convinced that proved you killed Sam Tjader."

"But the first shot was just a threat. The sheriff himself dug the lead out of the ceiling beam in the bank."

"Yes, that got Tjader to open the safe. But that doesn't account for the second shot fired when you were near the door."

"Judge, have you ever known a professional gunman to carry six beans in the wheel?"

"You mean, leaving the hammer set on an empty chamber?"

"Yeah. Don't you do that yourself when you carry a revolver?"

"Yes, I do. But I know many a man who, just prior to having to use his weapon, puts in that extra bullet."

"I never do. Come on, Judge, do you think Manitoba Joe Clark needs six bullets to rob the likes of Sam Tjader? I'll face any man on this earth with five bullets. Me or him, one will be dead after two shots. There ain't no need to tote six."

"There was a brass cartridge in both

empty chambers," the judge reminded him.

"Of course there was! I don't like dry firin' and I don't care if some hombre thinks I have six bullets. But it shames my gunman's dignity for Manitoba Joe to have to pack six bullets."

"The jury heard that argument and thought it insufficient."

"The jury was actin' under the duress of emotion, just like you accused me. Sam Tjader was their friend, their hometown banker. They assumed things in their high-strung state that they wouldn't in a normal situation. They weren't goin' to believe me, no matter what. But you, on the other hand, bein' a God-fearin' man, have got to think it through more logical like. You know there wasn't one witness that saw me shoot Sam."

"OK, then how do you account for the second shot?"

"At the time, I thought the bank manager found a gun and was shootin' at me. Why else would I try to stop a movin' stage? If I had known he was cold dead, I would have taken my good, sweet time."

Judge Kingston sighed. "Joe, let me tell you, I cannot intervene unless there is solid evidence or a procedural error. If you are innocent, you have a serious problem."

"If I'm innocent, all of Carson City has a serious problem."

"How's that?"

"The one who murdered Sam Tjader is still out there someplace."

The judge stared at the stout man. *Now that thought's going to plague me.*

"For God's sake, help me, Judge."

"For God's sake, I will consider what you've told me. But I'm also going to want you to do something for yourself."

"I cain't do nothin' in jail. You know that. I'm as trapped as a ragin' bear in a cage."

"You can confess your sins, Joe. The Bible says that the Lord is 'faithful and just and will forgive us our sins and cleanse us from all unrighteousness,' no matter where we are."

"It's too late for me, Judge. I've littered my path. There's no way to clean it up. I was born and bred to disdain churchgoin' folks."

"It's not too late, Joe. God doesn't lie. His Word is true for all men, no matter what."

"Well, I don't lie neither, and I'm tellin' you I didn't kill Sam Tjader. So, what are you goin' to do? Have you got a plan?"

"Just some questions." The judge stood up to leave.

"What kind of questions?"

"To begin with, I'd like to know which

42

anonymous Montanans hired Atley Musterman to be your lawyer, and why."

Manitoba Joe slammed his hands against the bars again. "I knew I could count on you! Dad gum it, I'm right about men at one glance. Always have been. You think I'm innocent, don't you?"

"No, Joe, I don't. I believe you had a fair trial and a just sentence. You deserve to hang for killing a good friend of mine, Sam Tjader."

"But you ain't convinced beyond a shadow of a doubt."

The judge turned away and strode quickly down the hall.

Chapter Two

The coffee tasted hot and strong as it trickled down the judge's throat. He tried to relax his neck and shoulders, then his whole body as he sat on the sofa, facing an empty, cold fireplace. He had loosened his black tie and unfastened the top button on his starched shirt. His dark gray wool vest flopped open against his strong, broad chest. He lifted his legs and propped shoeless feet on the brown leather ottoman then took another sip from the steaming porcelain mug and held it tight.

Judith came in from the dining room with a Dresden china cup and something in it that Mr. Cheney, the grocer, had called Ginger-Peach Spice tea. Her pale pink silk robe dragged across the rug, covering her bare toes. The white lace cuffs and high collar covered most everything else. Her

44

hair was still pinned on top of her head and her dark brown bangs curled and drooped almost to her eyebrows.

"You look like that bank robber after the stage coach horses ran over him," Judith said, sitting down on the opposite end of the sofa and tucking her legs beneath her. "What are you doing?"

He took another long sip of coffee. This time his hips, thighs, and calves loosened. Even his stocking-clad feet relaxed. "I suppose I'm just listening."

Judith took a sip of tea, then set the cup on the cherrywood table. She reached up and unfastened her dime-sized, round silver earrings and laid them on the table. "I don't hear anything."

The judge offered her one of his wry, straight smiles. It was so faint that Judith and Roberta were usually the only ones who detected it. "That's what I'm listening to. Sometimes silence has such a beautiful melody. Perhaps we should hold a concert of silence at the opera house this year."

Judith took another sip of peach tea. "That ought to be quite a draw. I wonder, when the concert of silence is over, do we stand and shout 'bravo'?"

Judge Hollis A. Kingston let out a quick

laugh and every muscle in his body released its tension. "I believe it's customary to compliment a concert of silence with rapid blinks of the eye."

"Like this?" Judith tilted her head, folded her hands under her chin and blinked a half dozen times.

"Judith Kingston," the judge said, chuckling, "are you flirting with me?"

"I certainly hope so. Is the concert of silence over? Sometimes they just drag on and on."

The judge took a deep breath and let it out slowly. "It was a bit hectic around here this evening."

"It was hectic all day. Your daughter calls this house a zoo, you know."

"This is a zoo with all the animals thrown into one cage," he added.

"Is that a complaint, dear Judge?"

"Not yet. But that reminds me . . . I got an interesting visit from Mr. Marshall of Marshall's Gallery. He's been contacted to do photographs that the illustrator will use for lithographs in Thompson & West's forthcoming *History of Nevada.*"

"Oh! And they want to include you, Judge Kingston!"

"No, they want to include us, Mrs. Kingston."

Judith sat up straight. "I'd feel very uncomfortable about being included in such a volume."

"Mr. Marshall absolutely insists that we include you. He wants us at the gallery on Monday."

"Maybe I'll get used to the idea by then. Are we going for a ride tomorrow afternoon?"

"Most definitely."

"Where shall we go?"

"I was thinking of New Hampshire."

"That bad, huh?"

"I was teasing. But I do look forward to a ride."

"Are Timothy and Alicia coming with us?" she asked.

"Not this time."

"Just Judith and the judge . . . how delightful."

The judge took another sip of coffee, held it in his mouth, then let it slowly flow down his throat. "Is Roberta coming home tonight?"

"I believe so. We haven't moved her bed yet. If she could talk Turner into it, they were going to try to patch those holes in the living room wall at her place. What do you suppose made those holes?"

"A clenched fist of rage."

"Oh, my." Judith reached across the sofa for his hand. It felt large, bony, firm, and warm. "Did you talk much with Roberta today?"

"A little before lunch." He squeezed her soft, warm fingers. "She said she wanted me and her to have lunch once a week after she moves out, and she'd cook the meal."

"That would be a culinary challenge. I tried to instruct that girl how to cook, but she was handicapped by her teacher."

The judge thought about Roberta's charred biscuits and mangled fried eggs. "I offered as an alternative to pay for a meal at the St. Charles."

"Did she talk any about Turner?"

"Only that he had been working long hours trying to meet the deadline at the mill."

Judith released his hand and plucked up a glass squirrel the size of a grapefruit. "Did you ever see anything more useless than this?"

"I'm sure it's expensive. Daisie Belle seemed delighted to give it to you."

"Yes, it does bring back such fond memories." She gently set the heavy glass figurine down and plucked up her teacup. "I trust Turner knows what he's doing."

"Did you talk to Roberta about it?"

"We had quite a discussion. Alicia sat on my lap and Douglas and Timothy played a vigorous version of marbles on the floor while Willie Jane and Marthellen practiced their duet for church. Until now, that has been my most tranquil moment of the day."

"What did Roberta have to say?"

"She's worried about Turner and their relationship . . .with working those long hours he's always too tired to do much. Some evenings he's too tired to even talk. She copes by reminding herself this is only temporary."

"I'm sorry I encouraged him in this mill project. I'm afraid it's been too hard on him and Roberta. There's a possibility he'll be defeated by it and lose heart."

"You're being too hard on him, Judge," Judith replied. "He's resilient and young enough to start over with some other challenge if that's the way it is to be. He has always struck me as a young man who portrays a kind of drama of his own, without music or a drum roll. I was amazed that Roberta wasn't drawn romantically to him much sooner."

"He's an ambitious young man," the judge admitted. "But you know what worries me about this refurbishing of the Consolidated Mill? What if the critics are right? What if this area cannot sustain another mill? All that effort for nothing."

"I suppose all businesses are full of risks," Judith said. "And there's usually doubts attached to any new beginning."

"Quite so. Anything related to mining is always an expensive risk. I worry about the financial backing. Longbake and Hearst both agreed to put in $75,000 to purchase and rebuild the mill. Then, after that less than sterling reception for Wilt Longbake, orchestrated by our daughter right here in this room last December, Longbake reduced his share to $50,000. Turner complained at the time that he wouldn't be able to rebuild everything for that. Yet now he's near completion, just like he wanted it. How did he do that for $25,000 under budget?"

Judith squinted at him. "What are you saying?"

"I hope the boy hasn't incurred an insufferable amount of personal debt."

"Are you worried about your little girl being married to a poor man?"

"I'm from Kentucky, remember? Poverty is worn with a badge of honor. Being debt-ridden is what troubles me."

"She will have to hire a cook," Judith announced. "And Roberta says that if the mill is a success, they intend to purchase Audrey Adair's former home."

"That's an ambitious goal."

"Do you think you should talk to Turner, as his future father-in-law?"

"Not yet. Every young man needs the freedom to find his own way. Turner is hard-working and mostly reasonable. I hope his efforts pay off, but they may not with this mill business. I certainly don't want my daughter starting marriage in so much debt that they'll never be able to try any other venture."

"Turner is not the only bright young man with a plan," Judith said.

"Are you talking about our David? My word, I didn't even see him today. Did you?"

"Only for a moment. He was busy working on his 'sherman' again."

"And how was my darling Alicia?"

"She missed her Grandpa Judge."

"Perhaps we should take those children with us on the ride tomorrow."

Judith smiled. "Why do your words come as no surprise to me?"

The judge gave her another of his slight smiles. "Did David come over to eat?"

"No, but I think that was because Barbara Day was here."

"My word, again?"

"She seems to like it here. You know what she told me? She said she always liked the name Judith. It reminded her of the queens in a deck of cards. Pallas is the queen of spades. Rachael is the queen of diamonds. Elizabeth I is the queen of clubs. And Judith —"

". . . is the queen of hearts," the judge said. "Everyone in Carson knows that. But I remember the names Argine and Esther in that pack somewhere."

"Maybe different countries have different names," Judith said. "Anyway, I believe Barbara has set her eyes on our son. And she's spent her entire life doing whatever she wants. The woman has an almost mystical appeal and a spirit that speaks her own language. I get the impression she's watching us watching her."

"But that's a preposterous pursuit. How does David intend to deal with it?"

"He plans on returning to India by October."

"But they won't allow him to take the children this time, being a widower."

"He figures either they bend the rules or . . ." She hesitated.

"Or we agree to raise them while he's in India?"

"That's the unspoken thought. How do you feel about that?"

The judge stared into the empty fireplace.

"I have absolutely no idea how I feel about that. And you?"

"Exactly the same. I keep hoping that I don't have to decide how I feel. Of course, there is one other way the dilemma would be solved."

"You mean, if David would abandon his missionary aspirations and stay here in Carson to serve the church across the street?"

"No. He would never be satisfied here. Nor would the congregation. There are grumblings already that his sermons are too pointed, too evangelistic, too challenging."

The judge felt his neck stiffen. "I thought that was the way sermons were supposed to be."

Judith nodded. "I think his sermons are some of the best I've ever heard. When he's preaching, I catch myself wondering, 'Is this our little David? The one who was fascinated with new gadgets and had fresh theories about everything under the sun? Where did he learn all of this spiritual insight? How did he become so skilled in speaking, so persuasive?' It amazes me."

"He still is full of storytelling," the judge said. "But he has grown more pensive and introspective over the years. It's marvelous to see his spiritual discernment. I often feel humbled to be his father."

"Did you ever tell him that?"

"No, I can't recall that I have, but I'm sure he knows how I feel." He cleared his throat. "Now, what way could he solve the children's dilemma and still serve in India?"

"He could remarry," Judith said, blinking her eyes.

The rented carriage rolled west on Sixth Street. Judge Kingston still wore his Sunday suit, but the silk top hat had been replaced by a broad-brimmed beaver felt. He stopped and waited for several men on horseback to ride past. Leather chaps covered their ducking trousers. Big spurs rested on the back of worn brown boots poked into long tapaderas. Their dusty drover hats, pulled low in the front, shaded leather-tough faces. Gloved hands rested on wide silver-capped saddle horns. Strapped to the men's waists were holstered revolvers and bullet belts where no brass cartridge ever turned green for lack of use.

The judge listened to the banter of the four men.

"I say we go on to Wyomin'!"

"Nah, I've been to Wyomin'. It's too windy. Let's head for Montana."

"I wintered in Montana once out on the

Yellowstone. Like to froze to death."

"How about Idaho?"

"Ain't nobody goin' to Idaho."

"Sounds perfect, don't it?"

The men nodded at the judge, then rode on.

Where will we go today? What would it be like to say that? What if I hadn't studied law? What if I'd never met Mr. Lincoln? What if I had come west as a teenager in '49? Or went to Texas in '65? Would I be riding down a trail today, debating Wyoming or Montana or even Idaho as my next destination? Of course, free-riding cowboys aren't candidates for an illustrated entry in The History of Nevada — *which might be another positive attraction.*

"Hey, Judge, are you parked or stuck?"

Lester and Twig Washburn lounged at the corner, each gripping a leash with small white dogs in tow. One glance told him the dogs were cleaner and better smelling than the Washburn brothers.

"Well, boys, looks like Daisie Belle got ahold of you," Judge said.

"It's their Sunday afternoon stroll," Twig reported. His wild and curly dark brown hair was crammed into an old bowler that looked ready to explode.

"Mrs. Emory pays us top dollar to walk them canines!" Lester added.

Twig flashed a tobacco-stained, toothy grin. "Yep, she opens up her pocketbook and gives us the top dollar!"

"What were you doin', Judge?" Lester asked. "You looked a bit distracted."

"I was sort of daydreaming, boys, waiting for the traffic to clear."

"I got to daydreamin' one time," Twig said, "and run a wagon right over the bluff out on Farmer Treadwell's place."

"You was drunk," Lester said.

"But I was daydreamin' too. I was dreamin' about me dancin' with Lola Montez, with her red hair floppin' in the breeze."

"Lola has black hair," Twig said.

"I told you, it were a dream. A man can dream about any color hair he wants."

"I suppose so. If you'll excuse me, Judith Kingston with the brown hair is waiting for me at home."

When he reached the front of the house, Alicia pranced on the concrete carriage step while Timothy swung round and round on the painted pipe hitching post.

"Did you see any panthers in town?" Timothy asked. "Some have come down from out of the hills. We'd better be armed and ready."

"Grandpa Judge!" Alicia called out. "I

get to sit next to you!"

The judge climbed down from the carriage and hugged his granddaughter. "Where's Grandma, sweetheart?"

"Willie Jane just came by to visit," Timothy reported, "and they are in the living room whispering about things they don't want us to hear."

The judge glanced toward the drawn curtains. *If I hadn't been dallying and stopped to visit with the Washburn brothers, we could have been out on our ride before Willie Jane caught us. That will teach you the dangers of daydreaming, Judge Kingston.*

Timothy spun around the pole twice more. "Can I drive the carriage today, Grandpa Judge? Please?"

"I might let you help drive."

"I am sitting by Grandpa," Alicia said.

"I'll ride up on the black horse," Timothy retorted. "Can I ride the horse, Grandpa? One time in India I rode a carriage horse for seven miles."

"I don't think this carriage horse likes riders. Timothy, step inside the house and tell Grandma Judith I'm out here with the carriage."

The nine-year-old sprinted to the front door, threw it open with a loud bang, and shouted, "Hurry, Grandma Judith, the last stage for Deadwood is pullin' out, and they only have two seats left!"

Judith scooted out the door, Timothy in tow. Willie Jane Farnsworth stood in the doorway.

"You children get in the rig," Judith said. "I need to speak to Grandpa for a moment."

"Give me the lead lines, Grandpa Judge," Timothy called out. "I'll drive it around the block once and settle down the horse."

"This horse looks permanently settled, son. Just wait and we'll all go." The judge turned back to his wife and looked into her worried eyes.

"Judge, it's Fidora. She's having her baby today, just like she predicted."

"Is there trouble?"

"Doc Jacobs sent Willie Jane to fetch me."

"Can't Willie Jane assist the doc?"

"It's not the delivery. It's Fidora who the doc is worried about. She's been bleeding a lot. And she asked if I could come be with her."

"My word, by all means. I'll have Roberta go with us on our ride."

"She went out to help Turner. They needed to work at the mill this afternoon."

"On a Sunday?"

"You know Turner."

"Did David go out to Dayton?"

"Yes, he and Reverend Hammond from the Methodist Church have teamed up to see about planting a church among the Chinese."

"Then it looks like Grandpa Judge gets the privilege of escorting the grandchildren by himself."

"Are you sure you don't mind?"

"Judith, there is a baby trying to enter this world and a mother who is in danger of exiting it. I believe you need to be there as a vessel of God's love and peace."

She stood on her tiptoes and kissed his cheek. "You're a rock."

He looked up at the two children waiting for him in the carriage. One sat patiently with small hands folded in her lap. The other stood on the carriage seat, an imaginary rifle at his shoulder, shooting pretend tigers off the roof of the house. "I thought you said I was a pushover," Judge said.

"It's all how you look at it." Judith squeezed his hand before waving at the children.

Judith and Willie Jane hurried south down Ormsby Street, trying to hold their long skirts out of the dirt. Thick white and gray clouds littered the deep blue Nevada sky as a cool Tahoe zephyr drifted down from the Carson Range to the west and blew wisps of their hair. A mild rain several days before had delayed the beginning of the worst of the dust season. They clutched their straw hats, even though both were tied down with wide ribbons.

"Fidora's not at her place on Ormsby Street?" Judith asked.

"No, she's at the St. Charles Hotel," Willie Jane replied.

"Good. Did Doc Jacobs insist she move up there?"

"No, Fidora rented a room herself a couple months ago."

"Well, I'm proud of her. I didn't know she —"

"Had the money? Some of the girls would surprise you how much they have saved."

"Since Roberta, then David and the children, came home, I don't have as much time to keep up with the girls. But Marthellen and I do pray for them by name every week."

"Most of them know that, Judith. The ones who care realize the only thread of decency they have left is stitched in place by the prayers of Judith Kingston and her housekeeper."

They soon reached the lobby of the St. Charles Hotel — one of the most elegant hotels in the state and the main stage stop in Carson City. Onlookers often stopped at that corner to watch the fashionable and famous of Nevada come and go.

Judith had not begun to perspire, but she knew her face was flushed. A young man with curly blond hair and garters on the sleeves of his white shirt greeted her from the counter. "Afternoon, Judith."

"Hello, Curtis, how's your mother doing?"

"She was out spadin' the garden yesterday mornin'."

"That's wonderful!"

"But her back went out and she's stove up in bed today."

"That's not so good. You tell her I'll try to stop by one of these days to check on her."

"She'd appreciate it. If you're goin' up to Fidora's, she's in room 201."

"Isn't that the Silver State room?" Judith commented. *Many of our state officials have stayed there,* Judith mused, *even our president, James Garfield. I wonder what they'd think if they knew . . .*

"Yes, ma'am," Curtis replied, "that's the one she wanted."

Judith and Willie Jane mounted wide carpeted stairs while noise filtered up from the Sunday afternoon crowd in the dining room

61

below. Willie Jane slipped open the big polished oak door of room 201.

A large crystal chandelier hung centered over a burgundy velvet sofa and a rosewood table. Burgundy curtains and valances draped the tall corner windows. Paintings of elegant Southern plantation homes and English dressage horsemen drew a sharp contrast to the Nevada desert setting.

Doctor Jacobs had the sleeves of his white shirt rolled up to his elbows. The shirt was still buttoned at the top, as was his gray wool vest. His tie and suit coat were tossed on a chair.

Willie Jane hurried to Fidora's side, while Judith went to stand next to Doctor Jacobs. "What's her condition?" she asked.

"Water broke an hour ago, but nothing since then."

"No contractions?"

"Nope, but when it does happen, it will be sudden."

"Is the baby still twisted?"

"Oh, yes, and mamma has already lost plenty of blood."

"What can I do for you?"

"Sit and talk to her, pray with her, because at any moment there will be the devil to pay."

Judith scooted a chair up to the opposite

side of the four-poster bed, across from Willie Jane. She examined Fidora's pale face and pale eyes. Judith knew this woman to be intelligent, but she could be impulsive, doing or saying things without thinking them through. Perhaps this trait caught her in her present predicament.

Fidora kept a steady gaze on Judith and reached out her hand.

"Thanks for comin', Judith." Her voice was deep, but softer than usual.

Judith took a deep breath and grasped Fidora's hand, which felt cold and sticky, thin and desperate. "You couldn't keep me away. Bringing babies into the world is the most exciting thing that ever happens on this earth."

Fidora closed her weary eyes. As she did, her chest sank and her cheeks shallowed. "Guess I'm kind of old to be havin' my first baby, ain't I?"

"How old are you, Fidora?"

"Twenty-three."

Judith bit her tongue. *Oh, dear Lord, she looks at least thirty-five or forty.* "Believe me, twenty-three is still young for birthing. I was your age when David was born." *But this is no time to mention the miscarriages before that.* "This is a very nice room for delivering a baby," she said instead.

"Ain't it, though? I picked it out myself."
Suddenly, terror flashed in Fidora's eyes.
"Judith, somethin's wrong."

"Every baby has its own timing," Judith
said. "We'll just have to wait for this little
one to be ready."

"I've been bleedin'. And I can feel
somethin' wrong in my belly. And I can see
it in Doc Jacobs' eyes."

"Just because we don't know what is
going to happen next, doesn't mean it will
be something bad. There are good surprises
too," Judith said.

"Like what?"

"What if . . . what if your baby is a strong,
healthy boy and needs a certain position to
kick from before he comes out. Once he's
ready, he'll pop out here and you'll be rockin'
him in your arms before the hour's through."

A wide, pained smile broke across
Fidora's pocked face, revealing straight
white teeth. "A strong, healthy boy, jist like
his daddy."

Willie Jane glanced at Judith. Both
women leaned nearer.

"So, his daddy is strong and healthy?" Judith prodded.

"Yep." Fidora's unpainted lips were ashen
and clamped tight. "And that's all I'm goin'
to say about that. Ever."

"Then that's between you and the Lord," Judith said.

"Me and Him has settled things up. I told you about that."

"Was that last December?"

"Yep. When you and me was sittin' in church all by ourselves and I was tellin' you about the major. I knew right then and there I still believed in Jesus and He hadn't given up on me."

"Yet you didn't quit the cribs?"

"Not right away. I was always scared of bein' poor, especially carryin' this baby. But I finally did quit, didn't I, Willie Jane?"

"Yes, you did, girl. I'm proud of you."

Fidora's breathing became labored. "Judith, when I was in the church that day, I made God a promise. I promised Him I wouldn't abort this baby like I did the others."

Judith sat still, trying to think of what to say.

"I ain't proud of my life," Fidora said. She closed her eyes slowly and ground her teeth. She clutched Judith's hand until her fingers were numb.

"Doc!" Willie Jane called out.

"I'm here," he replied from the foot of the bed, clutching his pocket watch. "Keep talking," he whispered.

"You promised to carry this baby full term. What else did you promise?" Judith asked.

"I promised I'd quit the cribs before Easter. I kept that one too. So, I reckon God will keep His end of the bargain."

"Just exactly what do you expect Him to do?"

"I asked Him if I could have a little bungalow in heaven."

"And what did He say?"

"He said all he had left was mansions, so I asked for just a modest one."

Judith smiled. "Oh, yes, that's exactly the kind of thing He would say."

Fidora tossed her head from side to side. Her mouth opened wide, but she didn't utter a sound as she clutched at Judith and Willie Jane. Beads of sweat popped out across her forehead.

"I can trust God, can't I, Judith?" she finally said.

"Do you believe Jesus is your Savior?"

"Oh, yes, I do! I really do!"

"Then, you can trust Him, honey."

On the third contraction, Fidora bit her lip. Drops of blood oozed to her chin. Judith took the corner of the bed sheet and wiped her clean.

"Judith . . . Willie Jane, you got to promise

me one thing . . . to find my baby a loving home."

Judith rubbed Fidora's arm at a steady pace. "Every woman feels this way. When we experience pain like we've never known before, we're convinced that we couldn't possibly survive. I believe that when David was being born I asked the judge to shoot me . . . I asked him several times."

"What did he do?"

"He kept saying, 'My word, Judith, pull yourself together.' And I screamed something like, 'If you tell me to pull myself together again, I'll shoot you. This baby is ripping me apart from the inside out and I am in no mood to be pulled together.' "

"You told that to the judge?" Willie Jane said.

"Yes, and some other choice things that the Lord is gracious enough to allow me not to remember. So, you hang on, Fidora. It's going to be a rough ride. Scream and yell all you want. I'll talk to the neighbors if they complain. But it will be worth it, honey. Believe me, the moment you see that sweet little one, it will be worth it."

The next contraction came with a hearty scream. Doc Jacobs yanked the covers off the bed and started giving orders: Water. Towels. Smelling salts.

There were more shrieks.

Willie Jane threw herself across Fidora's chest to keep her from sitting up while Judith braced her knees and assisted the doctor with the delivery. First, the feet, then the legs. Then a round, red slippery bottom.

"It's a boy!" Judith called out.

Another scream, a push, a shout and a groan. A faint whimper of a cry was heard as tiny lungs filled with outside air for the first time.

Judith cleaned the baby. Doc Jacobs cut the cord and attempted to wash the mamma.

Willie Jane grasped Fidora's hand and wiped her brow, panting out a description of the baby.

When Judith brought the infant wrapped in a flannel blanket to his mother and tucked him in beside her, Fidora croaked out, "He's beautiful . . ."

"Yes, he is, mamma, and he's strong and handsome," Judith said.

"Like his daddy?" Willie Jane prodded.

Fidora nodded. She admired the infant with pinched shut eyes, red face, and shock of dark brown hair.

Fidora moaned out each word. "I thought he would be bald."

Willie Jane hovered on one side, Judith on

the other. Doc Jacobs continued his frantic work at the other end of the bed.

"What's his name?" Willie Jane asked.

"Daniel," came Fidora's husky whisper.

"Oh? After his father?"

"No, after Daniel in the Bible. He was born in adversity, like when Daniel was in a lion's den. After this, things have got to get better."

"What's his last name?" Willie Jane pressed.

Fidora just shook her head. "No . . . no, I promised the Lord I wouldn't. Is the baby . . . all right?"

"Ten fingers, ten toes, two cute little ears and a broad nose like his mamma," Judith reported.

"I can't see him!"

"Honey, he's right here beside you." Willie Jane cuddled the baby closer to Fidora, who began to toss and turn.

"Doc," Judith called out, "what's happening?"

The doctor's shoulders sagged as he stood up. His eyes were dazed, his mouth hung dry and partly open. He wiped a bloody hand on a towel and shook his head.

Willie Jane turned away and began to sob.

Judith took a deep breath. *Oh, Lord Jesus, Lord Jesus . . . into thy hands —*

"Judith!" Fidora's voice was insistent, guttural.

Judith Kingston leaned down and kissed the woman's wet forehead. "I'm right here, honey."

"I can't see."

"You're tired. You need some rest."

"A good home . . . you promised to find Daniel a good home."

"You can count on me."

"Yes . . . yes . . ." Fidora's voice faded so low Judith couldn't hear.

"What did you say? Fidora?" Judith laid her ear on the woman's lips.

"It is worth it, isn't it?"

"Yes it is, honey. Now you just close your eyes and rest."

"Tell . . . tell . . ." Fidora struggled to say more.

Once again Judith put her ear on the woman's parched lips and heard, "Tell Turner . . . don't worry, all is forgiven."

Judith stood straight up again.

Willie Jane sobbed as Doctor Jacobs searched for a pulse, then closed Fidora's eyes.

Judith wanted to sneak out before daylight, but the bed felt so good. Fortunately, the judge had gotten up early again. It took so long to get her clothes on, all those buttons. She could see the tops of the hills out her window, clearly shadowed against the pastel blues and pale pinks of the May morning sky.

It was chilly, but pleasant to her mood. As she hiked to Mr. Stanton's livery, the firm breeze hugged her — a welcome gift to encourage her outing into the desert. The hills to the west were half covered with scrubby trees, like a man's face when he's trying to grow a beard. The hills on the other side were clean-shaven.

Mr. Stanton had "a gentle roan" ready for her. Judith traded for a mare with fire in her eyes. She enjoyed the powerful feel of the galloping beast as she whipped their way out of Carson and to the river. Judith hardly saw the palette of light and dark greens of the trees and bushes of the city. She was intent on the barren land, the comfort of the empty, arid desert. Today it would be her friend. Today they shared a common trait.

A hawk circled, then a flock of geese soared overhead. In moments, the sun would rise over the Pine Nut Mountains. She must hurry on her errand. Next time she would wear her house dress. Next time she would wear more comfortable shoes. Next time . . .

She went as far down the river as she

could away from Duffy's place. To the west she heard a dog howl. She jumped off the mare and drank in the solitude, enjoying the smells of sage and greasewood, the rippling isolation of the river. A dozen geese flocked along the bank.

Judith knew the wilderness rewarded stillness. She had come out here at other times of crisis and enjoyed watching the moving things. But today she was absorbed with one thought.

Jesus, you've always been my rock in this weary land, my shelter in times of storm. But Lord, I've got to tell the judge this vile secret. How can he endure it? How can we face it? What a cruel fate that I should be the bearer of such news. And how and when are we to tell Roberta? Why did this have to happen to us? Why? Oh, why? Oh, why?

Judith Kingston, the queen of hearts of Carson City, fell in a heap to the harsh, unforgiving Nevada sands and cried until she felt she could cry no more.

The judge laid down his pen and tried to straighten his fingers. For a moment, they seemed permanently cramped. He stretched them one at a time with his left hand before they regained movement. He glanced at the notes on his desk, then rubbed his gray mustache and goatee.

I used to write a dozen pages before my hand would cramp. Now, I'm lucky to get two. Mr. Gabbs used to do all this kind of thing for me. Ah, Spafford Gabbs, the consummate employee, the perfect clerk. I miss his British ways and efficient service. I'm afraid I took him too much for granted. But, of course, he needed to move on to higher and better things. Yet, why didn't I try to keep him by offering a higher salary or better title or . . . or what? And now there is this matter of my new clerk. She is, if nothing else, preoccupied.

The new clerk popped her head inside his office door. "Miss Kingston to see you, Judge."

"You don't need to announce yourself, Roberta."

"It's the other Miss Kingston."

A curly-headed six-year-old, wearing a slightly soiled long dress, burst into the office. "Grandpa Judge!" She leaped into his lap and planted a sloppy kiss on his cheek.

He hugged the girl and rocked back in the chair.

At 6'2", the young man who walked in behind the girl was as tall as his father. They shared the same high forehead, large ears, and rustic, frontier good looks. But the young man was clean-shaven. And he had his mother's piercing, dancing, fiery round eyes.

"David, what brings you and the princess downtown?"

"I need to make arrangements for Fidora's funeral."

"Will the county cover the costs? I'll be happy to help."

David pulled over a leather chair. "Actually, Fidora had it all taken care of. When Willie Jane cleaned out her place, she found a letter addressed to Charles Kitzmeyer, to be given to him in the event of her death."

"Funeral instructions?"

"And money to cover the expenses. She was quite thorough."

The judge held his bouncing grand-daughter. "To look at her, I wouldn't think she could plan her own birthday party."

"On my next birthday, I want a pony with black spots on his rump," Alicia announced.

"That can be arranged —" the judge began.

"Dad, we might not even be here," David cautioned.

The judge lifted Alicia and set her feet on the floor. She ran and dove onto the short leather sofa on the far side of the room. "Your daddy's right, honey," Judge said. "I'll buy you a pony for your birthday only if you are still living here in Carson City."

"Can we stay in Carson forever, Daddy? Please!" Alicia pleaded.

David's smile dropped. "That's bribery, Dad!"

"A grandfather spoiling his granddaughter is not a crime in the state of Nevada."

"Yes, your honor," David said with a laugh.

"Alicia, your daddy is right. We'll let the Lord decide. If it is the Lord's will for you to remain here, then you'll get your horse. If not, I know He'll have something even better for you."

"That sounds like one of daddy's shermans," the girl replied.

"Dad, did mother tell you about my needing to go to San Francisco at the end of the week for a couple days?"

"No, I don't remember that."

"I've got to talk to some folks who have a mission work in China. They might allow me to go there and take the children."

"China? I thought you wanted to go back to India."

"I do, but if that door is closed at the moment, I thought China might be a good alternative. Also, it borders India. It might provide an opportunity to get back there."

"But China . . . it's so . . . so . . ."

"Unreached? That's the point, I believe."

"But it's not even a British protectorate. What if something goes wrong? You've got the children to consider."

"I'll have to trust the Lord about that."

"Yes . . . but . . ."

"And so will you and Mother. I'm a missionary. That's what the Lord has assigned me to do. And he called Patricia, too. She gave her life for that calling. Am I to just give up, turn back, forget about the needs of the unsaved?"

The judge got up and put his arm around his son's shoulder. He was surprised how broad and strong it felt. "It's just difficult, David. Three years ago I put my arms around Patricia before you left for India. I never got to see her again. Next time, will it be you? Or Timothy? Or my little princess?"

"Dad . . ."

The judge took a deep breath. "We would be delighted to keep the children while you go to San Francisco."

"Thanks, Dad. Come on, Alicia, we have to walk home."

"I'm staying with Grandpa Judge."

"No you aren't. Grandpa has judging to do. Let's go home."

"Can Aunt Roberta come with us?"

"No, she has clerking to do."

"Well, I'm glad you don't have anything to do, Daddy."

A half-hour later, Roberta stuck her head in the door again. "Judge, Mr. Philip Campos is here."

The slightly balding man with red sideburns strolled in, wearing a charcoal gray silk suit with a pearl stickpin in his black four-in-hand tie. He held a gray top hat in his hand. His speech was precise and clipped. "Judge, did you want to see me?"

The judge reached over to shake the bank manager's hand. "I just stopped by for a visit this morning and didn't catch you in. I certainly didn't expect you to hike up here."

"It gave me an opportunity to stretch my legs. Besides, I've never been to your office before." His eyes scanned the volumes on the shelves against the walls. "I see, as I would expect, that you have an impressive library. I'm a voracious reader myself."

"I wanted to congratulate you," the judge said, "for your official acceptance as the new bank manager."

"Thank you, Judge. It was real good to be able to remove that interim label."

"You might be the youngest bank manager in Carson City history."

"I suppose so. Frankly, I hadn't even considered the possibility until . . . uh . . . after what happened to Mr. Tjader. And then I didn't want to seek a promotion based on another man's tragedy. It didn't seem right."

Like most of the citizens of Carson, Philip Campos came from somewhere else. The judge couldn't recall just where, though the slight accent sounded Eastern. He remembered Mr. Campos was a new father. Judith had given his wife a baby shower. Twins, they had, but one of them didn't survive.

"Someone had to take over as manager," the judge said. "Refusing the position wouldn't have helped Sam much."

"Quite right. And we're all much relieved that Manitoba Joe Clark is safely on his way to the gallows. Now, Judge, what can I do for you?"

"I'm reviewing a case and was unclear on bank procedure. I know that not all banks operate the same way, but I thought I might get a little guidance from you. What are your official bank hours?"

"Eight to four, Monday through Thursday. On Friday we are open until 8:00 p.m. On Saturdays, we close at 1:00."

The judge nodded. "Now, I know that Mr. Cheney, the grocer, and others come by

78

after hours, but you still open up to help them. Is that right?"

"Oh, yes. We have some major customers to whom we provide this extra service."

"How about before eight o'clock in the morning?"

"If someone were to let us know they would be coming by . . . say, someone with a large business, we would open up earlier if we were able."

"Does this happen much in most banks?"

"I don't know about other banks, Judge, but we do it all the time."

"Oh?"

Campos leaned over the judge's desk, then glanced back toward the half-open door. "You'd be surprised at the number of girls from the red-light district who keep their money in our bank. They know that if they keep their money at their place, some drunk will try to steal it from them."

"I suppose so."

"It's true, Judge. I'm not saying much for their moral character, but some of them are very shrewd with their money and have asked me to invest it for them."

"And they come to the bank during these early hours?"

"It's quitting time for them. And our regular customers would pitch a fit if we let the

79

girls line up with them, especially all dressed in their working clothes. We just thought it would be more discreet to take care of their banking privately."

"We?"

"Mr. Tjader is the one who started that little deal. But he didn't want to have to come to work early every day, so we traded back and forth. One of us would be there most every morning at 7:30 a.m."

"I see. I trust you have someone to trade off with now."

"Not yet. Frankly, Judge, I don't know which employees to trust like that. You see, unlike other transactions, this business takes place with no one else around to verify it. I'll have to wait until I can determine who has established that kind of confidence."

"Mr. Campos, you've been most helpful. I had no idea of the work that goes on in a bank other than what I normally see out front at the teller's cage."

"You're right about that, Judge. There's a lot that no one ever knows about." Philip Campos slid his hat on to go. "By the way, was that Mrs. Kingston racing out of town early this morning on a mare? I was quite impressed with her riding."

The judge strolled to the door with the banker. "Judith's jaunts around Carson are legendary," he said with a laugh. "But no one has ever accused her of early morning gallops. On the other hand, my present clerk has a penchant for recklessness."

Roberta strolled into the office a few minutes after Mr. Campos left. "Judge, I have these notes transcribed."

"Thanks, honey . . . I mean, Miss Kingston. Just leave them on the corner of my desk. Say, did you go on an early morning horse ride?"

"Good heavens, no. Why do you ask?"

"Mr. Campos thought he saw you galloping out toward the mill."

"It wasn't me, but it's nice to know the whole town is watching and waiting to bring you a report."

"Roberta, that's not what I meant."

"I'm teasing you, Daddy. I came to work early, you know that. I wanted to get this work done."

"I'm surprised you could finish all the transcriptions so soon."

She gave him a droll look. "I do understand legal terms, you know."

"I know. Have you decided to tackle law school?"

"No, I'm afraid it would be a little boring for me. Nothing personal, Daddy. Being a judge must be very rewarding, but a woman is not going to be a judge in this country, not in my lifetime anyway."

"Did you finish all the papers? This stack seems a little short."

"Yes, I finished. I cleaned them up a bit."

He groaned. "You did what?"

"Daddy, relax. I tightened up your sentence structure and deleted redundancies."

"But these are court notes," he sputtered, "not English class essays!"

"Now, Daddy, all of us could use a little editing now and then. Even David's 'shermans' could be tightened. Can I slip down to the hardware? I want to see if my peacock-colored paint came in."

The judge waved his hand. "Certainly. Go right ahead."

He waited until he heard the outer door close, then walked out to the front office. He knelt beside the wicker trash basket and retrieved page after page of wadded-up notes.

Peacock-colored paint? What in heaven's name is peacock-colored paint?

Chapter Three

Roberta's cream-colored silk robe was buttoned only at the collar as she swooped into the kitchen. It flagged out like a cape over her floor-length flannel nightgown.

"Daddy, I thought you'd be at work by now."

The judge glanced up from a stack of notes. "Good morning, darling. I've been working in my office here at home since 1:30 a.m. this morning."

She tore the crust off a piece of toasted rye bread. "On the Ormsby County vs. Tahoe Timber Company case?"

"No, I'll have to tackle that later today. This is a review of a previous case. There was something troubling about it, and I wanted to analyze the trial transcripts."

"Which case?"

"Manitoba Joe Clark's."

"I thought that was about the simplest case you had all year."

"Yes, that's what troubles me."

Roberta put down the toast and nibbled on the thin strip of crust. "Where's Mamma and Marthellen?"

"They toted some breakfast across the street."

"Daddy, it wouldn't hurt David to cook for his own children. In fact, I've heard him offer to many times."

"I know, but David has to get them both ready for school, and your mamma, well, she thinks having a good hot breakfast helps them learn better."

"If he moves them back to India, he won't have Mamma and Marthellen to cook for them."

"I think that's her point, darling. Your mamma is going to spoil him until the day he dies, just like she's going to spoil you. And just like she's going to spoil me. There's nothing we can do about that. She doesn't know any other way."

"I already told her she may not bring me breakfast after I move into my own place."

The judge grinned and took a sip of coffee. "Did you mention to her anything about lunch and supper?"

"No, Turner's hoping we'll have supper over here every night."

"We would enjoy that, of course. Did you get your room painted peacock blue?" he asked.

"Not yet. I've been helping Turner set up the office at the mill. Representatives of Senator George Hearst's will be here on Monday to inspect everything before they open it up. Turner is real nervous. His whole life is bound up in this venture. It's one thing to spend other people's money during a renovation. But now it's time to stoke the steam engines and turn on the machines."

"Has he got customers lined up?"

"He wants to just run some of Mr. Hearst's material from the Ophir up in Virginia City for a couple weeks to make sure everything is working. He says the customers won't commit until they see some results."

"It's a highly competitive business."

"Yes, but once Turner gets established, we're hoping he won't have such long days. A boss can choose his own hours." Roberta whirled over to the stove and poured herself a cup of coffee and added cream and sugar. "That's the good thing about being an attorney or judge. You don't have to put in such long hours."

The judge pulled off his reading spectacles and rubbed the corners of his eyes and edges of his forehead. He stared down at the stack of notes. *Starting at 1:30 a.m. doesn't constitute long hours?*

The back door swung open and a nine-year-old dressed in ducking britches, braces, and a smudged white cotton shirt tramped his dusty boots into the kitchen. "Grandpa Judge, come quick!" Timothy hollered.

"What is it?" the judge said, rising to his feet.

"Daddy needs help rescuing a damsel in distress. Hi, Aunt Roberta, do you have any bearclaws?"

"Not today. What did you say about David?"

"He's trying to get a lady off the church roof."

Roberta scurried to the back door while the judge slipped on his suit coat. "You aren't playing some sort of make-believe game, are you?" the judge inquired.

"No, really, Grandpa Judge. Douglas' mother is on the church roof and can't get down!"

Roberta stood out on the porch, surveying the scene. "I think Timothy's right, Daddy. Look!"

The morning desert air was chilly. Across the street, Judith and Marthellen held the base of a wobbly, homemade twenty-foot wooden ladder as a young man in duckings and plaid flannel shirt ascended toward a woman who straddled the peak of the steep church roof.

The judge took Timothy's sticky hand in his and jogged across the street.

"Can I climb the ladder?" Timothy pleaded.

"Absolutely not."

"In India, I climbed a rope ladder clear up to the outhouse."

I trust he has a few of the facts confused in that sentence. "This isn't India, Timothy," the judge replied as they dashed toward Judith.

"Grandpa Judge!" Alicia called from the front step of the parsonage. "Isn't this exciting? Daddy's climbing Jacob's ladder."

"Hello, darling." The judge released his grandson's hand. "Go over and sit with your sister," he ordered.

"But, Grandpa, I want to scale the tower and help save the princess from the band of thugs."

The judge squatted down next to the boy. "Listen, this could just be a diversion. What if they secretly wanted to kidnap Alicia, and with all of our attention over here they could snatch her? You'd better sit over there and guard your sister."

"Don't be silly, Grandpa, nobody would want to kidnap Alicia."

"Go over and sit on the step so you don't get your school clothes dirty," the judge ordered.

He joined the ladies at the foot of the ladder. When he grabbed the rungs, they stepped back, each shading their eyes with their hands as they stared up at the steep roof. "How in blazes did she get up there?" the judge asked.

"Barbara wanted to write a poem about the sunrise over Carson City. She decided the best place for inducing that creativity was by sitting on top of the church," Judith said.

"The woman doesn't have a brain in her head!"

"The world is hungry for inspiration . . . besides, the artistic mind is sometimes difficult to understand."

"So is lunacy," he muttered. "How on earth did she get up there?"

"Through the bell tower," Marthellen said. "My, that certainly looks tall from down here, doesn't it?"

"The bell tower is locked," the judge noted.

Judith shrugged. "That seems to be easily circumvented."

"Why can't she come down the same way?"

"David said he removed all the steps on the ladder above the bell. It seems a certain judge's grandson was fond of sneaking up there."

"Well, if the steps were removed, how did she get from the bell to the roof?"

"That's an intriguing question we're all anxious to ask," Marthellen said.

"Barbara Day has the tenacity of a faithful pilgrim traveling at all costs to a sacred shrine," Judith commented.

The judge stared up at his son, now perched just under the peak of the church roof. "But what does she stand for exactly?" he murmured.

Judith squinted up at her son. "All I want to know is how David is going to get her down from there."

"Hey, is this a private prayer meeting or can anyone join in?" Tray Weston said. He and Willie Jane Farnsworth climbed out of Chug Conly's hack at the curb.

"Need some help?" Conly shouted.

"Could you just wait a minute, Chug? We just might," the judge replied.

Tray stared up at the attempted rescue

while Judith and Marthellen took Willie Jane in tow and all three ladies walked out into the church yard.

Tray assisted the judge at the foot of the ladder. "Are they goin' up or comin' down?" he asked.

"We hope they are both coming down, however slowly," the judge replied.

"I reckon some ladies will go to extreme heights to attract attention," Tray drawled, then whistled as he stared straight up the ladder. "Now, there's a sight you don't see ever' day."

Barbara Day was flopped over David's shoulder like a grain sack. Her petticoats and bloomers were exposed to all below. When the judge turned his head away, he caught sight of Roberta still standing on the porch across the street, now joined by Turner Bowman.

"Tray Weston, you put your head down and wipe that smile off your face," Willie Jane shouted.

Tray bowed his head and looked at his dusty brown boot tops. "I don't reckon there's any graceful way to tote a lady down," he mumbled.

While David Kingston and his passenger descended one careful step at a time, the judge could hear Barbara Day humming a tune that sounded a lot like "Rock of Ages."

He braced his son's legs for the final steps. David quickly set Barbara on her feet to the sound of cheers and applause. Several carriages had stopped to watch the rescue. Out of one of the carriages waltzed Daisie Belle Emory, wearing a red hat, a red scarf, red lace gloves and red lipstick.

"What excitement so early in the morning," she gushed. "I just had to stop and see what was happening, although I'm in a hurry to meet with some senators' wives." She looked at the aproned Judith. "I thought you'd be going too, my dear."

At that moment, Barbara Day threw her arms around David's neck and attempted to kiss him. He spun his head to the side and she pecked him on the cheek instead.

"Barbara," David said, "you are safe on the ground. You can turn loose now."

She twirled around toward the crowd. "I suppose you all think me quite foolish."

"Barbara, you don't need to apologize," Daisie Belle called out. "We all do whatever it takes."

"I didn't get stuck up there on purpose," Barbara countered. "I was trying to capture a poetic moment."

"Aren't we all?" Daisie Belle retorted. "I'll give you a lift to Duffy's, if you like, and you can tell me all about it."

Daisie Belle and Barbara Day rode off as David Kingston rubbed the muscles in his shoulder. Even though the morning was cool, sweat dribbled off his face.

"Nice work, son," the judge said. "Where did you learn to carry someone down a ladder like that?"

"In Calcutta. There was a six-block fire. Hundreds and hundreds of people, mostly women and children, died. I had to learn in a hurry."

"Where'd that ladder come from? I didn't even know the church owned one."

"It belongs to Dr. Jacobs. He built it last summer when he painted his house. We needed it to clean some bats out of the back of the church."

"It's a good thing it was still here." The judge glanced over at his granddaughter, still sitting on the step. *Is that what she meant by climbing Jacob's ladder?*

Alicia waved. "Hi, Grandpa Judge. I'm all ready for school. Marjorie Walters wanted me to wear this dress today. Do you like it?"

"Of course I do. Where's your brother, princess?"

"I think he's charging at six-hundred leads," she called back. "I forget how it goes. May I please come and see you now?"

"Come on, darling."

She was in his arms before he finished the sentence.

"That was quite a feat, David," Judith said. "I marvel at your strength."

"I suppose we're strong enough to do those things we must do," he replied, a tinge of red on his cheeks.

"I certainly trust that is not something you must do again," she replied.

"I couldn't agree with you more, Mother. Barbara Day is a very talented but, shall we say, eccentric woman."

When Judith stared into her son's eyes, it was like looking in a mirror. *Just how acquainted are you with her talents, David?*

"Now, ladies," David said, "I believe our breakfast is getting cold on the kitchen table. And two youngsters need to get to school."

"Would you like me to warm it up?" Marthellen asked.

"No, I believe we've taken enough of your morning. Alicia, let Grandpa Judge go. We've disturbed the whole family plenty for one day."

The judge set the six-year-old down on the churchyard grass.

"Grandpa Judge, will you play horsey with me tonight?" she asked.

"Yes, but it's my turn to be the cowboy. You have to be the horse."

"Grandpa!" She looked up at Judith. "He is so silly sometimes."

David took her hand and led her back toward the parsonage. "Where's your brother?" he asked.

Judith spoke up. "He ran into the back yard yelling, 'Half a league, half a league, half a league onward, all in the valley of "debt" rode the six hundred,' " Judith reported as she led her troop back across the street.

"The valley of debt?" The judge chuckled, then sobered as he thought of Turner and Roberta. "With the decline in the mines, that might soon describe the entire Eagle Valley."

"Judge," Tray said, "me and Willie Jane need to talk to you and Judith about a private matter. Have you got a minute?"

"Certainly, let's step over to my office."

When they reached the side door, Roberta, still clad in her silk robe, paced inside the kitchen.

"I noticed Turner stopped by . . ." the judge began.

"Something drastic has happened and I need to talk to you and Mamma right now," Roberta declared.

"I was just going to visit with Willie Jane and Tray. Maybe —"

"Daddy, Turner brought absolutely crushing news. I have to talk to you right now." Roberta sniffed back tears, then sprinted to the stairway.

Judith's hands went to her cheeks. *Oh no! Turner's told her about Fidora's baby . . . oh, poor thing . . .* She trailed after Roberta.

"Judge, we can come back if this ain't a good time," Tray offered.

"Why don't you go in and have a cup of coffee with Marthellen? We'll be down in a minute or two," the judge suggested.

"I think we'll come back this evening," Willie Jane said. "Mr. Cheney is expecting me to open up the store this morning."

The judge took the stairs two at a time and followed the wails to Roberta's room. His daughter had pulled down a large dark green carpetbag and was yanking clothes out of her dresser drawer. Judith sat on the edge of the bed.

"What's this all about?" he asked.

"Daddy, it's horrible. Turner received a telegram this morning from that traitor, Wilton Longbake, who is in Sacramento right now. He says that he and George Hearst have decided to sell the reduction mill. He told Turner to pay the men off, padlock the buildings, and wait for further instructions."

"They spent $125,000 on this investment and now they're going to sell it before it operates one day?" the judge fumed.

"Apparently."

"But what are you doing?" Judith asked, as clothing scattered around them.

"Turner is catching the next train to Sacramento to confront Wilt Longbake. I need to go with him."

"Do you think that is wise?" Judith said as she stood up and gently touched her distraught daughter's arm.

"I have to, Mamma. Turner is convinced that Longbake never intended for the mill to open. He was just stringing Turner along in order to get even with me."

"It could have been a coincidence — purely a business decision that happened in spite of you," Judith suggested as calmly as she could.

"That's what I want to find out."

"Perhaps this is something Turner must handle on his own, dear."

"Mamma, have you ever seen Turner Bowman tote a revolver?"

"I can't say that I have."

"Well, he's wearing one today."

"Oh, dear." Judith looked over at the

judge with a pleading look.

"I have to go," Roberta said. "Can you help me pack?"

The judge paced his daughter's room. He couldn't help but think of more peaceful days when their grown daughter was a little princess, like Alicia. Back then they could protect her and forbid her. "But you can't travel with Turner alone," the judge finally said.

"I'll go with you," Judith offered.

"Mother, this is not a role for Judith or the judge. Turner and I must work this through ourselves. I feel a responsibility in this too. If it weren't for me, Turner would have his mill and Wilt Longbake wouldn't hate me so. He deceived and double-crossed us. Anyway, that's the way it seems. Either something suddenly caused him to change his mind or he intended to betray us all along. I wish I had never met that man and I earnestly pray that my dear friend, Peachy, sees the light before it's too late."

"David's going through Sacramento later in the week," Judith said, "perhaps he could . . ."

Roberta threw down a straw hat on the bed. "We have to go right now. When I get there I will, of course, stay in one hotel room, Turner in another. You can trust me, Mother."

"Marthellen will go with you," the judge announced. "She can visit her daughter, Charlotte, and her grandchild. She's been missing them very much."

"I can get along without a traveling chaperone, Daddy."

"I'm sure you can. However, it would bring great comfort to your mother and me if you allowed Marthellen to accompany you."

Roberta stopped her frantic packing and the judge encircled her with his long arms. "Please?"

"Okay, Daddy." She laid her head on his chest. "Why did this have to happen? Turner has worked so hard and I love him so much. I thought everything was going to be wonderful when the mill got completed. Now it's a disaster."

"Maybe it's part of the Lord's bigger plan, darling," the judge said.

And perhaps things would not have been as wonderful as you imagined, Judith reflected as she recalled Fidora's chilling words.

That afternoon, charcoal splotches lined the heavy gray clouds sailing across the Nevada sky. If the Pine Nut Range to the east had any height, a storm would have stacked up in Eagle Valley. Instead, the clouds briefly blocked the sun, then tumbled toward Utah.

Judith and the judge walked east on Caroline Street, arm in arm.

"Do we have any idea what we're doing?" Judith asked.

"Certainly. We just put our daughter, her fiancé, and our housekeeper and cook on a train to Sacramento."

"That's not what I meant. I wish we had gotten a chance to talk to Turner privately before they left. I was hoping to get a critical matter settled before he and Roberta —" Judith stopped a moment, then said, "For five days I've had those words eating away at me: 'Tell Turner all is forgiven.' " Judith slipped her fingers into his. "I have to tell him. I promised Fidora I would. I should have done it before now, but I thought it should be done in private. I've had no chance all week. I've hardly seen Turner. And all this came about so quickly. I came close to blurting it out to Roberta today, to cause her to slow down, to think this through . . ."

"You certainly couldn't do it at the funeral," the judge said. "I was startled that he came. It was awkward and I sensed his embarrassment too. Most of those attending were from the crib district."

"Mr. Campos from the bank was there. Maybe Fidora was one of those he was telling you about that had an account with him," Judith said.

They walked a block in silence, lost in their separate thoughts. "If Turner is the father," Judith finally said, feeling the pain of the words, "then the 'event' happened last September. That's when Roberta broke up with him and went back to college, and Consolidated Milling began cutting everyone's wages. It was not the most stable time in Turner's life."

"That's no excuse," the judge said. "Everyone sins, but a man has to take responsibility for his sin. If Turner is the father of that child, even though the mother was a soiled dove, the honorable thing would have been to marry Fidora and make the best of it. Adding to the sin was to abandon her and the infant."

Judith shuddered, thinking of what hearing Fidora's deathbed words would mean to Roberta. "There might be some other explanation for Fidora's words," she said.

"That possibility is the only thing that has kept me from punching that renegade young man in the nose."

"Judge!"

"I didn't really mean that, but you know how it upsets me. When a man absconds from his God-ordained duty, by either abusing or abandoning the women in his life, it brings out my anger quicker than anything else. And it upsets me to have my daughter be a victim of this sordid tale. First she was mistreated by Wilt Longbake and now, Turner Bowman."

"Judge, from the time that girl was born, you have known there would never be anyone good enough for her."

"My word, Judith, I'm not looking for perfection, just an honorable man with a great love for her."

"Until five days ago, we both thought Turner was that man. Maybe we should allow him to remain innocent in our minds until proven guilty."

"My mind heartily and completely agrees with that. It's my heart that won't quite draw in its horns," the judge confessed. "Now, let's hurry. Judge and Mrs. Kingston have an appointment at Marshall's Gallery."

Judge Hollis A. Kingston was rocking on his hands and knees in the living room when Tray Weston and Willie Jane Farnsworth eased through the back door.

The judge's tie and suit coat were tossed on a chair. His vest was unbuttoned.

A six-year-old princess straddled his back while her father and grandmother cheered from the sidelines.

Alicia's judicial steed plodded across the carpet, then bucked her into the sofa, to the squeals of delight from the young rider. "You know what?" she cried. "Marjorie Walters doesn't have a Grandpa Judge to ride on."

"Maybe you ought to spur him more, Miss Alicia," Tray teased.

The judge stood up and brushed off his knees and groaned. "Don't encourage her."

"One more ride, Grandpa Judge, one more ride!"

"We can wait," Willie Jane said.

"Oh no, you don't. You are divine providence come to rescue me."

"We have to go home now, anyway," David Kingston said. "There are youngsters who need baths tonight."

Willie Jane looked around. "Where's Timothy?"

"Last I saw of him, he was out in the alley with a box, stick, string, and fish head, determined to trap a tiger," Judith said.

"That big-game hunter will need his rain

gear," Tray informed them. "It's startin' to rain buffalo buckets out there."

"Tell Grandma and Grandpa goodnight, young lady," David instructed.

With chubby little fingers on their cheeks, Alicia gave Grandpa Judge, then Grandma Judith kisses on the lips.

Then she and David went out the side door.

"I'm sorry for the confusion of this day," the judge began as Judith offered their guests a seat.

"Judith explained it all to us . . . about the harried trip to Sacramento," Willie Jane said, as she and Tray settled onto the brown leather settee.

Judith sat on the edge of the green sofa. The judge took the stuffed leather chair by the hearth. "Have you decided to take those wedding vows?" he blurted out.

Willie Jane glanced over at a blushing Tray.

"Oh, my!" Judith clapped her hands. "The judge guessed it, didn't he?"

Willie Jane nodded. "Yes, but that's not all. I want to . . ." She stopped to swallow once. "Adopt Fidora's little Daniel." Willie Jane nervously fiddled with one of the tiny abalone shell buttons on the front of her beige dress.

"You mean, you both want to adopt him, right?" Judith said.

"Yes, Tray's agreeable to it. That's why we want to get married now," Willie Jane added.

"That baby needs a mamma and a daddy," Tray said.

The judge studied the couple intently. There was a moment's silence.

"Judge, you haven't said nothin'," Willie Jane said. "I know you might be thinkin' of the likes of the Mercedes Barega situation, but I ain't like her."

"Who's that?" Tray asked.

"Mercedes was a keeper of the cribs and was arrested a couple years ago for brutally mistreating a little Spanish boy named Juan, for whom she was a guardian," the judge said.

"I ain't that way, Judge. The Lord's changed me. Hasn't He, Judith?"

"Yes, He has," Judith said. "And I don't think you were that way even before He came into your life."

"I want to do right by Daniel," Willie Jane insisted. "Judge, you married me and Bence right here in your house just before he died. You figure you could marry me and Tray tonight?"

"Oh, my, not that quickly," Judith gasped.

"Willie Jane, that was a unique situation when Bence lay dying. But for you and Tray, we must organize a real wedding with a nice reception and everything."

"Would you help me plan it then?"

"Of course I will, but you can't get married with Marthellen off in Sacramento. She would be devastated. She thinks of you as one of her own daughters."

"You're right, Judith. I was just thinkin' of the baby. We could get the baby, couldn't we, Judge?"

The judge stood up, grabbed his black tie, and began to fasten it around his neck. "Let me spell out the procedure. Right now the infant is under the care of the court."

"That's you, right?" Willie Jane asked.

"In a legal sense. As you know, Doc Jacobs placed little Daniel with Mrs. Philip Campos. Since she lost one of her twins at birth, she certainly has the ability to nurse two babies."

Willie Jane fidgeted with an amethyst ring on her finger. "But that's only temporary, isn't it?"

"That's correct. The doctor is notifying the only known family member, an uncle who was last heard of living in Willow Bluff Texas."

"But he was the one that used to beat

Fidora," Willie Jane said.

"By law, we must contact the family. If the family declines to come forward to petition for the child, little Daniel becomes a ward of the state of Nevada."

"And you can approve him to be adopted by us," Tray concluded.

"I can approve his adoption or I can assign him to the children's asylum."

Willie Jane stopped fiddling with her ring. "But you would assign him to us, right, judge?"

"You two know how fond Judith and I are of both of you. So, there's no question what I'd want to do. But let me speak to you as a judge, not a close friend. You will need to be married. The family, if there be any, will have to refuse to petition for the child, and then any who wanted to adopt the child could file with my court and I would have the task of selecting from the applicants."

"I don't think anyone else would want to adopt Fidora's baby," Willie Jane said.

Judith noticed Willie Jane's tightly clutched fingers. The knuckles had turned white. "Willie Jane," she said, "it could be that Mrs. Campos would want to adopt him."

"A banker's wife adoptin' a crib girl's

baby? I don't see it. Besides, they already have the baby girl."

"I'm just saying that nursing a little one brings with it a certain attachment. Plus, Mrs. Campos lost her little boy during childbirth. She's liable to be emotionally drawn that way. Mrs. Campos didn't worry about the social stigma when she agreed to nurse him."

Willie Jane burst into tears. "But that ain't fair. If I could, I would have been the one nursin' him. Doc Jacobs even said we could use one of them glass nursing bottles with the glass tube through the cork and a rubber hose to the nipple. He said as long as we kept it boiled up clean ever' day it was almost as good as the real thing."

The judge rubbed his goatee and chin as if it would disperse the blush in his cheeks, then cleared his throat. "I'm not sure that will be how the case turns out. But we've got to let you know all the possibilities."

"But you'd rule in our favor, right, judge?" Tray said.

"As it stands, right at the moment, I would definitely want you and Willie Jane to raise little Daniel. And for that reason, because we are such good friends, if there were more than one applicant for the adoption, I might have to disqualify myself and let the

2nd District Judge rule on this."

Willie Jane's eyes grew big. "You would?"

"The judge wouldn't have any choice," Judith explained.

"Are you saying that we could get married and everything and then not be able to adopt the baby?" Tray said.

The judge nodded. "That's a possibility you must consider."

"Well, I don't care. I want to marry Willie Jane anyway. I love her, and you both know it."

"I trust Willie Jane knows it too," Judith said.

"I know it," Willie Jane whispered.

Judith lifted her eyebrows. "Well?" she prodded.

"It's just that . . ." Willie Jane looked straight at Judith. "Well, bein' married to a dyin' man for one hour is one thing; bein' married to a live man for the rest of my life is somethin' else!"

Judith laughed. "Oh, it is somethin' else, all right. What you need to decide is, do you want to marry Tray and spend your life with him whether or not you get to raise little Daniel?"

"I can't imagine my life without him. He has grown on me like crazy."

"Daniel?" Tray said with a gulp.

"No, you big dolt. You're the one I can't live without."

Tray's grin looked like a half-moon turned sideways.

"Does that mean we get to make wedding plans?" Judith asked.

Willie Jane nodded. "I reckon it does."

"Wonderful!" Judith jumped to her feet. "Oh, my, we'll need Daisie Belle's help," she added.

"Do you think she would?" Willie Jane asked.

"I think she will feel personally insulted if you don't ask her."

"Me? I thought you would ask her."

"We'll do it together."

"Tonight?"

"Eh, no, I think we'd better wait until to-morrow. She will have her makeup off by now, and Daisie Belle Emory will see no one, and I do mean no one, without her makeup."

Big black clouds rolled in from the north, loaded with hail and rain. Judge Kingston held onto his hat and bent forward into the fierce wind as he headed for the jail.

Manitoba Joe Clark remained seated on his bunk when the judge came down the hallway and stood by his cell. The outlaw's round, no-neck head rested on his hands, his elbows dug into his knees. The judge noticed the width of the man's legs, as huge as tree stumps. But Manitoba Joe did not at all look defiant.

"I ain't been screamin' and hollerin', Judge," he said.

"I am sure everyone appreciates it."

"They're movin' me to the state prison tonight. I ain't got a chance once they move me out there. You ain't even goin' to come see me once I leave town. Nobody will listen to me. I'll be forgot and hung and nobody cares."

"Joe, if I can promote justice, I'll help you, no matter where you are. But I'm still searching for something solid to hold on to. Your attorney, Mr. Musterman, refuses to talk to me, even though I said I was trying to help you. There is no legal way I can make him tell me who paid his fee."

Manitoba Joe raised his head slightly. "Bring him here. I'll get him to talk!"

"Go over it with me again, Joe. Tell me about that day," the judge coaxed. "There's got to be something we've missed."

"I told you ever'thing. There's nothin' left to say."

"Tell me again. If you didn't do it, there's got to be a way of hitting on who did. You're the only other witness."

"What do you want to know?" Joe said dully.

"What time was it when you followed Sam Tjader into the bank?"

"Seven forty-five."

"Are you sure it wasn't closer to 7:30? Mr. Tjader went in early some mornings for special customers."

"Nope, it was seven forty-five. I was watchin' the bank pretty close. I told myself if he didn't show by 7:50 I wouldn't rob the bank that day."

"Why is that?"

"Judge, one of my rules is that I do my robbin' before the citizens of the town start showin' up. That way, I don't take no chances on someone gettin' shot."

"Or some bystander plugging you in the back?"

"Yep, that too. Crowds is unpredictable. I ain't afraid of any man face to face. It's the shot in the back by a coward that chaws at me. 'Course, that's one thing about bein' hung. I won't have to worry none about bein' shot in the back anymore."

"Are you still certain there was no one in the bank when you busted in that morning, except Sam Tjader?"

"I told you that before."

"Well, I happen to know that sometimes Sam did early morning business through the back door. Was Sam in the back room when you entered?"

"Nope, he didn't have time to walk that far. I got the drop on him when he was by his desk."

"Did he glance toward the back room or make any movement in that direction?"

"Nope. Judge, I don't reckon there was anyone there. Why do you keep askin'?"

"It's very simple. If you didn't fire a second shot, someone did. Either someone was in the room, or Sam Tjader killed himself and then cleverly hid the weapon after he was dead."

Manitoba Joe's face was almost animated. "Maybe someone hid in the bank all night long and popped out after I left."

"That's beyond all reasonable doubt," the judge declared. "Remember, it was the jury's job to convict you beyond reasonable doubt. Why would anyone hide all night in the bank? If they wanted to rob it, they could have done it in the middle of the night. If they wanted to kill Sam, they could have done that on his way to work, then ridden up into the Sierras."

"I cain't explain it, Judge. I do know I looked all around, includin' in the direction of the back room, and I could see no one was there. If I had've, I would've got the drop on him too."

"Joe, it's very dark back in that room before a gas lamp is lit. If Sam Tjader hadn't had time to get back there, there couldn't have been a lamp lit as yet. Could it be that someone was lurking in the shadows of that back room?"

"No, sir. Look, Judge, I could've lied to you and said there was someone there. But I promised I'd tell you the truth. There was light from the alley comin' through the window. That's how come I knowed no one was back there."

"You could see what?" the judge asked.

"There was daylight beamin' through the window, Judge, that's all."

"Joe, there's no window in that back room at the bank."

"Sure there is. There's a window on the top of the door, and daylight was streamin' like heaven's rays and so was the wind. You remember the Chinook that day? I could feel the breeze. I noted to myself it didn't seem smart to have a window open in February."

"Joe, I'm telling you, there is a solid door there."

"Maybe they changed it now. It ain't

smart havin' a glass window on a bank door."

"Joe, I've walked down that alley behind the bank on my way to lunch at the Ormsby House every week for ten years. There has never been a window back there."

"Well, there was that day."

"Perhaps the whole back door was open?"

"Judge, I ain't blind, and I ain't makin' this up. There was a window in the top half of the door and there was no one back there. So, where does this put us?"

"Maybe your mind is playing tricks on you. You never mentioned this before. You destroy any credibility in your appeal if you state obvious falsehoods. I'm not saying this to make you mad, but there isn't any window on that door."

Manitoba Joe stared straight at Judge Kingston. "There isn't?"

"I'm sorry, Joe, there never has been."

Manitoba Joe's head fell again. His voice was gravelly and grave. "Then my mind is playin' tricks on me. It's all over. There's no hope."

"Joe, listen to me, you've been through many a bank robbery and many a gun battle. At some point, especially with hanging a certainty, you could start getting scenes confused."

He didn't look up. His head remained cradled in his hands.

"I'm sorry, Joe, I don't see how I can intervene in any way. The trial was fair. The jury was honest. The rules were followed. The verdict fit the crime. The witnesses told the truth."

"Ain't there nothin' you can do?"

"I can pray for your soul, Manitoba Joe Clark."

"I need all the prayers I can get."

"We all do, Joe."

"Is there any way you can come see me at the state prison?"

"I'll come out in a few days. It depends on my cases this week."

"I only got two weeks."

"I know."

"Well, thanks for listenin' to me, Judge. That's more than I thought I'd get."

"I have a strong desire for justice, Manitoba Joe. I'll have to take to my grave the weight of every innocent man I've mistakenly sentenced. I don't want to add you to that burden, if it can be helped."

Judge Kingston took the long way back to the office. The sky was still dark, but dry for the moment. The wind had dwindled to a wispy breeze. He swung around by the

Ormsby House and then slowly plodded down the alley behind the bank.

It was a twenty-foot-tall, two-story building. The second floor had 2×5-foot windows every six feet. The first floor was solid red brick except for an iron door, offset toward the north side of the building. The hinges were buried out of view from the alley. The door was as solid as a bank vault and reinforced with six-inch-wide plate-steel horizontal bands across the top, bottom, and straight through the middle.

The judge reached out for the cold, slippery brass doorknob. It didn't twist. When he pushed on it, it didn't budge. He turned and walked on down the alley.

If ever there was a door that doesn't have a window, it's that one. There's not even a keyhole. No one can get in that door. They can get out through the door, but no one can get in.

When he reached King Street, a familiar voice shouted from across the road. "Judge, wait up!"

Wearing a red flannel shirt and crisp, clean brown ducking britches, and carrying a tattered basket and rope-bound ragged suitcase, Duffy Day scurried between a freight wagon and a parked carriage.

"Did you see those lightnin' streaks, Judge? They plum scared me to death. But I didn't hide none. It's worse bein' inside than outside when the Almighty gets to thunderin'."

"Those new clothes make you look more handsome than ever," the judge said in greeting.

"They got a little wet, but I do believe you're right. Surely hope I don't cause no women to sin after me."

The judge cleared his throat and strolled west on King Street. "I'm sure that's something a young, eligible bachelor has to consider."

"I got my old ones in the suitcase, just in case I need to get comfortable real quick. Drake's wife, Barbara, helped me pick out the spankin' new ones."

"Looks like good choices to me."

"Yep, I peeked in through the window and nodded when she held up something I liked. And as soon as Douglas came home from school, we took him down and bought him some new clothes too. And that ain't all." He pulled out a round gadget similar to a watch. "I bought me one of these pedometers for a five-dollar bill. I hang it from the waistband of my pants inside and when I move my legs it causes this here machine to register a notch."

"What on earth for?"

"So's I can tell how much walkin' I do every day. It don't hurt for a man to know how much ground he covers."

"Did Barbara buy herself something too?"

"A new dress. I paid for it," Duffy asserted. "It's a head turner, it is. Jist the kind of dress Judith would wear."

The judge continued to stroll. *I don't believe Judith ever in her life wore a 'head turner.' Or has she? I suppose it depends on whose head is turning.* "What's in the basket, Duffy?"

"I got some pickled corn, stuffed olives, and a chili sauce from Cheney's. Barbara has taken a real likin' to eatin' like that. She says they eat that way in Indiana."

"Indiana?"

"Yep. Say, are you goin' home, Judge? Can I walk with you?"

"No, Duffy, I need to get back to the courthouse for a while."

"Then I think I'll stroll on over to show Judith my new duds. Did Marthellen bake any bearclaws this mornin'?"

"Marthellen's in Sacramento visiting her daughter."

"When is she comin' home?"

"I'm not too sure about that."

"A man kind of gets to missin' them bearclaws."

"Well, I'm sure Judith's cooked up something."

"I probably ain't that hungry."

"Is Douglas playing with Timothy?" the judge asked.

"Nope. I drove him and his mamma back out to our place. She didn't want him to get them new clothes dirty. And she needed to get back to her picture."

"Is she painting more landscapes?"

Duffy's pointed pink tongue rolled across his lips. "Eh, I reckon there is some land in it. She said it was Indiana."

"Did Barbara used to live in Indiana?"

"She ain't never been there before in her life. Your David's the one that's been there. That's where he buried his Patricia."

"Oh, India!" A wide smile played across the judge's face. "Is that what you meant?"

"That's what I been sayin', Judge. Maybe it's true that older folks lose their hearin' quick."

The judge scratched the back of his neck. "I suppose you're right. So, Barbara's doing a painting of India?"

"Yep, it's sort of in the background and then the big tall man is in the front."

"She's including a portrait?"

"Yep, and it's a good one, too. It looks jist like him."

"Just like who?"

"Why, your David, of course!"

Chapter Four

A small flash flood of a marshy lake had formed on the outskirts of town because of the downpour. Hundreds of birds littered the sky and trees and lawns. A light ground fog covered the landscaping at the Kingston house, but inside was a warm glow.

"And I thought it would be dreadfully boring until the Fourth of July pageant," Daisie Belle said. "Of course, there's always the possibility of Roberta and Turner, but we will need eight to ten months minimum to plan for that wedding. You did tell Roberta for me, Judith?"

The bright blue silk dress Daisie Belle wore was several years behind the style for New York, but she knew she could get away with it in Carson and refused to remove it from her wardrobe. She claimed the sound of the skirt's swish when she strutted across the room made her feel young again. Judith supposed it was the tease of the white lace bodice that made her hang on to it.

Whichever the case, as she waltzed into Judith's dining room with an armful of catalogs and sketches, Daisie Belle Emory demonstrated with each flounce that she was, indeed, still the queen of Carson City.

"I'm not sure anyone can tell Roberta what she should or shouldn't do about her wedding," Judith warned.

"Not even her mother?"

"Especially not her mother," Judith replied.

"Meanwhile, we shall pour all our energies into Willie Jane's wedding." Daisie Belle turned to the young woman and said, "Is that all right with you, dear?"

Willie Jane scooted up behind the two middle-aged ladies and scanned the catalogs now spread on the table. "I'm counting on you. But me and Tray don't need anything nobby. And with my background, I surely don't want to offend nobody."

"Your background?" Daisie Belle glanced at Judith. "Oh, you mean that you were a sinner before Jesus saved you? Weren't we all, my dear, weren't we all. Here's what I had in mind, but the decision is entirely yours, of course."

Daisie Belle pulled out a charcoal etching. "The wedding will take place on Saturday, June 4th, at 3:00 p.m. Is that satisfactory?"

"I think so," Willie Jane murmured. "I'm sure Mr. Cheney will give me the day off."

"Day off? John Cheney had better give you the week off. Judith will tell him about that," Daisie Belle announced. "That man has never turned down a request by Judith Kingston in his life."

Judith jotted down a note on the small pad she held in her hand. *Ask Mr. Cheney.*

Daisie Belle tapped a well-manicured finger on the papers scattered across the dining room table. "Now, the wedding will be held in my backyard, of course."

"Really? At your house?" Willie Jane gulped.

"Why, of course. I'll have Farmer Treadwell assist and we'll completely re-landscape everything. I believe I'll even install a pond and a small waterfall."

Judith glanced down at the charcoal sketch. *A waterfall? A person can build a waterfall? In Carson City, Nevada?*

"I thought we'd have more freedom and room there than in the church. And this isn't your first marriage, although it will seem like a first, since you were only married to Bence for an hour and never had an opportunity to consummate the nuptials."

"What do you mean? The judge was right there and made ever'thing legal." Wiillie Jane turned her head. "Didn't he, Judith?"

"Oh, it was quite legal," Judith said.

Daisie Belle patted Willie Jane's hand. "I thought perhaps pale rose pink and charcoal gray would be good colors for you. What do you think, Judith?"

"They would be very attractive, but that's up to Willie Jane to decide."

Both ladies turned to the future bride.

"Eh, yes, well, I reckon that would be nice. The gray would establish the formality, the rose pink would add a tease of frivolity. However, I refuse to wear white. I think a pearl or creme French silk would be much better. I have no intention of flauntin' my forgiveness from the Lord. And besides, the white should be preserved for those much purer than I, like Roberta.

"I thought, perhaps, the bridesmaids could wear three-quarter-length sleeves, with long black gloves. But then again, black gloves are out of style in the summer, except after dark, and you said you wanted the weddin' in the afternoon. I heard about a specialty shop in San Francisco that custom makes gloves. It's where Callie Truxell gets her lace ones, so perhaps if we put a rush on the order we could get them matchin' the charcoal gray." Willie Jane sucked in a deep breath and waited.

Daisie Belle stared at Judith, then back at Willie Jane, then down at her sketches. A wide, easy smile flowed across the natural beauty of her smooth face. "I must apologize for being so presumptuous. This young woman is obviously quite capable and competent to take care of her own preparations. I feel rather like a foolish, pushy old lady."

"Oh no, Daisie Belle," Willie Jane protested. "I really, really, want you to help me plan every detail."

"Oh, well . . ." Daisie Belle's blue eyes flashed, "in that case, let me explain how we will set up the chairs in the backyard. I am assuming from 150 to 200 guests." She pointed to the drawings. "Here is one idea. The grape arbor will go next to the waterfall right here beside the cavalcade of pink roses . . ."

Alicia yawned. "Grandpa Judge, can I sleep with you and Grandma Judith?"

"Princess, Aunt Roberta's bed is the most comfortable bed in the whole house."

"And you're the most comfortable Grandpa in the whole house!"

"Don't you try to butter me up, sweet-heart. You've got your face and teeth washed and your hair combed and prayers prayed. You need to go to sleep . . . in Aunt Roberta's bed."

"I miss my daddy," Alicia whimpered.

"He'll only be gone to San Francisco for a short while. He'll be home soon."

"I miss my mommy, too," she said, sniffling.

In the shadows of the darkened room, the judge wiped back the tears that stole down his cheeks. "I know it, punkin'. We all miss your mamma. She was one of the sweetest, kindest women on the face of the earth."

"She's with Jesus now."

The judge dabbed his eyes. "Yes, she is."

"Sometimes I wish I was with Jesus. Don't you, Grandpa Judge?"

He bent over and stroked her long, soft hair. "Yes, Alicia, I do. We'll all have our turn someday. Goodnight, princess." He brushed a kiss across her forehead, then walked quietly toward the door.

"Marjorie Walters has a mamma," Alicia said. "I love you, Grandpa!"

His breathing grew labored and the tears flowed freely now. He refused to turn back as he said, "I love you, Alicia."

He gently closed the oak bedroom door,

then pulled out a linen handkerchief from his pocket.

Judith slipped out of the adjoining bedroom. "Oh, my," she whispered. "I see she mentioned Patricia again."

The judge blew his nose. "I don't know how David can go through this every night. It must be crushing."

"I'm sure the Lord gives him the strength he needs."

Judith and the judge walked arm in arm down the stairway. "At least she didn't ask me tonight why her mamma had to die. I'm never more helpless than when she asks that."

"David is convinced the Lord wants to use Patricia's death to make him a more effective evangelist and missionary," Judith said.

"Well, he's much stronger than I am. I should be the one consoling him, and he consoles me. I didn't know it would still affect me so."

"You are a very sensitive person, Judge Kingston. And there probably aren't more than four people on earth who know that."

"Four?"

"David, Roberta, me, and Alicia."

"And Timothy?"

"Our Timothy is so absolutely thrilled with life, he hardly has time to notice others.

Do you have any idea what he has in bed with him tonight?"

"My word, he took something to bed?"

Even with her arm looped in his, she laced her fingers in front of her waist. "He has your old brass bunkhouse bell under his covers."

"A ten-pound brass bell?"

"He found it in the shed and snuck it into the house. It was under the covers, as if I wouldn't spot it."

"What is the purpose, pray tell?"

"He rambled something about summoning the troops at Ft. Laramie as soon as Crazy Horse crosses the river."

The judge rubbed his chin whiskers. "And what did you do with the bell?"

"I left it there and told him I was sure Crazy Horse wanted a good night's rest and that he couldn't ring it until after seven o'clock in the morning."

"Judith, why do you think he plays so many imaginary games?"

"I have come to the conclusion that it's the same reason you and I shed tears at the mention of Patricia. It's his way to deal with it. The real world can hurt."

They paused, still arm in arm, in the living room.

"Do we have a moment to sit and relax?" the judge asked.

128

"Not until I get the bearclaw batter fixed." Judith waved toward the kitchen. "I've had numerous requests."

"Who, besides Duffy Day?"

"Timothy, for one. I'm not sure they want my bearclaws, but they're hoping Marthellen's magic has left its mark. Come drink a cup of coffee and visit with me. We haven't had a lot of time together lately, Judge Kingston."

When they reached the kitchen, Judith pulled out a large pottery bowl. "Does it seem strange to you that Roberta, Turner, and Marthellen have been gone for four days and we haven't heard a word from them?"

The judge poured himself a cup of coffee, then eased into a chair at the breakfast table, his back to the night-darkened window. "Perhaps they're waiting for something to report."

"You'd think Marthellen would write," Judith fussed.

"There's hardly been time for a letter to get here."

"They could telegram."

"Telegram that nothing's happened?"

Judith sighed. "I know, but it's so difficult to wait."

"You want to be there making decisions for them."

"Of course not! Well, perhaps I do, just a bit."

"I believe we have enough here to keep us busy. How are you and Willie Jane doing with the wedding plans?"

"We have everything organized."

"So soon?"

"We released the entire matter to Daisie Belle Emory."

"Perhaps that's why she asked me the name of the new commandant at Fort Churchill. She mentioned something about a visiting army brass band."

Judith sorted through her spice rack. "I haven't heard that one."

"What does Willie Jane think?"

"She's quite amazed that Daisie Belle would want to do all of this for her."

"Daisie Belle Emory harbors less prejudice than any person in this entire state," Judge said. "Yet at first glance you would suppose just the opposite to be true."

"I think Willie Jane worries more about getting to adopt Fidora's little Daniel than she does the wedding," Judith said.

"There might be a good cause for her concern. Mr. and Mrs. Campos stopped by my office this afternoon. They heard that Willie Jane wanted the baby, and they wanted to officially petition the court for his adoption themselves, if the family so directs."

"Oh dear, have you told Willie Jane?"

"No. Would you like to do that?"

Judith took a deep breath and let it out slowly. "No, but it might be best if we told her together. It wouldn't seem quite like a judicial ruling that way. It will crush her spirit if she doesn't get that child."

The judge unfastened the top button on his white shirt. "I know, but the court will have to decide what's best for the baby."

"How well do you know the Camposes?" she asked him.

"Until Sam Tjader was killed, I hardly knew them at all. Philip Campos is a little young for that manager position and he always seems like he's trying to prove himself. Once he gains some confidence, he should temper a bit. How about Mrs. Campos?"

"She seems on the verge of tears most every time I see her. She's still struggling from the loss of the one twin."

Judge nodded. "She broke down in my office today at the mention of Willie Jane wanting to adopt little Daniel. Situations like this make me long for a nice, simple apex litigation case."

"Nothing in our lives is simple."

The judge took a sip of coffee, then pulled his black tie off. "Yes, I've noticed that adult

131

children take as much effort and concern as younger ones."

Judith surveyed the bowls and utensils lined up on her wooden counter. "Are you complaining, your honor?"

"I enjoy every moment of having them around, just as you do, my dear. Still . . ."

"Still what?" she prodded.

"I wouldn't mind a little time for just you and me."

She raised her sharply defined dark brown eyebrows. "Right now?"

"Well, I, eh, I mean . . ."

"Oh, my, for an older gentleman you certainly have retained your blush!" Judith went to the pantry and returned carrying a canister of flour.

"What I was thinking of was for you and me to take a few weeks in September for a vacation."

"A real vacation?" She set the flour can on the counter, then moved behind him and began to rub his neck and shoulders. "You mean, no legal convention, no political rally, no state boundary commission, no university regents meeting?"

"Just you and me, Judith."

"Do you think the state of Nevada can survive that long without their trustworthy Judge Kingston?"

"Do you think Carson City can survive without their darling Judith Kingston, queen of their hearts?"

"I think it would be delightful to give them the opportunity. Where would we go?" she asked.

"I think we should head west."

"To Sacramento? Then, we must go up to Rancho Alazan and visit dear Alena Merced! I believe her daughter, Martina, lives in Stockton since she married Mr. Hackett."

"How old's the baby now?"

"Baby Christina, dear Judge, is sixteen."

He shook his head. "Well, that's fine for a short trip, but I was thinking a little farther west than Sacramento."

"San Francisco? You know, we've never been there except to attend a meeting or convention. They say there are magnificent vistas on the north side of the Golden Gate. Perhaps we could take the ferry north, then rent a carriage and travel up the coast."

The judge shook his head again. "I was thinking a little further west than San Francisco."

"There's nothing west of San Francisco, dear judge, except the Pacific Ocean. What are you suggesting?"

"The Sandwich Islands."

"Hawaii? Are you serious?"

"It seems to me a week on the open sea and a couple weeks on a Pacific island might be quite a tonic."

"I can't believe you'd even consider that!" Each word seemed to dance out of Judith's mouth.

"I promised you, didn't I?"

"Yes, but that was thirty years ago . . . and we couldn't even find the Sandwich Islands on a map," she added.

"Well, I can find them now."

"But what if David still needs us, and Roberta still hasn't gotten married?"

He reached back and took her hand. "Let them schedule their lives around us for once."

"I just can't believe it. You really . . . this is so unlike you, Judge Kingston."

"I suppose there's still a surprise or two in the old man."

Judith scurried around the kitchen, gathering up the flour and sugar, toting them back to the pantry.

"What are you doing?"

"Putting everything back. I think it's about time to turn in, don't you, Mr. Judge-with-a-surprise-or-two-left?"

"I couldn't agree with you more. But what about the bearclaws?"

She turned off the gas lamp, then slipped her hand into his. "I'll buy some at the Boston Bakery."

Judge Kingston exited the Nevada state capitol building and strolled across the grounds. The leaves were still a pale green and the sky a clean blue, cooled by the steady breeze from the snow-capped Sierra Nevadas to the west.

In a month it will be hot and dusty, but now it's much too beautiful a day to be stuck in the closets of politics and the halls of justice. I'll leave my briefcase at the office, rent a carriage, and Judith and I will have a peaceful drive down to Genoa for a . . . No, she has the grandchildren. Then we'll merely take them along and . . .

"Hey, Judge, it surely is a beautiful day, ain't it?" Levi and Marcy dawdled at the open black iron gate on the southwest corner of the capitol grounds.

"I was thinking the same thing myself."

"Were you over there talkin' to Governor Kinkead?" Levi quizzed.

"Mainly, the governor was talking to me."

"He surely does like to talk, don't he?"

"I believe that's a prerequisite for the job. And today he had a lot on his mind. The Nevada Benevolent Lottery bill — passed at

135

the last Legislature and signed by him —
was declared unconstitutional by the Supreme Court here at Carson. I'm surprised
he didn't fly the flag at half-mast."

"I heard you were going to run for governor someday," Marcy said.

"Who told you that?"

"Roberta."

"Well, she's wrong. I'm the not the type."

"What do you mean by that?"

"I'd rather listen than talk."

"Well, listen to this, judge," Levi said.
"We rented the old Fat Boy place."

Marcy cleared her throat. "I believe his
name was Lawrence Caper."

"But no one knows where the Caper place
is. We all called him Fat Boy," Levi insisted.

"I told you, Levi, I don't want to be
known as the woman who lives in the Fat
Boy place."

Levi brushed back his thick, drooping
mustache. "Listen, Judge, we rented the old
Caper place and have been to town to buy
us a lounge, a mattress, and a spring-bed."

"Levi!" Marcy scolded. "Actually, Judge,
my parents sent us some money and we
were able to take advantage of Kitzmeyer's
sale to purchase a number of pieces of
household furniture."

"Well, I'm glad you got the, eh, Caper

place. The location is certainly convenient to both of your jobs."

"Marcy is only going to work another year, you know," Levi asserted. "Then she'll be busy makin' babies."

"Levi, you're embarrassing me."

"But, darlin', you can't be embarrassed in front of a judge. They've heard everything there is."

The three crossed Carson Street after tandem freight wagons pulled by seventeen mules and three horses plodded by.

"Levi, how's the new job coming?" the judge asked.

"I like it just fine. 'Course, I haven't been out at the quarry yet when it's blazin'est hot in the summer or freezin' in the winter. So, I reckon I reserve judgment. Did you know they transferred Manitoba Joe Clark out there?"

"Yes, I did. How's he doing with his new surroundings?"

"They keep them that's goin' to be hung off to themselves. I don't see him often. He ain't much to look at anyway, just a short, squatty man."

"Did he give the guards any trouble?" the judge asked.

"Nah, they said he was easy enough to get along with. I guess he's lost most his swagger."

The judge shifted his brown leather portfolio from one arm to the other. "He's quite an unusual fellow."

"He's a killer who shot Mr. Tjader in cold blood," Marcy said.

The judge thought of several replies but clamped his lips, then said, "Do you have any more purchases to make for that new home of yours?"

Levi nodded. "Yep. We got to pick out some pillows and sheets."

"Levi!"

"Eh, we need some . . . uh . . ."

"Household furnishings and dry goods," Marcy instructed.

"Yeah, some of them," Levi mumbled. "We'll invite you all out when we have the, eh, the Caper place fixed up."

Marcy and Levi turned south once they crossed the street. The judge headed west and came across Duffy Day lounging on the limestone courthouse steps. The small man, who rarely relaxed, seemed less wary and intense than usual.

"Afternoon, Judge."

"You've got the right idea, Duffy, sitting out here enjoying a beautiful May afternoon."

"Why don't you join me, Judge?"

"I think I will." The judge tossed his

138

leather portfolio down and sat on it like a cushion.

"Shoot, Judge, I've been askin' you to join me for years and you've always been too busy."

"And I'm still too busy. But sometimes a man needs to take a break."

They quietly gazed out on the city landscape around them. Two young boys kicked a dusty bottle. The judge watched a solitary heron's crooked neck and pale blue wings lift above the low bent branches of a cottonwood tree, giving graceful life and movement to the lazy scene.

A round-bellied man wearing a tight checkered suit made a brash exit out of the front door of the courthouse and scurried down the steps to where the men sat.

He straightened his bow tie. "I'm R. J. Tuttle, a salesman for the West Coast Sanitary Supply Company. Do one of you men happen to be the judge?"

Kingston glanced over at the clean-shaven but shaggy-headed Duffy Day. *He's a drummer and he has to ask which one of us is the judge?*

"That all depends, Mister Drummer, on what it is you need judgin'," the judge drawled as he straightened his silk tie. "My specialty is judgin' fried okra and boiled grits. There ain't nobody in the state of Nevada better than me!"

"Okra?" the man repeated.

Duffy cleared his throat. "I say, I'm Judge Hollis A. Kingston, first district court. Haven't I seen you before?"

"I don't think so . . ."

"You weren't the one convicted of fraud on that Reno towel scandal, were you? I believe there could still be a warrant out for you, Mr. Toolsky."

"No, that wasn't me. I'm not Toolsky. My name's Tuttle. I'm a salesman for . . ." The nervous man didn't finish. He backed down the steps, mumbling something about not judging a book by its cover and disappeared down the street.

Duffy roared with laughter. "I guess we fooled him, Judge. Did I do all right?"

"It was a frightfully good impression, Duffy. I'm amazed. But do I really sound that stuffy?"

"Yep, I reckon you do. 'Course, you didn't do all that good an impression of me," Duffy added. "You'd think a man from Kentucky could drop his g's and twang his ain'ts much better than that."

"I'm out of practice. But you could be running for public office one of these days."

"Shoot, Judge, when you look like me, it ain't all that hard to be smarter than I look. Say, did you know I had me a new girl-friend?"

"Don't tell me Lola Montez is back in town?" the judge chided.

"Lola? I'll let them Washburn brothers have her. This time I got me a real keeper."

"Where did you meet her?"

"Out in front of the Nice-N-Friendly Café. I was peekin' in the window at the bearclaws and she came out to see me. She works there, you know."

"That's great, Duffy. What's her name?"

"Sweet Lorna. I mean, her name is Lorna Clair, but I call her my sweet Lorna."

"What does she call you?"

Duffy beamed. "She calls me her sugarlump, but I don't reckon I want ever'one in town to hear that."

The judge smiled and stared across the street at the capitol building. "I won't tell a soul."

"She's just crazy about me, Judge."

The judge studied Duffy's simple eyes and crooked-toothed grin. *I'm not sure whether you or Timothy have the toughest time with reality, Duffy, but you certainly know how to enjoy the afternoon.*

He stood and picked up his portfolio.

"Enjoy the rest of the day, Duffy. I have to get back to my office and review tomorrow's cases. Be sure and introduce me to your girl-friend sometime."

Duffy leaped to his feet. "How about right now? Here she comes!"

The judge glanced up the sidewalk to see a pleasant-looking, dark-haired woman with brown eyes focused only on Duffy. "Hi, Sugarlump!" she called out.

As she came closer, her expression seemed a bit tight, and the quick look she gave the judge revealed a hidden story of tough times and hard living. She wore no makeup. She didn't try to hide the flatness or the lines.

Duffy cupped his hand to his mouth and said, "See, I told ya she'd call me that." He stepped toward the street. "Sweet Lorna, there's someone I want you to meet. This is my good friend, Judith's husband, Judge Hollis A. Kingston."

Her handshake was confident, firm, rough, and cool. "Judge, I'm so glad to meet some of Duffy's friends."

"Duffy has a whole lot of friends in this town," the judge said.

"So I'm beginning to find out. I've only been here three days and I've hardly met a soul who doesn't know Duffy Day."

Duffy's grin was as wide as the street. "Yep, I get around all right. That's how long we've been seein' each other — three days. I was hopin' to go by and introduce her to Judith."

Lorna lingered on the steps, her eyes scanning the block. "I have to be back to work at the café in thirty minutes. Couldn't we just sit on a park bench and visit while there's still an empty one over at the capitol? My feet are killin' me today."

The judge could see creases at her eyes and a sag under her chin. He figured her to be in her mid-thirties, with a little wear and hard work showing.

"I reckon we could at that," Duffy said, his face beaming.

"Why don't you two come over for supper tonight?" the judge asked. "I know Judith would enjoy meeting you."

"Judge, that's the nicest invite, but you know my sugarlump, he frets too much when he has to go inside a building."

"That doesn't bother you?"

Her smile was replaced by serious resolve. "No, Judge Kingston, it doesn't bother me in the least."

"Well, I've got another idea then. How about we have a little backyard cookout and picnic Sunday after church? Judith has been pestering me to fire-cook some smoked salmon."

"That sounds mighty fine, Judge," Duffy announced. "Can Barbara and little Douglas come along too?"

"Certainly."

"Thank you, Judge Kingston," Lorna said. "That was very thoughtful."

The judge stood on the step and watched as Lorna Clair and Duffy Day crossed the street together and passed through the gate to the capitol grounds.

Judith is never, ever going to believe this. I don't believe it myself. What is she up to? Who is this woman? Is she serious? She seems serious. It's a cinch Duffy Day is serious. But, Sugarlump?

"Grandpa! Grandpa! Grandpa!" Alicia shouted. She pushed open the Nevada Street door. "Come see Daddy!"

Judith met the judge at the kitchen doorway.

"David's back a day early?" he asked her.

"No, he's still in San Francisco." She followed him and Alicia into the living room.

"Where's Timothy then?"

"In the alley, trying to capture a mountain lion with a fish-head."

Alicia bounced in front of a four-foot-high, three-foot-wide painting of a handsome young man wearing a pith helmet and carrying a Bible. In the background was an outline of a map of India, complete with tiny portraits of different points of interest in the country.

The judge gasped. "My word! It's magnificent!"

"Did you ever see any portrait so real, yet so out-of-this-world?" Judith said. "It's our David, but he has such a cathedral-like, commanding presence."

"This is Barbara Day's painting?"

"She brought it by for us to look at."

"Look, Grandpa, here's Mamma. See? Right down here!" Alicia pointed to the lower end of the country where there was a small white Celtic cross printed with the name Patricia.

The judge slowly examined the picture. "Has David seen this?"

"No, Barbara wanted it at his house when he came home. She asked me to take it over to the parsonage. She didn't want to be around when he first viewed it."

"We must have it," the judge said. "We need to purchase it from her."

"I already thought of that. But she doesn't want to sell it."

"Cost is no object."

"She won't sell it for any price," Judith informed him. "She doesn't paint for money, she told me. She paints for love."

"Whatever the motivation, this is superb! We'll hire her to paint one just like it."

"I already tried, dear judge. There is to be one and only one, and she intends to keep it herself."

"But he's our son," the judge sputtered.

"Yes, your honor, but it's her painting."

"I'm stunned, and this has already been a quite stunning day."

"What else happened?"

"After lunch I met Duffy's new girl-friend."

"You met her? Daisie Belle stopped by to say she heard it was a serious relationship. What's she like? Where'd they meet? Does she understand how special Duffy is? Where did you . . ."

"I'll tell you everything after supper. By the way, we're having a little picnic for Duffy and his Lorna in our backyard Sunday after church."

Judith clapped her hands. "Oh, that's wonderful. I trust Marthellen will be home by then. Who's invited?"

"Just Duffy and Lorna and Barbara and Douglas and our family. And anyone else you want to include." The judge continued to survey the portrait. "If David goes back to India, we must have this painting, that's all there is to it. My word, this certainly tempts me to break the commandment about coveting."

Judith slipped her arm in his and stared at the portrait. "It makes me want to break the commandment about stealing."

The sun had just slipped behind the Carson Range, the wind had died down, and the air cooled to a pleasant sixty-five degrees. Judith opened the dining room windows, then heard steps on the porch.

"Are David and the children coming right over?" she asked as the judge swung open the side door.

Judge Kingston hung his hat on the peg, then pulled off his suit coat. "He brought Alicia and Timothy presents and wants to dig them out of his satchel first. Besides, I think he's a little dazed by the portrait."

"Where did you put it?"

"I propped it on the back of the sofa, as you suggested."

"What did the China Mission Board tell him in San Francisco?"

"He said he'd tell us both when he came over."

"You said he saw Roberta in Sacramento?"

"He reported they were waiting for an

eastbound train, and he'd explain that later too."

"Eastbound? Did he mean Reno? Omaha? New York? What is she doing? And who was waiting? Was it just her and Turner? Where's Marthellen?"

"Here they come," the judge said. "I do believe he brought them masks."

Judith scooted up to the window on the top half of the side door. "Timothy's is a Bengal tiger."

The judge slipped on his wire-frame glasses. "And Alicia?"

"It's either a princess, an angel, or a little girl who just got caught with her hand in the cookie jar."

The judge stood back as two children pushed through the door. "Look, Grandpa Judge, I'm the prettiest princess in the entire world," Alicia shouted from behind the mask. "Marjorie Walters will be wanting one too, but this is the only one in the world."

"Gr-r-r-r," said the ferocious tiger. "I'm goin' to eat the world's prettiest princess!" Timothy shouted.

Alicia squealed. "Grandpa Judge, save me, save me!"

She leaped up in his arms, while Timothy latched onto his leg. The judge staggered back.

"Perhaps you and I should go talk, dear," Judith said, taking David's arm, "and let the judge play with the children."

"Judith!"

She looked back at the hapless grandpa, then released her son's arm. "Then, again, perhaps not."

"All right, you two," David called out. "Leave Grandpa Judge alone."

Judith tugged Timothy off the judge's leg. "I'm sorry, Mr. Tiger, but no large ferocious cats are allowed in my house. It's bad on the furniture. But if I had a Bengal tiger in my yard, I bet he would chase off any cat or dog in the neighborhood, at least for a few minutes until supper time."

Timothy jumped up and yanked off his mask. "Can I go outside, Daddy?"

"You have to stay in the yard," David lectured.

Timothy pulled the mask back on. "That single fact might save the lives of countless neighborhood dogs and cats . . ." He exploded out the side door with a growl.

"Did you want to go out and play, too, princess?" the judge asked Alicia.

She shook her mask-clad face. "No, Grandpa, the Tiger will chase me!"

"Would you like to play Grandma's piano?" Judith asked.

"Will you help me, Grandma?"

"In a few minutes, dear. Your Daddy wants to tell Grandpa and me about his trip to San Francisco. We'll be in the kitchen while Grandma finishes preparing supper."

"Daddy went to Chinatown and bought us these masks," Alicia declared. "Can I keep my mask on while I play the piano?"

"Can you see out of it?" the judge asked as he set her down.

"Sort of, Grandpa Judge."

"Then you may keep it on."

Alicia skipped over to the piano while the three adults made their way into the kitchen.

With Timothy snarling in the yard, and Alicia plunking out "London Bridge Is Falling Down," on the piano, the men settled down at the breakfast table.

Judith began mashing potatoes at the stove. "What do you think of the painting, David?"

"I'm flabbergasted."

"We're all rather astonished," the judge admitted.

"I don't know whether to be inspired or embarrassed," David said. "It's the kind of piece done at the end of your career, not the beginning."

"It is very well done," Judith remarked.

"I'm not sure I ever looked that reverent," David said.

"It's an exact likeness," Judith insisted.

"Now you know what you look like in your mother's eyes," the judge said.

"Your father was put out when she refused to sell it." Judith poured more cream into the potatoes. "He offered her $100. I do think Barbara could make some money if she wanted to sell her art. She's that good."

"She's funny about that. She just won't sell any of her art," David said. "I certainly respect the integrity of her work."

"Even artists need to pay for groceries. Duffy could use help with expenses, especially since he has a steady girlfriend."

"He does?" David brushed his slightly shaggy brown hair back. "But I've only been gone a few days."

"You'll meet her Sunday afternoon," the judge said. "But forget that for now, we want to know what happened with the China Mission Board, and what Roberta is doing."

"Which would you like me to start with?"

The judge glanced over at Judith. "The mission board, obviously."

Judith stared down into the mashed potatoes. *It wasn't all that obvious to me, Judge Kingston. What about Roberta?*

"The news from the China Mission is mixed," David said.

151

"They don't have a place for you?"

"They want me to come. They need me in Shanghai, and I can take the children. I could serve as a headmaster for a school there for missionary children and children of the British and American consuls and staffs."

"That's nice, dear," Judith said.

"But it's not my calling, Mother. I need to be where I can preach and teach and evangelize."

"I'm sure they have those positions as well," the judge said.

"There is a great need. But they won't send a widower and his children out into the cities and villages. They'll send families, married couples, two men . . . in some cases, two women . . . but no single parent and children."

"Shanghai is closer to India than Carson City," the judge said. "Would you consider going that far to see what turns up?"

"I'm tempted, but that doesn't sound like a very good motive for going to China."

"We'd be delighted if you stayed here and served the church," Judith said. "We're getting extremely fond of having you across the street."

David smiled, then said, "I think some in the congregation are putting up with me because they know I'm only temporary. I heard a few grumbles about my 'Spurgeonistic sermons.' "

"Spurgeonistic?" Judith said. "That is an interesting word."

"Where does that leave things for you?" the judge pressed.

"I think I'll decline their offer, Dad. I know I'm supposed to give my life to India. The Lord must have some plan for getting me there."

"Grandma Judith, I have to go to the privy!" Alicia called from the doorway.

"Certainly, honey, why don't you leave your pretty mask in here."

"Would you go with me? I don't want to get eaten by a tiger."

"I can see how that could ruin your day." Judith turned to her son and her husband. "You two listen to me. I don't want you to say one single word about Roberta until I return. Do you understand?"

"Yes, ma'am," they replied in unison.

When Judith returned, she poured a lemon glaze on a bundt cake she had brought home from the Boston Bakery. "Now, tell us about your sister."

"I was at the station in Sacramento," David said, "and just happened to see her at the ticket window. She was buying tickets for them to depart today."

"Are they coming home?"

"No, they're going to Cheyenne."

"Why on earth Cheyenne?" the judge asked.

Before David could reply, Judith said, "Who is going to Cheyenne?"

"They're trying to catch up with Mr. George Hearst."

"*Who* is trying to catch up?"

"Is Hearst in Cheyenne?" the judge said.

"No, he's in Deadwood, Dakota Territory. Well, actually, he's nearby in a place called Lead. They expect to talk to him there."

"Who is *they?*" Judith said.

The judge rubbed his gray-and-black mustache. "Didn't they see Hearst in Sacramento?"

"Apparently, they just missed him."

Judith slammed her fist down on the counter and rattled the cake plate. "Listen, I want to know, and I want to know right now, who is traveling with whom? Is my unmarried daughter in a railroad car with a single man or not?"

"Mother, Marthellen is very much with them."

"Of course, dear," the judge said. "How could you think otherwise?"

"David, did Roberta tell you directly that

Marthellen was going on this trip with them?"

"I believe her words were, 'Tell Mamma not to worry, I am never out of Marthellen's sight,' end of quote."

"Roberta said that?"

"Yes, she did."

Judith felt the tension leave her neck and shoulders. "Now you may proceed."

"Where was I?"

"You had just said, 'No, he's in Deadwood, Dakota Territory . . . well, actually, nearby in a place called Lead. They expect to talk to him there,' " Judith informed him.

"Right. Turner had quite a scene in Sacramento. Wilton Longbake at first refused to see him, but Roberta managed to arrange a meeting. Longbake said simply that they were cutting back investments in Nevada and decided to cut their losses and sell the mill. Turner said he had invested $25,000 of his own money and —"

"That's how he finished the job!" the judge exclaimed.

"Turner Bowman never saved up $250, let alone $25,000," Judith said.

David shrugged his shoulders. "Perhaps he borrowed it?"

"Then he has a dreadful debt. Isn't this what I warned him about?" the judge fumed.

"I believe you warned me about it, not Turner," Judith said.

The judge threw up his hands. "And he has no way of paying it off!"

"He asked Longbake for the first $25,000 from the sale of the mill, but good ol' Wilton said Turner had no authority to expand capital expenses and would have to bear the loss himself."

"My word, what did Turner do then?"

"I believe he threatened to take Longbake out into the alley and beat the stuffing out of him, or words to that effect."

"How did Mr. Longbake respond to that?" Judith asked.

"He took the first train to New York and left behind a note saying they could discuss the matter with Mr. Hearst, who was in Deadwood, or Lead."

The judge lowered his chin and shook his head. "So they're just chasing after him?"

"It would seem so."

"Couldn't Roberta and Marthellen come home and let Turner settle this matter?"

"I think Roberta was concerned how Turner might settle it. She did not intend to let him travel alone."

"She's loyal, just like her mother," the judge murmured.

"She's possessive, just like her mother," Judith added.

The judge shook his head. "Poor Roberta . . ."

Judith ran the tip of her index finger around the bowl of lemon icing and licked her finger, then said, "Poor Marthellen . . ."

Chapter Five

The man with the silk hat wore a charcoal gray tie that sagged like his mustache. "I just had quite a talk with her and, other than her choice of men, she seems quite pleasant and normal."

"That's good, Mayor," the judge said. He was standing behind the brick outdoor firepit with a spatula in his hand. He glanced around at Dr. Jacobs and the sheriff, who both wore canvas aprons over their suits and held spatulas. "Do you suppose he's talkin' about Daisie Belle, Barbara Day, or Judith?"

"My word!" the mayor said. "I'm talking about Lorna Clair, Duffy's new girlfriend, of course. Isn't that why seventy-five people have crammed into your backyard, Judge Kingston?"

"I was kind of wondering why everyone showed up," the judge said. "All this time I thought it was this fine team of outdoor chefs that attracted them."

"If I drop another piece of salmon in the fire, it will be the last time I'm invited to cook," Doc Jacobs grumbled as he tugged on his tie to loosen it, then wiped his forehead with a towel.

"Duffy is barely able to provide for himself, runs off into the hills when he hears a gunshot, won't enter a regular building, and is so slow to figure some things out that he misses the point completely," the mayor said. "So there's only one question I've got about this whole thing of a girlfriend: What does that woman see in Duffy?"

He had not noticed Judith waltzing up behind him halfway through his tirade. "What she sees, dear mayor," Judith said, "is a simple, honest man with an open heart and legendary loyalty."

"That ain't all that much," the sheriff remarked.

"And that, dear Sheriff, is why there is no Mrs. Sheriff." She turned to the judge. "We have six more guests."

He unwrapped the package of fish that lay on the block of ice. "Who else is left in town?" he asked.

"The Johansens, the Rupperts, and the Porters."

"But they're from Genoa," the sheriff declared.

Judith held out a serving platter while the judge loaded it with grilled salmon. "They heard about Duffy's new friend and wanted to come take a look. I'm just sorry Mrs. Campos and the babies weren't able to make it. Mr. Campos said she was feeling poorly. I hope Daniel isn't wearing her down."

The judge inspected each piece of fish as he placed it on the tray, then glanced at the crowd. "Why didn't we just post signs up in Virginia City and Reno too?"

"I believe this was your idea, Judge Kingston," she said.

He scowled. "Was it a good idea?"

"It was a wonderful idea! Carson never has enough social activities."

"Now you're sounding like Daisie Belle," Doc Jacobs said. "I'm just thankful you didn't send invites up Virginia City way. We could have gotten guests from Gold Hill. They're having that outbreak of smallpox. Several have died, including one who committed suicide while in a smallpox delirium."

"Oh, my! I trust Mrs. Tjader and the children are OK in Virginia City. I'm going to have to keep her more diligently in my prayers." Judith took the platter of salmon, then studied the crowd. "Judge, have you seen Timothy?"

He waved his spatula toward the front of the yard. "The last I saw, he and Douglas Day were being chased through the yard by Alicia carrying a giant earthworm."

"Alicia chasing the boys? Good for her, but I can't imagine them being afraid of a worm . . . or a little sister."

"I think she was threatening to swallow the worm and they refused to look," the judge said.

The mayor made a gagging sound. "Swallow it? Our little Alicia?"

"Oh, she won't do it," the judge said. "I think it was the first time in her life that she had them on the run. She's enjoying it."

"I saw someone out front hanging upside down from a tree limb," the mayor reported. "Maybe Timothy is out there."

"No," Judith said. "That was Barbara Day."

"What is she doing?" the judge sputtered.

"She's modestly hanging upside down from a tree limb." Judith's brown eyes danced. "She claims that having the blood rush to her head improves her creativity."

"How on earth does a lady hang modestly, upside down?" the judge inquired.

Sheriff Hill stepped back from the fire and lifted a half-full glass of iced lemonade. "Now there's a woman who is definitely —"

"A wonderful artist?" Judith interjected.

"Yes, that, too," he replied.

"I need to get back to the serving line, gentlemen. This has been quite a challenge with Marthellen still gone. I don't know what I would have done without Willie Jane and Marcy pitching in."

"They both think of you as mamma," Doc Jacobs said.

The mayor plucked the spatula from the sheriff's hand and glanced under a large filet of salmon. "I believe this entire town counts on you mothering them, Judith," he said.

"At this particular moment, the entire town is hoping I have some more potato salad." She hurried back toward the house.

The men continued to grill fish and serve seconds as the large crowd mingled in the yard. All except the mayor. He slapped mustard on two slices of brown bread and laid a piece of cooked salmon on it. "Look out there, Judge," he mumbled between bites. "That's why I love the West. You don't find that kind of social diversity in the East.

Every type of person in town feels at home mingling around in this crowd. There's muscle, beauty, and jollity represented here. You are a definite competition for Farmer Treadway. All you need to do is add roast chicken, currant jelly, and archery shoots and you've got him beat."

"I've got all my deputies wanting time off next week," the sheriff said. "The Amities and the Railroad Nine are playing a baseball match at Treadway's park."

Doc Jacobs pulled off his apron, then folded it neatly. "I believe you boys can handle things for a while." He turned to the mayor. "The Kingston home says what beacons have always symbolized: safe journey, land ho, welcome home. It's the Kingston charm."

"Hear, hear," the mayor said. "And our Judith Kingston stands for everything that's right about Carson City." He pulled on his glasses. "Look over there at Daisie Belle Emory off to the side, visiting with the likes of Callie Truxell. What do Mrs. Emory and a red light-district, eh, businesswoman have in common?"

"They could be talking stocks," Doc said. "Daisie Belle told me the stock list looked very encouraging yesterday. Union's touching $29 on the board."

"I heard they was plannin' a weddin' shower for Willie Jane," the sheriff added.

The mayor gave a sharp nod of his head. "See what I mean, gentlemen? Only in Nevada."

Doc Jacobs took a swig of lemonade. "They could be talking interest rates and investments. Callie has saved up some dollars."

"And just how do you know things like that?" the sheriff quizzed.

" 'Cause Callie and a few of the girls are the only ones in this town besides Judith and the judge who pay cash for their doctor bills on the day they receive the services. Unlike some lawmen and city officials."

The mayor mumbled something unintelligible into the next bite of grilled salmon sandwich.

When the food was served and the crowd thinned out, the judge left his cooking chores to find Duffy Day. Duffy, his hair neatly trimmed, stood by himself in a three-piece suit and slightly askew tie, while several people huddled around Lorna Clair.

"Surely is a nice picnic, Judge," Duffy called out. "I didn't know it was going to be such a big snap like this. I thought we was the only ones comin' over. I surely do like parties. Ever'body bein' so friendly. I bet ever'body here has come over to me and my darlin' Lorna Clair and said hello, even some of them that normally ignores me on the street. Why do you reckon that is?"

The judge studied Duffy's wide brown eyes. "I imagine folks are usually busy on the street going and coming. They just have more time here."

Duffy grinned. "Yeah! That's it, ain't it? And here I thought they were jist comin' over to sniff out my darlin' Lorna."

"That's just what happens when you get a pretty girlfriend."

Duffy rocked back on the heels of his worn brown boots. "Yep, you're right about that. A plain old boy with a fancy woman at his side, I suppose that draws a look or two. I reckon you had to put up with that same thing all your life, ain't ya, Judge?"

The judge glanced across the yard where Judith visited with Daisie Belle and Callie. He couldn't see her at first, her graceful profile was hidden behind Daisie Belle. But then she stepped forward and his spirit soared. He didn't realize the intensity of his longing for her, to grab her up and take her away. "You are very right about that, Duffy."

"Think I'll get me some more of that there iced lemonade," Duffy announced.

"Why don't you offer to refill Lorna's glass as well?"

"Shoot, Judge, she's got good feet, she can jist . . ."

The judge glowered down at him.

"I think I'll go see if my sweet Lorna wants any more iced lemonade," Duffy said.

Grocer John Cheney grabbed the judge's arm. "Have you seen Judith? I need to tell her about the new shipment of pickled bay shrimp and cabbage I just got in. I know she'll want to sample them. Could you give her the message?"

The judge started to point toward Daisie Belle, but Judith was gone. Callie and Daisie Belle were visiting with Philip Campos.

"I'll certainly try to remember, Mr. Cheney," the judge said as he pushed on through the crowd. *I won't try very hard, of course.* He walked by the gaslight globe that stood on the corner post of the picket fence where Campos, Daisie Belle, and Callie stood.

"Now here is our dear judge and gracious host," Daisie Belle cooed as she slipped her arm in his and nudged him into their circle.

"I didn't mean to interrupt you," the judge said.

Callie's deep yellow satin dress was carefully buttoned high under her chin. Her pale face showed no trace of the usual makeup and lip rouge. The creases around her eyes made her look much older than twenty-five, but not out of place at the picnic. "Judge, we had jist finished talkin' and I was preparin' to leave," she said.

"Callie, I needed to talk to you about a case I'm reviewing . . . whenever you have a moment to spare."

Philip Campos bowed curtly. "Isn't that just like our judge? Always working, even on a Sunday afternoon. I need to check on my wife anyway, so if you'll excuse me."

Daisie Belle dropped the judge's arm. "I must be going too. I'm sure Judith will need help cleaning up." She patted the judge's cheek and headed for the house. The crowd parted for her like the Red Sea as she swished her way through . . . on dry ground.

"Callie," the judge said, "I'm reviewing a few things about the case at the bank."

"You mean, when Mr. Tjader was killed by Manitoba Joe?"

"My question is just about banking. Do you use the bank yourself?"

"Yes, I do. I ain't all that proud of a lot of things in my life, but I am savin' some

167

money, and one of these days I'll buy me a place and quit this work. I ain't rich like Fidora was, bless her heart, but I have saved a goodly sum."

"Fidora was rich?"

"I don't know what's rich, Judge, but she inherited some funds last fall when her mamma died somewhere down in Texas. And she's been savin' her own money for a number of years. She told me she invested a lot of it. She said when she retired she never wanted to have to work another day in her life. Ain't that somethin'? That's how she afforded that fancy suite at the hotel the last few weeks."

The judge leaned his hand against the picket fence. He felt a twinge in his back after two hours bent over the cookfire. He tried stretching out his shoulders. "I'm sorry Fidora didn't get to enjoy more of her wealth."

"Ain't that the truth."

"Callie, tell me about how you do your banking."

"You mean, through the back door and all?"

"Yes. How does that work?"

"It was mainly Mr. Tjader's idea. I think he did it just for us girls. He didn't have to. But he started openin' the back door of the bank early on some days so we could do some business before the other folks came in the front door."

"So you just go down the alley and through the back door?"

"That's the way it was with Mr. Tjader. When Mr. Campos started helpin' out, he liked things different."

"In what way?"

"Campos doesn't really want us girls in the bank. I reckon he's afraid we'll pick his pocket or pull a knife on him. He's not a very trustin' man. He always likes using the dutch door. Now, with Mr. Tjader dead, that's the only choice we have."

The judge stood straight up. "Dutch door? Callie, I inspected that door. It's solid steel."

"It surely looks that way, don't it? But the top half opens by itself. That center strip of iron just masks the division of the door."

"Are you sure?"

"Judge, I ain't got no reason to make up somethin' like that. Like I said, Sam Tjader thought that was a waste of time. I think he probably thought the old door was rusted together there anyway. He told me once they made it that way to provide a tempo-rary way to let some air circulate without lettin' alley dogs wander into the bank. It's sort of like a window. But he thought it a foolish idea because folks could come into the back room without no one out front knowin' about it."

"So the door opens and —"

"It don't open automatically. You got to knock on the door and let Campos know you're there. And you got to know the secret knock."

"Secret knock?"

"That was Mr. Campos' idea. Ain't that somethin'? Sam Tjader used to just leave it open and we wandered in when we felt like it. But Mr. Campos has us use this secret knock. It's one knock, then two knocks, then three knocks, then two knocks, then one knock."

"That's like a Morse code message," the judge said.

"Ain't it, though? Anyway, he opens the top half of the door and we use it like a teller's cage. Actually, it's kind of quick that way. Unless it's snowin'. He does let us come in if it's snowin'."

"But Mr. Tjader never used that dutch door?"

"Not when I was there. I cain't speak for the others. Maybe he treated some different, but I never heard anything about it."

"Did Tjader and Campos give you regular

deposit slips and duplicate receipts?"

"Tjader used to, but Campos said we might as well do it in a more simple way. Since Mr. Tjader died, Mr. Campos keeps records in a black ledger. He has a page for each of us girls. He records the deposit, we both initial the ledger, then he gives us a small receipt. It's a simple system, but it works. But why are you askin' all of this, Judge? Manitoba Joe has already been sentenced to hang."

"I like to review capital punishment cases. I certainly don't want to make any procedural errors," the judge explained.

"You mean, if you made some error, a murderer like Manitoba Joe Clark could go free?"

"That's one possibility."

"I surely wouldn't want that to happen. Sam Tjader always treated us fair. There probably ain't ten girls in town who save money, but for those of us that do, it's nice to have a banker like Sam."

"How about Campos?" the judge asked.

"I don't like him too much, Judge. I reckon he's OK, but I've spent a lot of years decidin' instantly whether I like a man or not, and I just don't like him."

"So, are you going to stop doing business at the bank?"

"I thought about it, but I can't withdraw my funds until September."

"Why's that?"

" 'Cause Mr. Campos invested my funds into some bonds that won't mature until October. But I get 11.2 percent on them, which is almost twice as good as the bank rate of 6 percent."

"You're a smart businesswoman, Callie Truxell."

"If I was real smart, I'd find a new line of work."

"Callie, back before Sam's death, which days did he come in?"

"Sam worked Mondays and Fridays."

"Then Mr. Campos opened early on Tuesday, Wednesday, and Thursday?"

"Nah, he just did Wednesdays back then. They never opened early on Tuesday and Thursday."

"What? Never?"

"Like I said, Judge, there aren't that many girls wantin' to bank. And now, Campos has cut back on that. Just Mondays and Fridays."

Since Sam Tjader was killed on a Tuesday, none of this probably applies after all. But that's what I needed to find out. "Callie," the judge said, "I'd be interested to know in the fall how your investments do."

"You figure on redirecting some of your savin's, Judge?"

"I just might."

"I think I'd better scoot back to my place and cover up some of these wrinkles. This is about the longest I ever went without makeup since I was twelve. Tell Judith thanks for invitin' me. And tell her I'll try to make it over for the quiltin' lesson next week."

He watched Callie shove her way through a crowd of boisterous men at the gate who seemed too busy to notice her, and too stubborn to step aside.

The yard was half empty when the judge slipped into the front door of the house. Judith sat on the edge of the couch, drinking a cup of tea. Daisie Belle Emory sat across from her in the leather chair by the empty fireplace, wearing a Bengal tiger mask.

"I see Timothy has shared his treasure with you," the judge said.

"Yes, and it's given me a wonderful idea. Next year at the New Year's ball, we will all have to wear animal masks! Won't that be delightful?" Daisie Belle giggled.

"I will not wear a squirrel mask," Judith declared.

"My, she does hold a grudge," Daisie Belle said. "And after that exquisite Tiffany glass figurine I brought her. Now, Judge, what do you think about an animal costume party?"

"It sounds like a zoo," the judge replied.

"Oh . . . oh . . . that's brilliant, dear judge! A zoo. Carson City needs a zoo! We can have a wildlife ball this summer and all the funds raised will go for a Carson Zoo!" Daisie Belle jumped to her feet. "Is the mayor still out there?"

"I think so."

"I must go tell him our dear judge's wonderful idea." She hurried out the front door.

The judge glanced over at Judith. "My idea? That's preposterous!"

"Now, Judge, Daisie Belle is going to be Daisie Belle. There isn't much we can do about that. And now that you're here, could you step over to the parsonage and ask David if he has any eggs? I'll need to borrow a few."

"Eggs? I think everyone's through eating."

"We'll need them for breakfast. I had to use more this afternoon than I planned for."

"I'll do it later, when everyone has cleared out."

"Judge Kingston, about a half hour ago I saw Barbara Day climb down out of her tree and hike over to the parsonage. Neither she nor David have been seen since."

"A half hour ago?"

"At least, if not an hour. Meanwhile, Timothy and Douglas are trying to hang themselves upside down in that same tree and Alicia is upstairs lying down on Roberta's bed."

"Is she tired?"

"I think she's convulsed with the pangs of what Dr. Jacobs calls cholera morbus."

"She ate too much smoked salmon?"

"I think she ate too much earthworm."

"She actually *ate* it?"

Judith held the bodice of her dress out in front of her and tried fanning herself with it. "At least she ate half of it. I was a little confused by the story I got from Timothy."

"I'll go up and check on her," the judge announced.

"No, you'll go across the street and borrow some eggs while I go and say goodbye to our guests."

"Right . . . eggs. Are you sure we should be pushing like this into David's business?"

Judith locked her fingers in front of her. "Yes, I'm sure."

"What if they're discussing spiritual issues and I interrupt them?"

"What if they aren't?" Judith replied.

The parsonage was a white single-story

wood-frame house sitting just north of the church yard. It was heavily landscaped and gave the building a sense of privacy and seclusion.

The judge rapped lightly on the front door, then waited. He fastened the top button on his white shirt, then straightened his tie.

He knocked again.

This time he glanced through the dogwood bushes back across the street toward his house. People still milled in the backyard. He could see Daisie Belle fluttering about, but didn't spot Judith.

Undoubtedly, she is watching what I do, whatever it is I am doing.

He opened the front door and peeked into the small but very neat living room. "David?" he called out. He stepped inside and raised his voice. "David?"

Barbara Day's huge portrait was still propped up on the back of the couch. He took a step toward the hall, then stopped. He thought he heard muffled voices from the back of the house.

What am I doing? This is another man's house. He's an adult. He makes his own decisions. Besides all that, he's a man of God. I can't just barge in here. My word, I'm not sure I want to know anymore.

The judge slowly backed out the front door and closed it quietly. *I do believe Judith can come ask about eggs later on. This is none of my business.*

He had just stepped off the porch when he heard footsteps from around the side of the house. "Dad?"

Squinting through the shrubbery, the judge spotted a shirt-sleeved David Kingston.

"I see you're out in the backyard," the judge said.

David stepped around to the front. "Yes, Barbara Day came over. I'm afraid it was a little hectic for her, and me, over at your place. Are the kids behaving themselves?"

"I believe so. The princess has a tummyache from eating an earthworm," the judge reported. "I think we're all amazed she would do that."

"I'm not. She was the one who would try every exotic dish in India," David said. "She was a trouper that way. Timothy wouldn't touch them at all, but she will try anything."

"I trust she's had her fill of worms. Anyway, your mother sent me over to fetch some eggs."

"She's still cooking for that hoard?"

"I believe she's concerned about breakfast. You know your mother."

David led the way into the house. "Yes, I do know Mother," he said. He returned from the small kitchen with a basket of eggs. "And you can tell Mother that Barbara and I are sitting in the backyard."

The judge carried the basket back to his house while thoughts tumbled in his head. *Even though the only place to sit in the back-yard is a wooden swing made for two, I will tell her you were sitting back there and hope she doesn't conjure up visions of you jostling each other on the slatted bench. But I'm not at all sure I should tell her you had red lip rouge on the back of your neck!*

Timothy called him from the birch tree near the intersection of Musser and Nevada streets. "Grandpa Judge, watch this. I can drink lemonade while hanging upside down."

"I don't think you should —" the judge began.

"Hand me the glass, Douglas," Timothy called.

Timothy negotiated the clear glass container to his lips. He tipped it back, then immediately spit out the lemonade. The glass crashed to the ground. Timothy coughed and swung down.

The judge grabbed him up and patted him on the back. "Are you all right?"

"Uh, huh." Timothy coughed again. "I poured it up my nose!"

"I think you'd better not try that again."

"Yeah," Timothy said and nodded. "Douglas, where's your mother? Let's go tell her we learned how to hang upside down in a tree."

"She's over in your backyard," the judge reported.

"Is she hanging from a tree limb over there?" Douglas asked.

"No, I think she's visiting with Timothy's daddy."

"Boy, that sounds boring," Timothy said.

"Why don't you boys go on over and tell her what you've done," the judge said.

"Nah, we'll see her later. We wanted to hang around and see if Alicia vomits up the worm," Timothy announced. "I said it would come up in one piece, but Douglas thinks it will just be tiny little worm chunks."

"You aren't going to see anything. If she does bring it up, it will be thrown away without any inspection," the judge declared.

"Really?" Timothy whined.

"Yes, so you might as well go tell Douglas' mother about your feat."

"Our feet?" Douglas queried.

"Go ahead," the judge urged. "Maybe

there's a limb you can hang from in the backyard of the parsonage."

"Yeah!" Timothy yelled. "We can challenge your mother to a contest."

Both boys raced across the street.

When the judge went inside the house, Levi Boyer and Tray Weston were in the kitchen with Marcy and Willie Jane, helping Judith wash dishes.

"Levi, I was afraid you had to work all day and miss the party," the judge said as he set the basket of eggs on the counter.

"I am workin', Judge. I just came by here to get the sheriff, and maybe a piece of pie."

"Is there trouble at the prison?"

"Somebody shot Manitoba Joe Clark from up on the bluff behind the prison," Tray said. "They fired long range."

"Did they kill him?" the judge asked.

"Nope, just clipped him in the leg. It ain't too serious, but Joe's as mad as a hornet in a hailstorm."

"How could they see anything from that distance?"

"A man could spot Manitoba Joe from fifty miles. There ain't no one who looks like him."

"Is the doc up there?" the judge asked.

"He's on his way. That was my first stop."

The judge peered out toward the front

street. "Have you got a carriage or a horse?"

Tray lapped his thumbs in his vest pocket. "I have the warden's carriage."

"Good. You can give me a ride."

"Right now?" Tray whined. "I haven't had my pie."

"Hurry then, or bring it with you. I'll drive."

Judith walked the judge to the door, then handed him his hat. "How was everything next door?" she asked.

"David and Barbara were sitting in the backyard visiting."

"Visiting about what?"

"I don't know. I didn't ask that."

"Were they sitting on the lawn swing together?"

"I don't know. I didn't see Barbara. David hiked around to get me the eggs. Maybe she was hanging upside down from a tree."

"Modestly, I trust. What do you think we should do about it?"

"About what?"

"About David and Barbara."

"They're adults," the judge said. "We aren't supposed to do anything about it." He paused. "But I did send Timothy and Douglas over to play in the backyard."

She threw her arms around his neck and kissed his cheek. "You're a good man, Judge Kingston."

★ ★ ★

The warden of the Nevada state prison paced the hallway next to the infirmary. "Judge, I was going to send Tray right back to town to ask you to come out. Manitoba Joe is asking for you."

"I thought he might be. How's he doing?"

"He will be limping for a couple weeks," the warden explained. "Doc figures the bullet was purt'near spent when it reached him."

"That's quite a distance away," the judge said. "It takes a marksman to hit anything from that far."

"By the time I got two guards up there to scout around, there was no trace of anything. It's mainly hard rock, and they couldn't distinguish any tracks. The sheriff went up to look around before sunset."

Doc Jacobs came out of the infirmary and into the hall. "I thought I heard your voice, Judge."

"How's the patient?"

"Mad and mean and insisting that I go get Judge Hollis A. Kingston immediately."

"I meant, how's his wound?"

"Nothing that iodine, gauze, and a month of rest won't cure. 'Course, Manitoba Joe doesn't have a month."

The judge started toward the door. "I'll go talk to him."

"I'll send a guard in with you," the warden offered.

"Why?" Doc Jacobs blurted out, "you got him handcuffed to a bedframe."

Manitoba Joe Clark was lying on his back, dressed in prison duckings and a white boiled shirt. His tight pantleg was cut off at the knee and his stubby calf was wrapped tight in gauze. His bald head was propped up on a wool blanket. Both hands were handcuffed to the metal bedframe.

"Joe, how's the leg?" the judge asked.

"I've been stung by scorpions that hurt worse than this. But it proves my point, don't it?"

"That you didn't kill Sam Tjader?"

"Whoever did it was tryin' to put me away."

"There's a whole town full of people just two miles west of here who really liked Sam. Some of them were talking about yanking you out of jail and lynching you. It doesn't seem too far of a stretch to imagine that one of them got a little soused and sat up on that hill to take a potshot at you."

"But if I'm right . . . that I didn't kill Tjader, then the killer is still at large, and this proves he's still in town."

"Even if we can prove it wasn't some

183

drunk who just fired toward the prison at random, it would only prove that someone out there wants to kill you. Do you think there are any people in the western states that would like to see Manitoba Joe dead?"

The prisoner ran his tongue around his full lips. "I don't reckon there are more than four hundred, maybe five hundred, men who would like to shoot me dead on sight."

"It's a definite hazard in your line of work."

"Well, I ain't used to feelin' so helpless. They got me chained down like a turkey the day before Thanksgivin'."

"I've talked to the warden. They aren't going to take you out to the quarry any more."

"Yeah, he's determined to keep me alive so he can hang me."

"I also talked to Governor Kinkead. He's aware that I'm looking into your case. I want him in town in case we need some last-minute intervention. But I want to be real honest with you. The governor said the people of Nevada are so incensed by Sam Tjader's murder and so anxious to get rid of Manitoba Joe Clark that there would have to be overwhelming hard evidence to the contrary before he would ever step in."

"Have you discovered anything?"

"I might have found out about your 'window' in the storeroom. I just heard this afternoon that the back door divides like a dutch door in the middle. The top half could have been open."

Manitoba Joe whooped. "See? I wasn't making it up."

"Nope, you weren't. Of course, Tjader could have hiked over there and opened it up."

"He didn't have time. I went in right behind him."

"But it doesn't mean that anyone was in the back room."

"Judge, ain't that enough to get this hangin' postponed?"

"At this point we don't have one single bit of evidence that anyone else was back there."

"You believe me, don't you, Judge?"

"If the hanging were taking place today, I could not in good conscience stop it. The best I can tell you is that I need more evidence. First, I want to solve this mystery about the half door being open. I will try to find out something before your execution date. But at this point, I'm not very confident."

"That ain't exactly what I want to hear, Judge."

"Manitoba Joe Clark, I cannot make up facts or evidence. But I pledge that I will keep looking."

"What about that two-bit lawyer of mine? What did he say?"

"He refused to talk to me. He boarded a train and left town."

"Don't that tell you somethin'?"

"Joe, I've seen many an attorney ride into town, lose a case, and ride out the next day. My best advice to you is still to settle up with the Almighty."

"I've been talkin' to Him a little lately."

"And?"

"He ain't talkin' back. I told you, He gave up on me."

"If I believed that, I'd give up on you too."

"What do you mean, Judge?"

"If I thought for one minute there was no chance of your ever believing in Jesus Christ, then there would be no purpose in postponing the inevitable. It surely would make my job a lot simpler. Sam Tjader was a good friend of mine, and I'd like to know his death has been properly vindicated. It would be real easy just to walk away from this prison and go back to my house and sleep until daylight without worrying about this case. But the truth of the matter is, I don't believe God has given up on you, and if you need an extra week to figure that out, I'm trying to get you that extra week. So don't tell me He's not talking to you, because He's talking to you right now if you'd open your ears to listen."

Manitoba Joe glanced up at the infirmary ceiling, then shut his eyes. "That's really why you're doin' it, ain't it?"

"Yes, it is."

"Shoot, Judge, I do wish I could've sat down and had this talk with you about ten years ago. I've done some mighty stupid and thoughtless things since. Seems like all these days in jail all those deeds keep bubblin' to the top. I can't erase 'em."

"Without God's holy help, we're all smeared on the inside with stuff too awful to imagine," the judge said. "That's what the Bible says."

"They got me chained to a hospital bed. I can't control anything I do."

"You can control your mind and your heart."

"Are you through preachin' at me?"

"I'm going to see if the sheriff learned anything about who shot at you."

"I don't suppose that will cause the governor to postpone the execution."

"Nope, but it might cause him to speed it up." The judge got up to leave, then reached into his suit coat pocket and pulled out a small leather pouch. "Here's some tobacco, Joe. If they ever unchain you, enjoy it."

"Thanks, Judge, I'm mighty obliged."

"I'll be back in two days."

"I'm countin' on it. Eh, Judge, I reckon I don't deserve it . . . but pray for me, if you take a notion."

"That's something I can guarantee."

"Here I am chained to a bed, locked in prison, shot in the leg, waitin' to be hung." Manitoba Joe shook his bald head. "What could be worse than this?"

"Unless you get serious with God in the next few days, I've got a feeling you're going to find out."

The papers on the judge's office desk contained over twenty thousand words on why Federated Silver should be awarded an additional 175 feet of mining claims on a horizontal tunnel 6,000 feet below the surface of Mount Davidson. Next to it were a similar stack of papers spelling out why The Little Shamrock Mine was the rightful owner of that 175 feet.

The judge studied the two piles of papers.

Justice. I want to make sure justice triumphs. But this is two greedy companies fighting over more silver. Where is the crying need for justice in this case? Someday, Judge Kingston, you will need to retire. You're getting weary of mining litigation. At least this week it seems so —

"May I come into the office unannounced?" Judith asked.

The judge stood up. "I seem to have lost my clerk, though I'm not sure she asked for time off."

Judith strolled over and kissed him on the clean-shaven part of his cheek. "You look very judicial this morning."

"I'm supposed to be studying these two mounds of papers, and I keep thinking about Manitoba Joe Clark."

"Do you believe he's innocent?"

"I don't know, but I do think for the first time in his life old Joe is thinking some eternal thoughts. I guess I'd expect one like him to curse and scream all the way up to the gallows. What can I do for you?"

"I'm on my way to the grocery store. Mr. Cheney has some bamboo shoots from Burma he wants me to try. I also thought I'd pick up our mail, but our box was empty. I figured you had it here at the office."

"I sent Duffy down to get it almost an hour ago. He said he wanted to stop by and thank you for the grand picnic, so I asked him to deliver the mail. He's always done that before."

"What do you suppose distracted him?"

189

"Either the Washburn brothers chased him out of town, or . . ."

Judith waltzed over to the window and stared down the street. "Or he got distracted by his sweet Lorna. I'll go by the café on my way home."

The judge walked over to his hat rack. "I'll go with you."

"I don't want to draw you away from your work."

"What? Is Duffy Day the only man allowed to be distracted by the girl of his dreams?"

Judith grinned. "Why, Judge Kingston, am I still the girl of your dreams after all these years?"

"Is it September yet?"

"Are you dreaming of Hawaii?"

"I'm dreaming of you and me on a slow boat to get there."

Duffy Day was not at the Nice-N-Friendly Café. Nor was Lorna Clair. But the Kingstons' mail was stacked on the counter. The judge toted it out to the sidewalk where Judith was waiting. "The boss sent Lorna down to the depot to pick up supplies and Duffy offered to help."

"He's enjoying himself," Judith said.

"Yes, but I still don't have Lorna figured out."

"Maybe she truly likes him. What did we get in the mail?"

"You got a letter from Marthellen."

"Was there one from Roberta?"

"No."

Judith snatched Marthellen's letter from his hand. "Let me see it."

"Perhaps we should wait until —" The judge's words were cut off as Judith began to read.

Dear Judith and Judge . . .

I'm writing you a quick note from Cheyenne. I'm sure David has made it home and filled you in on what's happening. Mr. Longbake has proved quite impossible. He truly seems to want to make life miserable for both Turner and Roberta. I pray for Peachy's sake there is more to it than that.

We are awaiting a stagecoach ride to Deadwood and Lead. We've been warned that it is a rough trip, but Roberta is clinging to Turner. She thinks she's the only one on earth who can tame him. She may be right. I don't know who would be more of a renegade — Wilt Longbake or Turner Bowman — if it weren't for Roberta.

In the meantime, I feel like I'm the tail

on a kite on a very blustery day. I just keep trying to hang on.

However, I'm having the time of my life. I can't believe I'm here, and you're there. There is some talk that we could miss Mr. Hearst in Lead. He is reported to be going to Chicago. Roberta says we'll follow him to the ends of the earth, if need be.

Turner won't quit until he gets his $25,000 loan out of the sale of the mill. I've never seen a man with such a trapped look. You'd think he was stuffed inside a dressmaker's dummy or Jonah's whale.

I'll write to you from Deadwood or Lead. I hope the matter is resolved and we can head home soon. I have dozens of stories to tell you.

Roberta asks about David and the kids. Turner was wondering how Fidora's little baby is faring. In all his troubles, I'm surprised he even remembers little Daniel.

From the Cheyenne depot,
Marthellen Farnsworth

Chapter Six

The bright mid-May sunlight was just up over the Pine Nut Range in the east. It filtered through the lace curtains into the living room, illuminating the suspended dust in the air and racing shadows down the wall.

The judge plodded off to the office after a near sleepless night.

David sent the children to school, then drove out to the state prison to hold services for the inmates.

Marthellen and Roberta were someplace in the dreary Black Hills of the Dakota Territory.

And Judith sat alone on the green velvet settee, a cup of lukewarm tea in her hands, her cold, bare feet tucked under her. Her old flannel robe covered her old flannel gown.

Her hair hung limp, uncombed, across her shoulders.

There were no tears left.

Lord, we've been through a lot together in Nevada. When we moved here eighteen years ago, David was nine. Roberta was two. Nevada was wild and primitive . . . lawless . . . violent. It was an awful place to move a young family and try to set up a home.

But it was our place, our calling.

David has his beloved India.

We had Carson City.

For two years I was terrified every moment of every day. I kept a loaded shotgun by the door. I would never let the children out of my sight. If the judge was five minutes late coming home, I just knew he had been savagely murdered.

But slowly and gradually You taught me that I could overcome those fears. As I trusted in You, I could face the Nevada challenges. Year after year after year, I've grown in confidence of Your provision and Your leading. There isn't a building in this town that I wouldn't march into, and not a person in the state I wouldn't confront face-to-face.

You have led me into and through every type of difficulty and obstacle. I didn't flinch when guns were drawn, when my name was cursed, when the judge's life was threatened time and again. I've withstood it all. With Your con-

tinued help, I can face everything.

Everything but this.

I just don't know why I feel so overwhelmed. What if Turner is the daddy of little Daniel? What if he neglected Fidora in her time of great need? What if he has the heart of a renegade and irresponsible deceiver?

He is not the first on the face of this earth. Nor the last.

Life goes on.

My life goes on.

Roberta's life goes on.

I must write her and inform her of what I know. "Tell Turner, all is forgiven," that's what Fidora said. It's plain enough. I will tell Roberta to come home at once. Turner can chase Hearst or Longbake, or whomever, by himself.

But I can't do that. I can't tell her anything. I can't make her do anything, even if I did tell her.

I can't even make me do anything.

I don't know why I've been crying so. I don't know why I'm sitting here alone. I don't know why I can't make myself get up and get dressed.

Perhaps all my strength has been built on straw, and this is the final stroke to topple my resolve. I don't want to be here. I don't want to feel this way. I don't like this part of me. I just want to go to sleep and not wake up until everything is wonderful.

I'm tired, so tired. It's been a long battle. The enemies of the world, the flesh, and the devil have surrounded me before. And now, a little skirmish that in previous years would have hardly diverted my faith has crushed me.

I just don't know what to do. I don't know what to think. I don't know what to say. I don't even know how to pray.

I wish the judge and I were on that boat right now. I don't want to get dressed. I don't want to go outside. I don't want to have to face today, let alone tomorrow.

A sharp rap on the front door caused her to flinch and spill cold tea on her robe.

And I especially don't want to talk to anyone right now.

Judith slumped down in the settee and covered her head with a forest green velvet pillow.

Go away! Judith Kingston is not at home. And I don't know when she'll be back!

The rapping continued with short, crisp knocks.

Judith sneaked into the kitchen at the back of the house and the knocking ceased. She darted into Marthellen's darkened and deserted room and peered out at the alley. She saw no one.

There is nothing wrong with my having some privacy. I do not live in a glass house. I do not need to be inspected. I am going to creep up-stairs, crawl into bed, and pull the covers over my head and stay there.

Forever.

Judith went back into the kitchen and slid her tea cup onto the polished oak counter. She thought she saw movement in the yard. She inched over to the breakfast table and slowly pulled back the curtains.

The woman standing in the flower bed, her face pressed against the glass, jumped back with a shout.

Judith raised her hand and waved as if being forced to be a reluctant volunteer. Then she cried. And cried.

Daisie Belle Emory erupted through the side door, wearing daffodil-colored satin and smelling of roses. There was an artificial bloom on her cheeks.

"I see you're having one of those days," she asserted as she marched toward Judith.

"I never have these kinds of days," Judith sobbed.

"I have them all the time, dear Judith, so welcome to the club. Now, come with me."

Judith clutched her robe tightly under her chin. "Where are you taking me?"

"I'm taking you upstairs. You are going to wash your face, then I'll help you get dressed. We'll comb and pin up your hair and try a few drops of Dr. Hall's Female Remedy in your eyes."

"In my eyes?"

"You don't think the sparkle in Daisie Belle's eyes comes from her love life, do you? Heavens, if I waited for that I'd be blind." She tugged Judith up the stairs.

"I can take care of things," Judith mumbled. "I don't need you to —"

"Obviously, you cannot take care of things. And obviously you need my help. A vulnerable Judith Kingston . . . I like that. And, dear Judith, there is one thing you can count on. No one, and I do mean no one, will ever hear about this from me."

She led Judith into her upstairs bedroom. "I presume there's water in the basin. You yank off that old gown and robe with the tea stains. I'll pick you out something cheery to wear."

Judith stared across the room but didn't move.

"It's really quite simple, dear Judith, either you pull off those things and wash up, or I'll do it for you. And believe me, I am quite capable of doing so."

Judith let out a deep sigh and slowly unbuttoned the worn flannel robe. Daisie Belle pulled open the smaller of the two wardrobe closets.

"That's the judge's," Judith said.

"Don't you just love the way men's clothes smell? It's so . . . so . . . manly." Daisie Belle closed the wardrobe and opened the one next to it. "Oh, yes, the royal blue. You must wear it today. Every time you wear it, I die of envy."

"You do?"

"There's something about the way it captures your eyes. What I'd give to have eyes like Judith Kingston."

Judith tucked the collar inside her gown and began to wash her neck and face. The cool water made her breathe faster. Her mind seemed more alert. "My eyes? You must be kidding me. Daisie Belle, you have the most beautiful eyebrows and eyelashes in the city of Carson."

"But I'm trying for the entire state. That's the point. I work at it, just like I work at everything." She carried a pair of white patent leather lace-up boots. "You will wear these," she announced. "You see, dear Judith, I spend a lot of time and money to look like this. I choose my wardrobe carefully. I practice strolling into a room with a slight swank."

"You do?"

"I wasn't born with that, my dear. Some days it takes thirty minutes just to fix my eyes. But it's all worth it, because when I stroll into a room, heads turn."

"You always look magnificent," Judith agreed.

"Thank you, my dear. But let me tell you what is truly magnificent. I watch the crowd when you enter a room. You could be wearing a schoolteacher dress in mud brown, with black India rubber galoshes on your feet and a gingham bonnet on your head, and every head in the room would turn. Do you know why?"

The first smile in over fifteen hours spread across Judith's face. "Because of the galoshes?"

"No!" Daisie Belle said. "Your eyes. Not your eyelashes. Not your eyebrows. Not your sweet face. Not your curly bangs. Not your plain dresses. When you walk into a room and flash those dancing brown eyes, everyone in the room perks up."

"You're exaggerating."

"Hah! Envious? Yes. Exaggerating? No." She motioned to Judith. "Now, hurry up, and I'll help you lace up your corset."

"I don't want to wear a corset today."

"Of course you don't want to wear a corset. You don't want to wear anything but your old flannel gown. But you're going to wear it anyway. We're going out to lunch at the Ormsby House and I want you to look your best."

"I really don't want to go anywhere," Judith said with a sigh.

Daisie Belle handed her a cream-colored corset. "That's already settled. Either you put this on modestly, or I'll put it on you indecently."

"Daisie Belle!" Judith fussed. "You're embarrassing me."

"Good . . . good . . . a little blush looks good on you today. Now, tell me all about what has crushed the spirit out of my dear Judith." Daisie Belle yanked the strings on the medium-length sateen Prima Dona corset.

"I haven't worn this in years," Judith said.

"I'm sure that's because you have to watch the judge's heart. You wouldn't want an old-timer to get too excited, would you?"

"Daisie Belle!"

"You avoided the subject. What happened? It must be a family matter. The only other time I have ever seen you this crushed is when you got news that Patricia was dying. My word, no one has died, have they?"

"Oh, no . . ."

Daisie Belle finished tying the satin strings, then plucked Judith's dress off the bed. "Now, I can't imagine that the impeccable Judge Kingston caused this melancholy. He would die before he caused you any pain. So that leaves David. Oh! He didn't run off and elope with Barbara Day, did he?"

"Of course not!"

"Well now, that just leaves dear Roberta."

Judith took a deep breath and dropped her chin.

"What on earth has she done?"

Judith jerked her head up and held her breath to let the insult settle. "Nothing!"

"You definitely look better with color in your cheeks." Daisie Belle strolled over to the mahogany jewelry box on the dresser. "Where do you keep your good jewelry?"

"That is my good jewelry."

"Yes . . . well, I'm sure I can find you something. Now, tell me all about it."

When they finally reached the Ormsby House, Judith felt like she was dressed in costume for one of Daisie Belle's plays. Even though they both would never see forty-nine again, she did notice that every one of the mostly male heads in the dining room turned and watched them stroll up to a table next to a window facing Carson Street.

"I think I might like sitting in a less conspicuous place," Judith murmured. "I don't normally go out dressed like this unless it's to one of Governor Kinkead's balls."

"Yes, and you always have that slightly balding, tall, good-looking older gentleman on your arm. That's too bad, dear Judith. You're stuck with me. We shall sit at the window. The Ormsby House needs to redecorate. It's much too dark and dreary in here. We will be the fragrant flowers in a moldy old peat bed."

"I don't exactly feel like a fragrant flower."

"Well, you certainly look the part. For the life of me I don't know why I gussied you up so. It only makes me feel plain."

Judith laughed. "That's a lie, Daisie Belle Emory."

"Well, yes it is." Daisie Belle giggled. "I've never felt plain any day in the past twenty years. But it did make you laugh. Now, we will leave Roberta and Turner in the Lord's safe hands. You and the judge raised a bright, handsome young lady. It is time to trust her wisdom and her judgment."

"Is this the same bright, wise daughter of mine that fell for Wilton Longbake's condescending manipulations last fall?"

"No, it isn't that girl, because this Roberta learned from that Roberta and made a wise decision right before

Christmas. This Roberta has much more experience."

The waiter stood patiently at their table. His eyes brightened when Daisie Belle turned to him. "Anthony, tell Maurice that I want the Saturday special for two with just a touch of lemon sauce on the grilled lamb, and have him chop the peppers and onion very fine in the rice."

"It's not Saturday," Judith whispered.

"Oh, dear Judith, for me it is always Saturday."

The waiter disappeared quickly. "If you let them cut the peppers in large chunks, there will be some stuck to your teeth the next time you meet the king."

"The king?"

"Well, you know what I mean. Oh look!" Daisie Belle waved through the window to a woman walking on the sidewalk. "There's Willie Jane."

Soon the younger woman with the pale gray cotton dress was seated beside them.

"You must stay for lunch," Daisie Belle insisted.

"Oh, no, Mr. Cheney needs me back at the store. Besides, I feel like a scrubwoman sitting next to you two today."

"We just felt like putting on something pretty," Daisie Belle announced. "Now, how does Tray like the wedding plans?"

Willie Jane hung her head. "Well . . ."

"He has different ideas?"

"Oh, no . . . that ain't it." Willie Jane sighed. "He thinks all the plans are very nobby. But we kind of —"

"You had a fight?" Daisie Belle asked.

"Oh, no, Tray doesn't hit me. He treats me real nice."

"Let me guess," Judith said. "You're getting very nervous about being married, and now you find that everything Tray does or says annoys you?"

"Yes! Did he tell you that?"

"Oh, no, I haven't seen Tray in days. You just have normal wedding jitters."

"I'll tell you what normal is," Daisie Belle said. "Normal is walking down to the depot with money in your hand for a one-way ticket to Omaha."

"Really?"

"Honey, marriage is a great unknown. If we dwell on how unknown it is, it's terrifying," Judith said. "If you didn't think that way, I would say you aren't thinking about it seriously enough."

Willie Jane took a deep breath. "I am surely glad to hear you say that. But what am I going to say to Tray? I acted very contrary this morning. He's such a rock. He doesn't have a second thought about this marriage at all, and I'm running around all panicked."

"Why don't you tell him you love him more than anything in the world, but you're scared to death you might not be able to live up to his expectations," Judith said.

Daisie Belle took up the challenge. "And that you're so anxious for the wedding day that you're afraid of rattling on about things of little importance to him."

When she paused for a breath, Judith jumped back in. "And tell him that if you could, you'd marry him this afternoon. But since you can't, ask him to be tolerant of your anxiety."

Willie Jane stared at the women. "I can't believe this . . . two mothers! Thanks for the advice." She jumped to her feet. "I have to go now."

"You still have a few minutes, just relax," Daisie Belle said.

"I have to stop by the bank and put some money back . . . for that train ticket to Omaha." Willie Jane's grin revealed two slight dimples.

The cook at the Ormsby House, Maurice, personally brought out the ladies' dinners and waited by the table for Daisie Belle's smile of approval before he returned to his duty.

"Oh, I found you, and you're together!" Marcy Boyer called out. "This is such a marvelous day!" She scooted up a chair between the ladies. "You will never guess what I discovered this morning!"

"You're expecting a baby?" Daisie Belle blurted out.

Marcy's round eyes widened, and her perfectly smooth cheeks broke into a tooth-revealing grin. "Yes! Isn't it the most exciting thing that ever happened in the world?"

Judith reached over and squeezed her hand. "It's wonderful. And here I thought you two were going to wait a year before starting a family."

"It just happened."

"I think it's tremendous news," Daisie Belle said. "What does Levi say?"

"I'm sure he will be as thrilled as I am. But he's at work and I haven't had a chance to tell him yet."

"Did you check with Doc Jacobs this morning?" Judith asked.

"Yes, I went right in first thing, but he didn't even examine me. He said to wait a few weeks before a check-up. I suppose he knows what he's doing."

"He's had lots of experience," Judith said. "When is the baby due?"

Marcy giggled. "Nine months from last night."

Judith blushed. Daisie Belle dropped her fork on the china plate.

"I just know I'm pregnant. It's funny how a woman can tell. I just woke up this morning knowing it."

Daisie Belle cleared her throat. "Well, every once in a while a woman is mistaken. Dear, it doesn't hurt to wait for the doctor's examination before you tell Levi."

Marcy Boyer danced her fingers along the top of the chair. "I took the day off from work and I'm going to look for some baby things."

"Marcy, don't be in too big a hurry to spend money," Judith warned.

"Yes," Daisie Belle agreed, "men need to ease into these ideas. Why do you think the Lord has us carry that baby for nine long months? It's to get the men ready to be a father."

"Oh! You're right. Maybe I won't buy anything. But I can look."

"That's a good idea," Daisie Belle said. "Besides, we will want to throw you a shower a few weeks before the baby's arrival. You must leave us a few things to get for you."

"I never thought of that. I think I'll stop

by the post office and write to my mother. It will be her first grandchild. She'll be thrilled." Marcy hurried out of the crowded restaurant.

Daisie Belle leaned forward and whispered, "When Marcy said they had planned to wait until next year, did she mean wait until next year to . . ."

"At least she knows the exact moment of conception," Judith said.

Daisie Belle sat straight up and stabbed a bite of lamb with lemon sauce. "We are going to change the subject. All of this is very fine and dandy conversation for a married woman like you, Judith Kingston. But for a widow like me, it only means another very lonesome, sleepless night."

They were spooning small bites of caramel custard dessert when Duffy Day startled them by tapping on the hotel window. He wore a neat, dark gray shirt with seams low on the shoulder, an almost straight black tie, and fairly new tan ducking trousers with leather braces.

"Duffy has my mail," Judith said. "I'll go out and get it."

"We can send the waiter," Daisie Belle suggested.

"I wouldn't do that to Duffy."

"He does look very neatly dressed."

"Shaved and a haircut. Lorna Clair has made a difference in that man's life." Judith hurried out to the hotel lobby.

Duffy waited for her at the curb. His floppy felt hat was in one hand, several letters in the other. "You look like a cow all slicked up for the county fair," he said.

Judith bit her lip. *Lord, I have to keep reminding myself that Duffy means that as a compliment.* "And you look very nice today, Duffy."

"I spent the morning with my sweet Lorna. We was shoppin'."

"Did you have a good time?"

Duffy rocked back on his heels. "I bought her that ring. Did you see it yet?"

"No, what kind of ring did you buy her?"

"A diamond ring that cost 105 cash dollars."

"An engagement ring? So soon?"

"We've knowed each other a whole week. That's longer than I ever knowed any woman in my life." Duffy dropped his gaze to the sidewalk. "But it seems like we've known each other our whole life. Do you know what I mean, Judith?"

"I believe I do, Duffy. That is very exciting news."

"I never ever thought any woman would want to marry the likes of me, let alone a woman so beautiful."

Judith glanced across the street at the state capitol and noticed the Stars and Stripes snapping in the desert breeze. *Well, Lord, I'm glad most of my tears are gone. Take care of Duffy. He's such a gentle, trusting man. Don't let him get hurt in this.* "Is that my mail, Duffy?"

"Yep. The judge asked me to bring the mail to you at the Ormsby House."

"He knew I was down here?"

"He said you'd be settin' right out at the window with Daisie Belle Emory. And there you were."

"I wonder how he knew that?"

"The judge is a real smart man, Judith."

She took her mail. "Yes, isn't he?" *And he can be very manipulative, too.*

Back in the restaurant, several men huddled around Daisie Belle's table. They tipped their hats and dispersed when Judith approached.

"What did Duffy have to say?"

"That he bought his sweet Lorna an expensive engagement ring," Judith reported.

"Oh, no . . . is he setting himself up to be heartbroken?"

"I don't know. I pray not. He's certainly not heartbroken at the moment."

"She will taste the wrath of Daisie Belle

Emory if she's playing games with our Duffy."

"Speaking of playing games," Judith challenged, "just what time did the honorable Judge Kingston call on you this morning?"

Daisie Belle raised her hand to her mouth. "Whatever do you mean?"

"I mean, the judge came by your house early this morning and said dear Judith was in a fit of melancholy and you should go over and cheer her up."

Daisie Belle grinned. "Did it work?"

"Yes, but it was conniving."

"No, it wasn't. You didn't ask why I happened to be up and out so early."

"I should have been more suspicious with you prowling through the bushes and snooping in the windows."

"You had a concerned husband."

"I'll take care of him later."

"I imagine you will."

"Meanwhile, I'm going to read my mail. There's one from Peachy."

"Do read it aloud," Daisie Belle said.

"It's an invitation."

"A wedding invitation? She really is going to marry Zeeb Longbake?"

"On July 19th at St. John's Church in New York City, with a reception following at Vanderbilts' . . . *and* another reception the next week at the San Francisco estate of Mr. George Hearst."

"Our little Peachy has done quite well," Daisie Belle said.

"And I trust she will be happy," Judith said. "I hope Duffy will be too. I'm tired of forecasting doomed and troubled relationships. I trust they are all delightfully, deliriously happy."

"Even Roberta?"

"Oh, yes, especially Roberta."

For the first time in twenty-four hours, Judith mentioned her daughter's name without tearing up.

It was midafternoon when the judge came in the side door, hung his hat on the peg, then strolled across the kitchen to kiss Judith on the back of the neck.

"You're home early, Judge Kingston."

"They settled out of court."

"The mining litigation case?"

"Yes, they filed a twenty-thousand-word petition, and a twenty-thousand-word rebuttal. I studied it for a week, then they settled out of court. Sometimes I feel like I'm wasting my time."

"Well, I'm glad you got off early. I was afraid you came home just to see if your melancholy wife had straightened up."

"The thought did cross my mind."

"I'm much better, thank you. I don't understand why that hits me all of a sudden. It's as if every once in a while the Lord needs to remind me that I'm not nearly in control as much as I think I am."

He slipped his arms around her waist and kissed her on the lips. "I trust you didn't mind me recruiting Daisie Belle."

"It's just what I needed. How are you dealing with the situation?"

"I still think we need to confront Turner and allow him an opportunity to speak before . . ."

"Before what?"

"Before we tar and feather him and run him out of town. But first we must get them home."

"Shall we telegraph them to that effect?" Judith asked.

"I've thought about it. I keep thinking any day now they'll walk through the door. By the way, do you have any idea how that lower limb in the willow tree got broken off?"

"I believe that was when Timothy and Douglas tried hanging upside down on it at the same time." Judith handed the judge a cup of coffee.

"I didn't see them out in the yard."

"They went down to the park with their homemade slingshots. Timothy is going to capture a rare Himalayan black bear. Alicia is upstairs reading *Stuart Brannon and the Crippled Gypsy Princess.*"

"Does she know how to read a book like that?"

"She likes looking at the illustrations."

"I take it we have the kids for the afternoon?"

"Yes, David's gone, you know."

"What do you mean, he's gone? Where did he go?"

"Judge, he explained all of that to us before. He wanted a little time to think and pray, so he went up to Lake Tahoe for the night. He'll be back tomorrow around suppertime. Don't you remember him asking us?"

"I guess I don't. Did he go alone?"

"I think so."

"You think? Have you seen Barbara Day around town this afternoon?" the judge quizzed.

"No, have you?"

The rap at the front door sent the judge scurrying through the dining and living room. Judith tugged off her apron from over her pale peach cotton dress and followed him. She overheard the judge and Tray Weston talking in hushed tones as she went up the stairs to check on Alicia.

Barefoot, she was sprawled across the bed on her stomach, studying an illustration of a man fighting a bear with nothing but a stick, while a beautiful black-haired girl on crutches hid behind a pine tree. Alicia looked up with wide eyes. "Someday, Grandma Judith, I'm going to marry Stuart Brannon!"

"I'm afraid he will be a very old man when you're big enough."

"Well, I can't marry Grandpa Judge because that would put you out of work," she declared.

"Thank you for thinking of me."

"And I can't marry Daddy."

"No, that wouldn't be a good idea."

"He told me when Mamma died that he was never, ever, ever going to get married again," Alicia said.

"That sounds pretty definite."

"That's why I'm leaning toward Stuart Brannon. I hope he doesn't marry the crippled gypsy girl." She turned the pages slowly. "Or my best friend, Marjorie Walters."

"Judith?" the judge called out from down below. "We've got a message from Roberta."

As soon as Judith dashed down the stairs, the judge said, "Deputy Weston brought us a telegram. He was at the station when it came in."

"What does it say?"

"I haven't read it yet, but do you know why Tray was at the station?"

"He was nervous about the wedding and had a tiff with Willie Jane this morning and was considering buying a ticket for Omaha to get away. Now read Roberta's telegram."

"He was running to San Francisco, but how did you know that?"

"Willie Jane is scared too. Let me see the telegram."

"My concern is, are they getting married because they want to, or in order for Willie Jane to adopt Fidora's baby?"

"Judge Kingston, either you read that telegram from my daughter, or I'll be forced to shoot you and read it myself. Are you afraid of what's in there?"

"Perhaps." He handed it to her. "You read it."

"Judith & Judge Kingston: Daddy, please go to Mill office. Turner's desk. Upper right-hand drawer. Mail 'Expenditure Ledger' to Mr. Jacobson, 701 La Salle Street, Chicago, Illinois. On our way to Chicago. Explained everything in a letter. Turner is very troubled. Got to be with him. Love, Roberta."

Judith turned the telegram over and looked at the blank back side as if expecting something else. "That's it? Send ledger to Jacobson? Who's Jacobson? What are they doing in Chicago? Why haven't they come home? How can I write to my daughter when I don't even know where she is?"

"She said a letter will explain."

"How long will it take for a letter to arrive from Deadwood? It's primitive up there. The letter could get lost. I want to know what's going on right now."

The judge walked to the back door and plucked up his hat.

"Where are you going?" she asked.

"Since I took off work early, and you're doing fine, I thought I'd just go out to the reduction mill and find Turner's ledger."

"Do you have a key to the office?"

"No, but I'll take the sheriff with me. I'm sure we can find a way in."

Judith paced across the back porch. "I'm not doing all that fine. I think I'll go with you."

"What about the children?"

"All right, I'll stay at home with my grandchildren and wait for that letter from my daughter."

"It won't be here today. Probably not tomorrow either."

"Then I'll just sit and wait."

"Are you sure you're all right?"

"Perhaps I'll take the ledger to her in Chicago," Judith said. "I need something to do."

The judge opened the Nevada Street door and nodded at a woman walking up the sidewalk. "You can visit with Barbara Day, who is not at Lake Tahoe."

The Consolidated Reduction Mill was the newest of the three at Empire, perched along the Carson River six miles west of Carson City. It had operated only a few months before labor unrest and a well-placed bomb sabotaged the machinery. For five months Turner Bowman had pushed a crew of twelve to rebuild and retool the mill.

But now, less than a week left in the rebuilding schedule, the mill sat idle like a giant racehorse still at the starting line, while the other mounts stretched their legs on the straightaway.

Sheriff Hill drove the carriage up to the mill's front gate. "I have a key to the gate," he announced, "but the office is another matter."

The judge pushed open a window at the side of the office and slipped in that way.

"Judge, you get what Turner needs. I'll wander around out here and see that every-

219

thing else is on the square," the sheriff said. "The way it was suddenly shut down the other day, no telling what they forgot to lock."

Sketches and draftsmen's designs lined every available wall. Turner's desk was littered with drawings of pulleys, giant pistons, and stamp machines bigger than a house. In the top right-hand drawer was a black leather ledger labeled "Expenditure Ledger #1," and under it, an identical black leather book labeled "Expenditure Ledger #2."

Two books? Which one does he need? I'll send both, but what if one is for potential investors to review and the other isn't? Is Turner going to receive them? Or some Jacobson man on LaSalle Street?

The judge plopped down in the oak captain's chair and shoved some of the papers aside.

He opened the top ledger and followed each entry with his finger. *Re-building of Consolidated Mill, Empire. Nevada, December 1880, Turner Bowman, contractor. Capital infusion after purchase: Mr. G. Hearst $75,000. Mr. W. Longbake —*

Here the Judge noticed that $75,000 was crossed out and $50,000 was written in the margin.

He followed each entry with his finger.

Page after page after page.

It was on page 34 that he noticed an item on the top of the page: *Additional capital infusion: $25,000* Why the asterisk? What does it mean? Where did he get this money? Is this the big debt he's chasing right now?*

The judge read the entry over and over.

Suddenly he dropped the book and looked up. *February 12th? That's the day after Sam Tjader was killed!*

He continued to search the book but his eyes seemed to be skipping over the words. *How did he get that money? If it's a loan from the bank, then Campos will have record of it. If not . . . no, no, something isn't right, here . . .*

He flipped open the second ledger. On page 16 he found a listing as "Debt Retirement." There was a careful ten-year plan for paying off George Hearst and Wilton Longbake, but no mention of the additional $25,000.

He doesn't have a plan for paying back the bank? Maybe he had the money saved. Maybe it's his own. But last December he was so broke he couldn't buy Roberta a Christmas present. If he didn't owe it to anyone, why chase Hearst and Longbake across the country? Of course, if he didn't owe it to anyone but could convince Hearst and Longbake he did, by showing this *ledger, for instance, then he could get away with $25,000. But if that's all he wanted, he could have taken it and skipped the country before repairing the mill. But if the rebuilding plan went astray, he needs to pull out as much cash as he can. Somehow, I've got to see the bank records. I've got to know this was a legitimate loan. Why would Turner have me come get these . . . unless he just didn't think I would look through them? Maybe he doesn't care what I think. Perhaps he's hoping for an instant repayment, then take off to a new location . . . with my daughter.*

"Judge, did you find what you wanted?" the sheriff called in the window.

Judge Kingston stood and picked up both ledgers. *I may have found out more than I wanted.*

"I'm headed back out to Duffy's," Barbara reported. "I'll take Douglas with me."

Judith stood in the doorway. "He and Timothy went down to the park with their slingshots."

"I'll go fetch him," the younger woman said. "Would you like to walk with me?"

"I'm sorry, Barbara, I have to stay here."

Barbara Day stared into Judith's eyes. Judith admired her dainty features and heart-shaped mouth, like an elfin fairy who might at any moment fly away.

"You don't want to walk with me?"

"Alicia is upstairs napping," Judith explained. "And the judge had to go see the sheriff. I can't leave her by herself."

Barbara's voice softened. "I was hoping we could talk."

"Well, do come in. I'll fix some tea." Judith stepped back from the door.

"I don't drink tea. Or coffee. They destroy creativity." Barbara glanced down at the wooden steps. "Could we just sit out here and visit?"

"Certainly." Judith sat at one end of the porch, Barbara at the other. Both faced Nevada Street, the parsonage, and a May sun that was midway in the sky. There was a swirling breeze coming down from the Carson Range, strong enough to flutter Judith's bangs and drift dust into her eyes. "I hear you and Douglas and his father lived in Alaska."

Barbara played with her braids. "Those were our happiest days together. My memories there include cabbages in our garden that grew to seventy pounds; crabs that measured three feet across on the beach. Once we saw a chunk of glacier the size of the capitol building thunder into the sea while we were on a boat. The only time I ever saw my husband tremble was when we went over a bridge there. From the center the dizzying view below made him ill. I wanted to stay and paint a picture of it, but that was impossible."

"What did you want to talk about, Barbara?"

The younger woman twisted her long braids around, swung them on top of her head and pinned them. "How come you and the judge like everyone in this town but me?"

Judith felt like someone had stabbed her in the side. "What?"

"From the day I arrived, right after Drake's death, I've felt like you don't think I'm worthy to live in this town."

"But . . . but that's not true," Judith said.

"You think I don't take good care of Douglas. You believe I'm taking advantage of Duffy. And now you think I'm not good enough for your David," Barbara insisted. "I feel your judgment hanging over us about who we are and who we ought to be."

"I have concerns, yes, but no spite or malice intended." *Oh, Lord, have I been so distressed with other concerns that I haven't sensed how I've been coming across to Barbara?*

"That's not the way I see it."

"Barbara, you are a very straightforward,

blunt person. I'm not quite used to that, so let me explain things my way."

"Start with how I raise Douglas. What am I doing wrong?"

"Barbara, it is not a question of right and wrong. All of us do things differently. And if our way seems to work, we think others should do it that way too. I like the way you encourage Douglas to try new things, to experiment with life, to learn and grow in his abilities. But there doesn't seem to be any parameters. He has no bedtime, no discipline, no emphasis on study in school. I know he's just a little guy, but I worry about him."

"Douglas has more skills for his age than any child around. He can compete with your Timothy, who is three years older."

"Yes, but he can't even read at Alicia's level. He's quick to follow and imitate, but doesn't often take initiative, and is sometimes so sleepy he takes a nap right on this porch."

Barbara's head and voice lowered. She seemed to study her worn brown boots. "Douglas sleeps well, but he's always been sleepy in the daytime. I don't know what to do about that."

"Perhaps Dr. Jacobs could examine him?"

"Specialists in Santa Barbara couldn't

figure it out. They said he would grow out of it . . . maybe."

"Well, forgive me for being presumptuous about that subject," Judith said.

"Did you see the ring Duffy bought for his Lorna?" Barbara asked.

"I haven't seen it, but Duffy said it was beautiful and expensive."

"Where do you think he got the money?"

"I supposed he sold some hogs."

"I gave him the money," Barbara announced.

Judith's eyes opened wide.

"You seem surprised. Didn't you think I had any income? Didn't you think I love my brother-in-law? Why are you so astonished?"

"I guess because I had not been exposed to other signs of your concern for Duffy. The only time I see you is when you're engaged in bizarre behavior . . . perched in a tree studying a nest. Stuck on the peak of the church roof. Hanging upside down in a tree in my front yard. I only know you in those types of situations and you only know me in reaction to such times. So, perhaps neither of us knows the other very well."

"I suppose you are right."

"I believe I've jumped to some conclusions about you. And perhaps you have jumped to some conclusions about me. Please forgive me for my failures. I've been rather distracted with David's losing Patricia, whom we loved very deeply. It has affected the judge and me more than we imagined."

"Can we talk about the third item?"

"You and David?"

"I love your son, Mrs. Kingston. I've loved him from the first day I met him. I've never known any man to be so sensitive and yet so strong in his convictions. And I've never known any person, male or female, who was so convinced of exactly what God wanted him to do with his life."

Judith stretched out her legs. "David decided that he was going to India when he was about Timothy's age. The catalyst, I believe, was the death of Jenny Clemens, a playmate of his. It affected him deeply."

"That's what he told me too. Now, why is my friendship with David anathema to you?"

"That isn't the word I would use."

"That's the way David describes your feeling. I'm sure that's why he went to Lake Tahoe. He wanted to pray about what place I have in his life."

Judith rubbed the back of her neck. "Barbara, can I ask you some personal questions? I believe they will help me understand you better."

"Go ahead."

"Did you divorce Drake Day?"

"No. We were separated when he got sick because I had an opportunity to go to Mexico and paint a mural. By the time I got word about his condition and found that he was here in Carson City, he had died."

"Why did Drake have Douglas, and not you?"

"Have you been to Mexico lately, Judith?"

"No, I haven't."

"There are some places that I feel are too revolutionary and violent for a child. Do you believe me?"

"Yes, I do. Now I have another question. Do you know Jesus as your Lord and Savior?"

"Yes. Do you know Jesus as your Lord and Savior, Judith Kingston?" she challenged right back.

"Why, of course I do," Judith stuttered. "That was rather rude."

"As was your inference."

"Perhaps so." Judith sighed. "But it was a very important question to me. David is a missionary. His whole life is committed to God. It's important that his mate have a heart-knowledge of God."

"My mother was a Bible believer. I've always known that our Creator is the Jesus of the Bible, and that He is perfect in character, and glorious beyond thought," Barbara Day explained.

"But we cannot trust our daily problems and temptations to a God way out there," Judith said, "a God we don't personally know. To truly know God, we must perceive Him from our own spirits. We have to speak to Him, make peace with Him, receive communication from Him. We must lift our whole hearts to Him, not just a little part."

"Not everyone can know God like you do," Barbara said, her voice tense. "You expect too much of me."

Judith sighed. "I don't seem to be able to say anything to you that doesn't cause friction. I've had a very emotional day, for which you are in no way to blame. I might be better off visiting with you another time so I won't have so much to apologize for."

"Like when?"

"How about when David and the judge are present? At the moment, I feel much too emotional and protective of my children to have an unbiased discussion." Judith stood up. "I was sincere when I asked your forgiveness for misjudging you. Whoever is right for David is a decision that he will make for himself. I trust my son's judgments, perhaps even more than I trust my own. But I do have one last question for you. Are you convinced that you are the one God has selected to help David achieve his life task of ministry in India? Will your partnership help him do that?"

The antagonism instantly melted from Barbara Day's suntanned face. "That has been troubling me the most," she admitted. "I believe that is the real reason David needed to get alone and pray."

After Barbara left, Judith wandered out in the yard to the tree Barbara had climbed. She looked high up in the branches, wondering what it would be like from there. She thought of the friends of her childhood who climbed trees while she sat against the trunk, reading a book.

She reached her hand out. The bark felt smoother than she expected. *I have never climbed a tree in my life.* She cradled a foot on the lowest branch and pulled herself up.

Chapter Seven

Still wearing his judicial robe, and carrying a leather satchel crammed full of documents under his arm, Judge Hollis A. Kingston entered his office and stared at the empty chair behind a clerk's desk stacked with papers.

I need a new clerk. I need a clerk now, but I can't dismiss my own daughter. If it were anyone else, I'd fire them. This is not working out. Perhaps I could hire Spafford to come in after hours and catch things up.

The sheriff appeared in the doorway. "Get out of your robe, Judge, and grab your shotgun; I need you to come with me."

Judge Kingston quickly unbuttoned his robe. "What's going on?"

"Sounds like two Montana drifters rode into town and got into a shooting match with Manitoba Joe's lawyer, Mr. Atley Musterman. Apparently they don't approve of Joe's representation."

"But I thought he was long gone from here," the judge declared.

"He came back for some reason, and these guys must have followed him. Somebody said they complained they didn't feel they got their money's worth."

The judge jammed on his felt hat and picked up the dust-covered shotgun propped in the corner next to an orangewood cane and two umbrellas.

When they exited the courthouse, the sound of a gunshot came from the south. They jogged along Carson Street toward a crowd milling in front of Jack's Saloon.

Duffy Day dodged a farm wagon loaded with hay, then called out, "What happened, Judge?"

"Duffy, go get Doc Jacobs!" the sheriff yelled. "Chances are, we're going to need him."

The group of men gathered just outside the saloon divided to allow the sheriff and judge into the brick building. The room was half full of men huddled at the back door and staring out.

"They're back in the alley, Sheriff!" an apron-clad bartender called out.

"Be careful, Judge, they're all drunk. No tellin' who will get shot," someone else shouted.

The sheriff shoved his way to the back door. The judge, a good six inches taller, followed.

"That two-bit lawyer is down the alley to the right. Them Montanans is to the south," the bartender reported. "They were sittin' over in the corner talkin' and drinkin' for an hour, then that attorney jumps up and pulls a gun. He makes a run for the back door, with them two on his tail. There was shootin' in the alley but I don't think anyone is shot . . . yet."

When the sheriff crouched at the doorway, the bartender said, "Don't go out there, Sheriff, they'll shoot you!"

As soon as the sheriff crawled out on the concrete step leading down to the cobblestone alley, a gun fired. Splinters from the door lintel rained down on the sheriff and judge.

"Get back," someone yelled. "This ain't your fight."

The sheriff hiked out to the middle of the alley. "You just attempted to murder the sheriff of Ormsby County, boys. That makes it my matter."

"We didn't know you was a sheriff," one of them hollered.

"You know now."

"We wasn't aimin' at you, Sheriff. We ain't that bad at hittin' what we target."

"I appreciate that, boys. Maybe the judge will take that into consideration. He's right behind me." The sheriff faced the two Montanans while the judge covered Atley Musterman's position.

"Lay down your guns," the sheriff ordered. "You're under arrest for unlawful discharge of firearms and disturbin' the peace."

"Cain't do that, Sheriff. Musterman called us out here and challenged us to a gunfight. We won't back away with him pointin' a pistol at us. He puts his down, then we'll follow."

"Did you hear that, Musterman?" the judge called out. "Toss down the gun and stand up."

"I can't do that, Judge, they'll kill me for sure."

"What's this all about?" the sheriff demanded.

"We found Musterman in a saloon in Reno. We hired him to come down and file an appeal for Manitoba Joe. But he came into Jack's an hour ago sayin' he got a better offer not to file an appeal. His answer was to outbid 'em. So we got mad, 'cause we figure he was tryin' to gouge us. Ain't no one in this town who gives a dung heap what happens to Joe."

"So, we threatened to slice him up and feed him to the dogs if he didn't do it for the agreed price. He pulled his gun and shot at us. We ran out to the alley."

"Is that true, Musterman?" the judge yelled.

"What part of it?"

The judge took a couple steps closer to the cowering attorney. "That someone in town offered you money not to file an appeal?"

"Could be."

"Who paid you?" the judge demanded.

"That's privileged client-attorney information, and you know it, Judge."

"He's not a client unless he's hired you for legal representation. If he just offered you money, that's called a bribe. Who is he?" the judge prodded.

"Could be anyone in town," the bartender called out. "Ain't none of us want Sam Tjader's killer to get off the hook."

Someone near the back door yelled, "We'll take up a collection in here and match them Montanans' offer."

The sheriff slowly walked toward the gunmen, who were squatted behind packing crates. "Boys, you aren't backin' a very popular cause. Maybe you ought to jist mount up and ride back to Montana."

"Joe's our friend," the thinner of the two, with dirty blond hair, declared.

"That's nice that even bank robbers and murderers have pals, but you ain't helped Joe one bit. If you gun down this lawyer, no matter how worthless he is, folks is goin' to want to lynch you with your pal Joe by nightfall," the sheriff said.

"Hire yourself a different attorney," the judge shouted.

"Make him give us back our money!" one of the Montanans hollered back.

Judge Kingston walked over to where Musterman, dressed in a dusty black three-piece suit, was squatted behind a rain barrel. "You took a higher offer and won't refund their money?"

"I spent most of it," Musterman admitted as he waved his hands, including the one with the revolver. "I got a little drunk last night and had bad luck at the Faro table."

The judge glanced down the alley behind Musterman, as if watching someone. When the attorney turned around, Judge Kingston creased the man's hat with the shotgun barrel and he slumped to the cobblestones.

"Musterman, your luck hasn't improved any today," the judge remarked.

"What happened down there?" the sheriff called out.

Judge lifted his voice and announced, "The lawyer decided to put down his gun."

Doc Jacobs caught up with them in the sheriff's office. He examined the conscious, but ailing, Atley Musterman. He then met the judge at the sheriff's desk.

"How is he?" Judge Kingston asked.

"Just like I always said, attorneys are the thickest-skulled individuals on the face of the earth. You didn't even break the skin, but he does have a substantial lump. He's threatenin' to sue you."

"But I saved his life."

"For a ten-dollar fine, he can go free," the sheriff stated. "You want to talk to him before I turn him loose?"

The judge nodded and walked to the open cell where Musterman sat on a bunk, holding his head.

"I ought to sue you!" Musterman growled.

"Let's see, you threatened an officer of the court, discharged a firearm in the city limits, and refused to surrender your weapon when commanded to do so. I have at least twenty-five witnesses, including the county sheriff. I believe that would be six months to a year in jail. If the higher sentence was chosen, you'd serve your time at the state prison. Now, Mr. Counselor, if you still want to bring a lawsuit against me, then go right ahead."

"I didn't say I was going to. I said I ought to!"

"I'll tell you what you have to do. You have to pay those boys back their money. You owe them a hundred dollars. I presume that whoever else hired you also paid you in advance, so all you have to do is pay these boys with some of that money."

"I won't have the money until the bank opens tomorrow."

"I want to know when I can have that money laying on my desk in my office tomorrow morning," the judge demanded.

"I'll get it to you by 7:30 a.m."

The judge studied Musterman. *The bank doesn't open until 8:00 a.m. I don't know if you knew what you were saying or not.* "That's fine. I'll tell the Montanans to meet me in my office at 8:00 a.m. You'll have the hundred dollars then."

"I could just ride out of town," Musterman boasted.

"That's true. And I could show the Montana boys what trail you took. It's up to you. Pay them off and forget it, or keep looking over your shoulder till they find you."

"I'll pay them off," the lawyer muttered.

"Good choice. I'm sorry for the blue lump on your head. I was convinced it was the only way to keep you and them out of a gunfight. The ice company still has some river ice. Buy yourself a chunk and bring that swelling down."

"Is the sheriff going to turn the Montanans loose now?" Musterman queried.

"He's got to. They paid their fine, just like you. But I'll have a talk with them first. That'll give you time to go hole up and sleep this off until morning."

"Yes, sir, I think I will."

"Musterman, I think you better decide whether you want to be an attorney or a gambler. As it now stands, I will reject you from practicing in my court and recommend the same to the other district judges. Pull yourself together, Atley, or you're going to lose your career."

"I don't need any more lectures," Musterman retorted, then stalked out of the cell past the judge, the sheriff, and the doctor.

"What about them two in the back?" the sheriff quizzed.

"I'll go question them. It will give Musterman a moment to get out of sight."

The two men stood in the rear of the unlocked cell, smoking cigars. They were wearing huge oversized bandannas, and their pantlegs were stuffed inside the tops of their boots.

"Are we free to go now, Judge?" the short, stocky one asked. He wore unpolished cowboy boots and had a rugged, weathered face. His hair used to be red but was bleached out from years under a Montana sky.

"In just a minute. Musterman is going to get your money out of the bank and have it in my office in the courthouse by 8:00 a.m. You stop by after that, and I'll have the hundred dollars waiting for you."

"Thanks, Judge." They headed for the iron bar door.

"There's a couple of other things," Judge Kingston said. "First, don't hang around town tonight. Go out to Dayton or up to Washoe City or out to Moundhouse, but don't hang around town. Sam Tjader was an extremely popular bank manager. He had a wife and children and was active throughout the community during the time he was here. People in this town are convinced that Manitoba Joe Clark killed Tjader. They may not take kindly to his friends."

The thin Montanan stepped over to the judge. "Manitoba Joe didn't kill that banker."

"How do you know that?"

" 'Cause we've known him for over ten years. Joe has never in his life shot at a man who didn't shoot at him first. That's his style. They've got to make the first play. When we got word that Manitoba Joe was in jail for shootin' an unarmed banker, we knew it was a lie."

"Is that when you first hired Musterman to be Joe's lawyer for the trial?"

The thickset man rubbed his unshaven chin. "We didn't hire him first time."

"Shoot no, Judge, we didn't hire him then," the taller one added. "We was spendin' time in the Bozeman jail and heard about it from another prisoner. By the time we got out, we thought we were too late, but we came down anyway. That's when we happened onto Musterman at the Reno saloon, braggin' that he was Manitoba Joe's lawyer."

"Did he tell you who did hire him?"

"Nope, he wouldn't say. But from the looks of the way things went, I don't think it was a friend of Joe's."

"You could be right. Stay out of town. Come to my office in the morning. And if you still want to try and help Joe, I'll give you the names of a couple attorneys up in Virginia City who might come down and take up Joe's case. No lawyer in Carson City will touch it. Like I said, Sam Tjader was a popular man."

Judith was carefully hanging up the judge's robe when he returned to the office. "Looks like you left in a hurry," she said.

"The sheriff wanted me to set a fine for a couple of boys from Montana who were disturbing the peace." He jammed his hat on a peg and returned the gun to the corner beside the umbrellas.

"While carrying a shotgun?"

"Just a precaution."

She began brushing the robe. "I heard a tall, slightly balding gentleman cold-cocked a drunken gunman in the alley behind Jack's Saloon. Would you know anything about that?"

"He wasn't exactly a gunman, more like an educated misfit who doesn't like people much." He walked over to Roberta's desk. "Look at all of this! I need my clerk."

"That's why I'm here. I've come to file some things for you."

"You don't have to do that."

"Of course I don't. I can choose to listen to you grouse and grumble about your absentee clerk, but I'd rather file."

"Are Timothy and Alicia still at school?"

"Yes, and David's home."

"How was his time at the lake?"

"He said he really sorted things out and made some decisions."

"What kind of decisions?"

"He's going back to India."

"Without the children?"

"No, he's taking them. If the board won't accept him, he will raise his own support and go anyway."

"Raise his own finances? No one just launches out like that."

"He said that doing the right thing, no matter what others think, is a lesson he learned from his father."

"Well, yes . . . but . . ."

"He's coming for supper. You can discuss it with him then."

"Going off to India on your own like that sounds risky."

"His last tour was not without risks."

"I know, but I worry about him every day he's over there."

"And, dear Judge, you worry about him every day he's here. He went out to see Barbara to tell her his news."

"Don't tell me he's planning on her —"

"Coming over for supper? Yes, I invited

her and Douglas. Duffy is busy with his sweet Lorna."

"Is David taking Barbara with them to India?"

"You'll just have to ask him tonight." Judith fussed with the papers on the desk. "In the meantime, you might want to read a long letter from your other child."

"You have a letter from Roberta? Why didn't you say so!"

"I just did. Besides, I've already read it." Judith rolled open the top drawer on a large oak archive cabinet behind the desk and began to file papers.

"What does she say?"

"Why don't you read it aloud?"

Dear Mamma and Daddy,

So much has happened in the last week it's hard to know where to begin. I'm sure you have heard from Marthellen, so there is nothing to say about the scene in Sacramento, except that Wilton Longbake is a complete jerk. Instead of 'Zeeb', they should have nicknamed him 'Judas.' I'm thrilled to have gotten away from that situation.

Peachy has been in my prayers every day. I keep thinking I should write her, but I'm not sure she would appreciate what I have to say, and I can't wish her false sentiments, nor should I try to control her life. She must live with her own decisions. Besides, she knew plenty before she ever moved to New York. I do know she will be good for Wilt's children.

I know one of the reasons that wealthy couples and royalty have such huge dining tables and each one of them sits on the ends. Sitting that far from each other saves the marriage. That way you don't notice if he eats his peas with a knife, eats his soup with a fork, or puts catsup on his eggs. Perhaps Peachy will survive, for Wilt Longbake insists on long tables.

We arrived in Cheyenne on Tuesday and had to spend the night there before finding room on the stagecoach to Deadwood.

Daddy, I know how you love historical artifacts . . . guess what I bought for you? The cutest little girl, named Angelita, had to earn some money for her sick grandmother and was selling the four bullets that were in Jack McCall's revolver after he shot Wild Bill Hickok up in Deadwood. Her grandfather was at the Number 10 Saloon when it hap-

pened and he secured them from Mc-
Call himself. But her grandfather died in
a hotel fire, and the bullets were her last
souvenir memory she had of him. She
hated to, but needed to sell them. I
didn't think $2 was such a bad price for a
piece of history.

"Good grief," the judge snorted, "we
waited a week to hear how some pint-sized
huckster sold her an old bullet?"
"Keep reading, dear," Judith said.

The stagecoach ride to Deadwood was
an unbelievable event. Eleven of us were
mashed in there for two days of foul language and tobacco juice. It must have
been similar to the stories you tell of the
Comstock in the old days.
Mr. Hearst was not in Deadwood or
Lead. He owns a mine called the
Homestake in Lead, just a few miles
from Deadwood. Turner was very disap-
pointed. He is such a bulldog to do
things right. I don't believe I've ever
loved him more than I have this week.

"A bulldog to do things right?" the judge
fumed. "It sounds like he's convincing her
to buy more than just a phony $2 bullet."

Judith continued to file papers that had piled up on Roberta's desk. "Keep reading, dear."

While we were waiting for a stage to Fort Pierre, so that we could follow Mr. Hearst to Chicago, we visited with some people who own a hardware store across the street from the hotel. Todd and Rebekah Fortune are in their late twenties or early thirties. His father was one of the pioneers in Deadwood. You should hear the funny stories that are told around the woodstove at the hardware. You would really like them, Daddy.

"Get to the point, Roberta . . . get to the point."

Rebekah Fortune's father is a Chicago banker with some wealth and many connections. She said he had mentioned building a mill down in Arizona, near some God-forsaken place called Tombstone. He wants to buy a working mill, tear it apart, and move it. Turner telegraphed him, and he asked us to come to Chicago. So that's when I telegraphed for you to send the ledger. You sent both, but Turner said that was fine.

The trip to Fort Pierre was flatter than the one from Cheyenne, but oh what horrible dust. It made Nevada's Forty-Mile Desert seem like a picnic on the Truckee River. We took a steamboat to Iowa and the train into Chicago. At the moment, Marthellen and I are at the LaSalle Hotel waiting for Turner to finish his meeting with Mr. Jacobson and his partners.

Turner did reach Longbake and Hearst in New York and they telegrammed that they both wanted their investment back, but if they had to take a ten percent loss to disperse of the property they would. One of their Chicago attorneys is handling their end of the negotiations.

I told Turner this is the end of the trip for me and Marthellen, no matter what happens. We will leave tomorrow and should be home in a day or two after you get this letter. If negotiations go well, Turner will be released from his obligations to the mill and will be traveling with us.

The judge glanced up at Judith. "She's finally coming home! Perhaps by tomorrow."

"Please continue," Judith said.

He's talked about asking you if he could have my job as your clerk, Daddy. I'm thinking I'd rather not work after we're married.

"He wants to be my clerk?" the judge boomed.
"You did offer him the job once."
"Yes . . . yes . . . but that was before . . ."
"Keep reading, Judge."

Turner has such lofty and noble ideas. Do you know what he suggests doing with some of the money? He wants to set up a trust for Fidora's little baby, Daniel. Isn't he a great guy, mother? Sometimes he reminds me so much of Daddy.

"Me? There is nothing about that renegade that's like me! Of course he wants a trust. He feels guilty."
"Guilt is a good emotion, Judge."
"He's got a lot of explaining to do before he'll ever be my clerk!"
"There's a little more to the letter."

If they do not make a sale, Turner talks about going to New York, but I could not face Wilton again, and doubt whether I could face Peachy either. So . . . your wandering daughter (and clerk) will return soon. I'm glad David is so steady and solid. You deserve one child you don't have to worry about.

Mother, you always told me I would find a man to love forever. Turner truly does bring out the best in me. I believe I have chosen that man. After knowing him for years and years, just this week I feel like I truly understand him.

"What's that supposed to mean?"
"Finish the letter," Judith said.

I can't wait to get home and start planning the wedding. Turner feels like the failure of the mill to open might be God's perfect timing. If it would have opened he would be working day and night and have little time for me. As it is now, if the clerk's job is still available, he'll have the same hours as Daddy. Wouldn't that be wonderful?

I've never been happier in my life.

I love you two very much.

Roberta

"He's a rascal, a scoundrel, a knave, a

rogue, and a miscreant!"

"Miscreant?" Judith raised her eyebrows. "But our daughter has never been happier."

"Well, I can change that . . ."

"Why?"

"Are you telling me none of this bothers you?"

"All of it bothers me. A trust fund for Daniel? When I read that part, I thought I'd faint. But we've got to make the best decisions that are allowed to us from this point on. We've got to encourage Roberta to determine her best choices, and we've got to encourage Turner to do what's right. All of your fuming, all of my tears, all of our judgments will not change events that have happened in the past."

"What are you suggesting?"

"That our daughter is coming home, perhaps by tomorrow. We will talk everything through without getting emotional. We will make sure we have all the facts she knows, and she has all the facts we know. Then, she will decide her next step and we will support her in that."

"I'm not hiring a philanderer and . . . and . . ."

"And what?" Judith challenged.

The judge paced the office. *I cannot tell her of the sudden appearance of $25,000 in his* *ledger. Not until I know more!* "He could be a libertine and a deceiver," he blurted out.

"No verdict, Judge Kingston, until after all the testimony is presented."

"I am shocked that you're taking this so well."

"So am I," she replied.

It was well past 9:00 p.m. when Judith finished washing the dishes. She found the judge sitting in the dark of the living room.

"What are you doing?"

"Listening to myself rant and rave."

"I didn't hear you."

"I meant how I sounded earlier."

"I thought you did quite well during supper."

"Even when Barbara ate the gladioli and kept talking about going to India?" the judge asked.

Judith brushed her bangs out of her eyes. "Having the pickled seaweed sprouts get caught in your throat three different times did seem a little suspicious to everyone."

"I wasn't thinking of supper. I was thinking of how upset Roberta's letter made me. There are some crucial, and I do mean crucial, details we must find out from Turner before things go further. In fact, there could be criminal activity."

Judith sat on the brick hearth. The only light filtered in from the gas lamp in the kitchen. "What are you talking about?"

"I didn't want to tell you this, but it's heavy on my mind. You know how I've been reviewing the Manitoba Joe Clark case?"

"What does that have to do with Turner?"

"That's what I'm trying to find out. The only thing I've discovered is that I believe the back door of the bank was partially open the morning Tjader was killed."

"And?"

"And someone could have been in the back room and witnessed the holdup. And what if Manitoba Joe is telling the truth? What if he fired one shot into the ceiling beam, but not the second one?"

"Then someone else shot Tjader to make it look like Manitoba Joe did it?"

"Precisely."

"Yes, your honor, but you aren't giving me a motive or linking Turner with it."

"I would suppose the motive to be money."

"But the robbery money blew all the way to the Carson Valley. The bank had to invalidate all those notes."

"What if other money was stolen but didn't get blown away. There would be no way to document the amount."

"OK, someone happened by chance to be in the back room or side room. Why the suspicion on Turner?"

"In the records of the milling company, I found an entry buried on page sixteen of an infusion of $25,000 capital that did not come from Hearst or Longbake."

"We've known that all along."

"Yes, but the date on the ledger was February 12th, the day after Sam Tjader was killed and the bank was robbed."

"That's a tragic coincidence, but not an indictment for murder."

"I know. It's all circumstantial. That's why it's eating at me. This afternoon, I stopped by the bank to talk to Philip Campos."

"Surely you didn't say you thought Turner was a murderer?"

"No. I can't even make myself consider that. But the mystery deepens."

"Oh?"

"I asked Campos when Turner's loan was due, that he would be coming back soon and I was checking a few things out for him."

"And what did Campos say?"

"That Turner was refused a loan. He even had Tjader's daily log to show when it was turned down: February 9th."

"Two days before the holdup?"

254

"Precisely. And not only that, Campos says that he was the only one in the bank that day and Turner got so mad about having the loan rejected that he almost got into a fight with Sam Tjader."

Judith clutched her hands in front of her waist.

"Tjader then threatened to summon the sheriff and, according to Mr. Campos, Turner Bowman vowed to shoot Tjader."

"Did Mr. Campos tell this to the sheriff when they investigated Sam Tjader's death?"

"No, because they caught Manitoba Joe red-handed. The crime was solved. He sluffed off Turner's remarks and cursing as an unfulfilled threat."

"Cursing?"

"Campos said Turner swore at Tjader up and down the lobby of the bank for not giving him the loan."

"I've never heard Turner Bowman curse."

"Judith, there seems to be a side to this young man that grows darker and more sinister every day."

"But how could we be so totally wrong about him?"

"Campos could be mistaken. But if Manitoba Joe did not kill Sam Tjader, then someone did. If I prove Manitoba didn't do it, the case is reopened. And if Turner made threats against Tjader, and a few days later has an unaccountable sum of $25,000, he would logically become a suspect."

"This is crazy! I don't believe Turner Bowman is a murderer."

"I don't either. But if he were guilty of the other wrongs, murder is often the culmination of a series of sins. One thing leads to another. And that's why I'm sitting here in the dark. Two weeks ago, I wouldn't believe that Turner could be the father of Fidora's baby. Now I'm starting to believe it. How long until I'm able to believe that he's also capable of murder? I don't know, I just don't know."

"What will you do now?"

"That's what puzzles me, Judith. If I forget everything, ignore the whole matter, a very mean, violent man named Manitoba Joe Clark will hang, and Sam Tjader's murder will be settled. Then everyone is happy."

"Everyone?"

"The town wants Manitoba Joe dead. Roberta gets Turner. Turner can establish a trust fund for Daniel, with no one the wiser."

"Willie Jane won't be happy unless she has Fidora's baby," Judith said. "But how about Judge Kingston? Will he be happy with doing nothing?"

"I'll be miserable the rest of my life."

"Judge, we can't do anything until Roberta and Turner get back. We have to ask him all these questions and see how he explains them."

"It will crush Roberta."

"The truth is always healing in the long run."

"I know, but some days I long for a more peaceful, simple existence."

"What if this is the simple life, Judge Kingston?"

"That is a gruesome thought."

"I say we leave it all with the Lord, and go on up to bed for now."

"Leaving it with the Lord, my dear Judith, is what I've been trying to do for the last hour."

"I'll sit it out with you then."

"No, you go on up. One of us needs to have enough energy to take care of the grandchildren tomorrow."

"And welcome home a very happy daughter."

His tie was loosened, his vest unbuttoned. His coat hung neatly on the back of a dining room chair. After taking off his boots, he propped his feet on the low cherrywood table. Soon, his chin was slumped down on his chest, his eyes closed.

Judge Kingston was asleep in the brown leather chair in the living room when pounding on the front door brought him to his feet.

In the moonlight he spotted the shadowy outline of a man on the front step. He stubbed his toe on the corner of the sofa, then staggered to the door and pulled it open.

"Tray?"

"You sleep in that suit, Judge?"

"Not usually. What's the matter?"

"The sheriff sent me to fetch you. Someone shot and killed that lawyer, Atley Musterman, down in front of the Paradise Hotel."

"I'll get my boots." The judge disappeared into the dark living room. "Was it those Montanans?"

"Nobody saw it, but the sheriff is trying to find them."

"I told them to go out to Moundhouse or up to Washoe City."

"Somebody said they saw them at Callie Truxell's place earlier in the evenin'."

The judge emerged from the doorway. "We should have left them all in jail."

"That's what the sheriff said when he sent me to fetch you."

Even though it was close to 3:00 a.m., there was a crowd of angry men in front of the sheriff's office when Tray and the judge pushed their way in.

Two deputies guarded the back door, two more at the front. The sheriff and Doc Jacobs conferred at the desk. Callie Truxell and another woman huddled at the woodstove, drinking black coffee.

The judge tipped his hat at the women. "You gals doing all right?"

"We just want to go home, Judge," Callie replied.

"I'll see what I can do." He marched over to the men at the desk. "What do we have, Sheriff?"

"A mess. Why can't all murders be simple like Manitoba Joe shootin' Sam Tjader? Catch the bad guy. Convict the bad guy. Hang the bad guy. That's how I like justice."

"What's he mumbling about, Doc?" the judge asked.

"About an hour ago, as far as we can tell, someone shot Atley Musterman in the back, down by the Paradise Hotel. He died instantly."

"Any witnesses?"

"Oh no," the sheriff retorted. "No one saw anything. No one even came out to check on the gunshot for ten . . . fifteen minutes."

The judge glanced around the room. "Were the Montanans in town?"

"I got them in that back cell now. I found them both over at Callie's. She and the other gal claim they were there the whole evening."

"And they didn't go anywhere during that time?"

"Not even to the privy."

"Then they have an alibi. You have to turn them loose."

"Not so quick, Judge. Callie, her friend, and the two Montanans were asleep when we broke in on 'em."

"That's her business, Sheriff. Unfortunately, not all sin is illegal in Nevada."

"The men were awake enough to grab for their guns. What if they slipped out after the girls fell asleep and snuck back up there for an alibi?"

The judge lowered his voice. "What does Callie say about that?"

"She sticks by her story."

"Let me talk to her."

The judge scooted a chair to the woodstove. He glanced at the heavier girl with the round face and long black curls.

Callie spoke softly. "Penny, this is my friend Judith's husband, Judge Kingston. Penny's new in town, Judge. Look at us.

They didn't even let us get properly dressed or pin up our hair or nothin'. We didn't do anything, Judge. They shouldn't wake up people in the middle of the night who ain't done nothin'."

"Callie, you told the sheriff the two Montanans were with you and Penny all evening."

"They came about ten o'clock. They was still there when the sheriff banged on the door and the deputy climbed through the window."

"And they didn't go downstairs for a drink or a smoke or anything?"

"Nope. I told the sheriff the same thing."

"Callie, if these men were devious, if they tried to pull one over on you, would it be possible for them to have slipped out of your place after you girls fell asleep, then snuck in later for the purpose of an alibi?"

Callie shook her head no. "Look, Judge, no man ever climbed into my bed when I didn't know about it, and no man ever climbed out when I didn't know about it. Ever. These two didn't leave."

The other woman nodded her head in vigorous agreement.

The judge stood up and motioned to the deputy at the door. "Tray, go get a carriage. Take these ladies home."

"But it's only a few blocks," he grumbled as he glanced over at the sheriff.

"You heard the judge," the sheriff said.

When the judge had joined Doc Jacobs at the sheriff's desk, the lawman said, "You believe the girls?"

"Yep. They don't have any reason to make it up."

"Yeah, well, like I said, why can't all the murders be simple ones?"

"Doc, was Musterman killed with only one bullet?" the judge asked.

"Yep. Just one."

"Seems kind of strange for two violent men to stalk one man and then only one pull the trigger. One is a murderer and the other a witness to a murder. That doesn't make too good a partnership," the judge said.

Sheriff Hill rubbed his eyes. "You don't think they did it?"

"No."

"Well, then, who did?"

Doc Jacobs spoke up. "Could have been any man that liked Sam Tjader and was mad at Atley for defending the banker's killer."

"Where are the Montanans' guns?" the judge asked.

The sheriff pulled two bullet belts, revolvers, and holsters off the wooden peg on the wall. "These are them."

The judge tossed the holstered guns over his shoulder. "Let's go back and talk to them."

The Montanans slouched in the small cell, hands gripping the iron rails. "Judge, we didn't do this. We didn't shoot the attorney," the thin blond one said.

"How long were you at Callie's?"

"Must have been about ten o'clock 'til the sheriff beat down the door," the stockier one declared. "We should have listened to you and rode out of town."

"Yes, you should have. Whose gun is this?"

The thin man ran his fingers through his hair. "That one's mine, Judge."

Judge Kingston cocked the hammer back to the first click, then spun the chamber.

"There's a spent brass cartridge in one of the chambers," the deputy at the back door called out.

"Are they both this way?"

"Yep."

"Are you saying two gunmen from Montana shot at Musterman, but one missed? They didn't fire these guns. The bullet belts are completely jammed full. These boys never loaded up with six bullets. They keep the hammer on empty, then leave a cartridge there to protect it in case it is accidentally dry-fired. Isn't that true, boys?"

"Yes, sir, that's true. A man could get bucked off his horse and shoot himself in the leg if he ain't careful," the taller man declared.

"Sheriff, you've got to turn these men loose," the judge said. "There is no evidence against them. No one saw them around town after ten o' clock. They have solid alibis and their guns haven't been fired. As far as people wanting Musterman dead, he didn't have many, if any, friends in this town. I think he had properly insulted everyone."

The sheriff gestured toward the front of the building. "That crowd out there knows they're friends of Manitoba Joe's. They won't let these two just ride away."

"Sure they will. When Tray ushers Callie and Penny out to the carriage, every sober and intoxicated eye will be on those two ladies. Have one of your deputies usher these boys out the back at the exact same time. Then ride them to the north edge of town before you turn them loose."

"I reckon that'll work," the sheriff said.

"Sheriff, what about our hundred dollars that lawyer owed us?" the tall Montanan asked.

"I'll check on it when the bank opens. But don't count on it. Nobody's going to pay a dead lawyer."

"How much money did Musterman have on him?" the judge asked.

"Eleven dollars."

"Then give it to these men. I heard Musterman admit to owing them a hundred dollars." The judge then turned to the two men and said, "Boys, get out of town. Go to Reno. Somewhere. This time pay attention to me. I'm not getting up in the middle of the night for you again."

"Yes, sir. We'll ride north. But what about Joe? What's to become of him?"

"If we find some additional evidence, there could be a hearing. With a little luck, he could have his sentence reduced to twenty years. But if there isn't any evidence to the contrary, he'll be hung as scheduled and there's not one thing you can do about it except pray."

"We ain't exactly the prayin' type, Judge."

"You might want to change your ways. It doesn't look like you've been all too successful the way you're going."

Chapter Eight

May sunlight glimmered through fast-moving clouds, changing from moment to moment like flickering light from a camp-fire. A stiff morning wind plucked at the judge's hat-brim, making him tug his hat lower, and he buttoned his dark gray suit coat over the top of his vest. After walking a block, he unfastened his coat to flap in the breeze.

Early traffic, mainly freight and delivery wagons for the stores lining Carson Street, brought provisions for another day of customers and busy chaos.

He glanced across the street at the state capitol grounds and the black iron fence that surrounded them and thought of the capitols around the world.

Judith and I really must travel more. We

266

spend our whole lives embroiled in this one small part of God's sphere. It would be nice to walk down a sidewalk where no one knew who we were. Sit at a café window and watch a crisis someone else had to settle. Have nothing to trouble my mind at night but the last passage of Scripture I read and which flower bulbs to plant in the fall.

Lord, I'm tired.

I need a little rest.

A little resolution.

In Your time, of course.

He pulled a watch out of his vest pocket and stared at the roman numerals. *Seven twenty-eight a.m. I do believe it's time to check a few things out.*

The judge strolled west on Procter Street, then turned north into the alley. To the left were the back doors of Thomas Carriage and Repair, Mrs. Gratney's chicken coop, the white block warehouse of Eagle Valley Ice Company, and the abandoned cabin of Uncle Ted Pidsmere.

To the right was a huge two-story, red brick building with no outside stairways, no windows on the lower level, and a steel back door with three wide horizontal bands reinforcing it.

The judge pulled black deerskin gloves out of his suit coat pocket and tugged one on his right hand. He glanced both ways at the empty cobblestone alley, then put his left hand on the brass doorknob. He slowly tried turning it to the left and to the right. It didn't budge.

He lifted his gloved hand, hesitated, then struck the door.

One knock.

Two knocks.

Three knocks.

Two knocks.

One knock.

He stepped back and waited.

And waited.

He's certainly not hovering by the back door, anxiously waiting for Atley Musterman. Of course, Campos might not be here. Or he might know about Musterman's death. Or it could be that Callie's story is all a charade, a bit of drama for the old judge. Maybe there is no secret knock. No back entrance banking. No split back door.

The judge stepped back up to the door and once again repeated the pattern of knocks. He thought he heard a footstep.

A muffled voice pierced through the door. "What do you want?"

His hand over his mouth, the judge said in a demanding tone, "I want my $200!"

The top half of the big door swung open.

A white-faced Philip Campos stood there, clutching a short-barreled .45.

"Judge Kingston?" he gasped.

"Mr. Campos." The judge tipped his hat, then pulled off his gloves. *He was obviously not expecting anyone to show up wanting $200.*

"What do you want?" Campos jammed his revolver into a concealed chest holster under his navy blue suit coat.

"I want to talk." *Do you always carry a concealed pistol, Mr. Campos?*

"Now?" the bank manager stammered.

"Your employees won't arrive for a half hour, isn't that right?"

"Eh, yes."

The judge waved his arm in the open doorway. "And this isn't a normal day for you to come early to bank the girls' savings?"

"What girls?"

"The crib girls. The girls from the tenderloin who use the back door of the bank. You do remember your customers?"

"They show up on Mondays and Fridays."

"So, let's talk, Mr. Campos. May I come in, or would you like to discuss this from the alley?"

Campos swung open the bottom half of

the heavy door. After the judge strolled in, Campos began closing both halves of the heavy door.

"Leave the top half open, Mr. Campos. That way we'll have a little light back here. This is a stuffy room without a window. I wonder what this was built for?"

"It was meant to be a boardroom, or something like that." Campos pointed toward the bank lobby. "We can go out front to my desk, Judge."

"Let's just sit back here at this old table and enjoy a little fresh air coming in from the alley." The judge sat down, then pulled off his hat and laid it in front of him.

Philip Campos moved over to the table. "It's a little dangerous leaving an open door at the back of a bank. There could be more Manitoba Joes prowling around."

"Oh, I don't know," the judge said. "You have a very efficient .45 caliber sneak gun. Besides, it's only 7:30 a.m. You haven't opened the big safe yet, have you?"

Campos slumped down in a chair across from the judge. "Well, actually, the safe is open." He glanced nervously out the back door. "Now, why the rouser at the back door, Judge?"

Kingston leaned forward. "You mean, the comment about $200?"

Philip Campos waited, the tic under his eye twitching.

"I'm here on behalf of Mr. Atley Musterman. I believe you owe him $200."

"But, he's dead! I mean, you were right there at the sheriff's office last night . . . so I hear."

The judge watched Campos carefully. "You're right, Musterman is dead. But I have often represented the claims of dead people."

"Are you talking about his estate?"

"Yes."

"Musterman didn't have any funds in this bank, I can assure you of that. I would doubt if he had any money in any bank. I believe that man gambled away every dime he ever made."

"You knew him fairly well?"

"No, but I heard rumors."

The judge leaned back in the birch chair and glanced toward the alley. "I believe you're right about his gambling and his ability to save. What I was interested in collecting was the $200 you offered him not to press an appeal for Manitoba Joe."

"He told you that?"

"The sheriff and I had to disarm him yesterday afternoon. Where do you think I learned about that secret knock?"

A fairly cool breeze blew in through the open door, yet perspiration broke out on Campos' forehead as he drummed fingers on the gray painted table. "I suppose you're wondering why I would offer him that money? Well, it's like this. I'm like the majority of people in this town. I wanted Sam Tjader to get justice. I know it was foolish, but I honestly do not believe it's illegal to bid for a lawyer's services."

"I don't suppose you know who paid Mr. Musterman to represent Manitoba Joe during the trial?"

Campos examined his neatly trimmed fingernails. "I presume that was Mr. Clark himself."

"You didn't have anything to do with it?"

Campos dropped his hands on the table. "Judge, I've never made it any secret that I want Manitoba Joe to hang for the heinous crime against my dear friend, Mr. Sam Tjader. Why on earth would I ever want to pay an attorney to defend his murderer?"

"Mr. Musterman's incompetence comes to mind."

"I had no knowledge of Musterman's ineptitude until the trial."

Judge Kingston leaned forward. "No matter how ineffectual Mr. Musterman was, he was murdered last night. Someone will be accountable for his death."

"Could it be, Judge Kingston, that you contributed to that action?"

"Just how did I do that?"

"By making such a public display of the counselor's vicissitude, you might have helped him to become a target for those who are unable to get at Manitoba Joe."

"Mr. Campos, I put my life on the line yesterday to disarm a gunfight that certainly would have led to violence. Your remark is shallow and vindictive."

"Other than trying to shame me for my foolish actions, Judge Kingston, why exactly did you come here?"

"I told you, I came here to collect Musterman's $200."

"But, he's deceased. He can't serve as a lawyer now."

"You didn't hire him to be a lawyer. You hired him not to be a lawyer. He can do that quite efficiently now. I believe he will keep his part of the agreement, don't you?"

"But why do you want the money?"

"It seems Mr. Musterman has two outstanding expenses. First, there is the matter of his burial. A hundred dollars ought to cover that nicely, even if the body must be shipped to another location. And second, he owed the two Montanans $100. I was there when he promised it to them."

"But this is highly irregular," Campos complained.

"So is paying a lawyer not to file an appeal. Think of it this way, Mr. Campos . . . suppose Mr. Musterman had not met that fatal bullet last night. Then he would have come to the door this morning, you would have handed him $200, then he would have given the Montanans half of that. They need those funds to hire an attorney. You're not trying to back out of an agreement just because of Mr. Musterman's unfortunate demise?"

"But those Montanans are in jail for killing Musterman."

"All the more reason they need an attorney." *How is it, Mr. Campos, that Callie told you I was at the sheriff's office, but didn't happen to mention the Montanans sneaking out the back door?* "I find it curious that a moment ago you said Musterman may have been killed by enemies of Manitoba Joe, and now you say it was the only friends he has in the world."

"Well, I certainly don't know who did it."

"Nor do I. And the $200?"

"Yes, well, I'll go get the money . . . it will take a moment to open up the safe."

"I thought you said the safe was already open."

"Oh . . . yes, quite right. All this interrogation has me rattled." Campos stood and headed toward the main lobby of the bank.

"While you're getting the money, would you please retrieve the black leather ledger you keep the girls' accounts in?"

Campos turned in the doorway. "What?"

"That ledger you keep for Callie, Fidora, and the girls."

"That's private bank property. I can't divulge such information. Not without a court order."

"I'm the judge, remember?"

"Yes, but I need to have the court order in my files. What would the bank trustees say?"

"Are you denying me access to that ledger?"

"I have no choice."

"What are you hiding, Mr. Campos?"

The bank manager's face flushed a dull red. "That's an insult, Judge. There's no shame in following standard bank procedure, and I will not have you come in here and badger me." When he jammed his hand into his suit coat, the judge expected the drawn revolver. However, Campos drew his hand out, empty.

He disappeared and quickly returned with the money. "I believe this concludes our business, Judge."

The judge waved the bills in his hand. "Don't you need me to sign for this?"

"That isn't necessary."

"But how will you keep record of where this money went?"

"Judge, stick to the courtroom. I will not tell you how to run your business. You don't tell me how to run mine."

"Mr. Campos, I do not take other people's money without a written record of such a transaction. I'll wait while you write a receipt."

Someone in the courthouse had stacked the District #1 Court mail on the now-clean clerk's desk. The judge plucked up a top letter from Willow Bluff, Texas. He was re-reading it when Sheriff Hill strolled in.

"Judge, you and me have to stop workin' day and night. We'll never live to be old men at this pace."

Judge Kingston glanced up from the letter. "Sheriff, we already are old men."

"Ain't that the truth. When they came and woke me up last night, my first reaction was to tell them to let 'em shoot each other, I'd handle it in the mornin'. Maybe I ought to retire."

The judge lifted his eyebrows. "What,

and give up all this fun?"

"I can't find one solitary soul who saw that shootin' last night. Musterman was at the Paradise Club borrowin' chips and drinks and sayin' how he had money comin' in today, and there would be a lot more after that. He told them he was on a permanent retainer."

"With skills like Musterman's, that could only be blackmail. Who retained him?" the judge pondered.

"I reckon whoever paid him not to represent Manitoba Joe."

"But that was Mr. Campos at the bank. I interviewed him this morning."

"You don't say! He wants Manitoba Joe to hang that much?"

"Doesn't everybody?"

"Ever'body but Judge Hollis A. Kingston, the man who sentenced him in the first place. Like I said, nothin's simple around here."

"Some things become even more complex, Sheriff. I received a witnessed letter today from Fidora's last known relative, an uncle in Willow Bluff, Texas. He states that the family has disowned her and wants no part of any of her sinful possessions."

"That little baby is a sinful possession?"

"I suppose so."

"So, you'll have to make a ruling about the Camposes or Willie Jane and Tray taking custody?"

"If I can't get the father to step forward."

"Do you know who he is?"

"No, but I still have a few people to grill, so to speak. I really didn't search very hard until hearing from Fidora's family. Now, did you come in to keep me awake, or do you have another gunfight beyond your target range and need a crack shot like me for backup?"

"Crack shot? The reason I let you tag along is that I know you couldn't hit the side of a barn, and no one'll get hurt. Besides that, you make a good-sized barricade in case I need to dodge bullets."

"Always happy to be of service."

"I came by to tell you them Montanans didn't go to Reno last night. They went up to Virginia City. Said you could contact 'em there. They wanted to find an attorney like you mentioned."

"That's good. I got their money from Campos."

"How did you do that? He's tighter than a fig in February with his own money."

"He was a little reluctant. Say, didn't Mrs. Tjader move back to Virginia City after Sam died?"

"Yep, she and the kids live with her mother in a green two-story house on Bonanza Street. Why?"

"I think I'll stop by and pay my respects as long as I'm going to Virginia City to give the Montanans their money."

"Are you goin' to take the train?"

The judge pulled out his watch. "If I can get there in eighteen minutes, I will. First, I've got a couple of favors to ask of you."

"What do you need?"

The judged pulled a printed form from the top left drawer of the clerk's desk, then pulled the glass stopper out of a bottle of India ink. With pen in hand he hurriedly scratched several words in the blanks and scrawled his name across the bottom. "Witness this court request, then serve it as soon as you can to Mr. Campos at the bank for the surrender of a black leather ledger that contains bank records for the crib girls."

"They got accounts?"

"A few of them do, and I want to see them."

The sheriff studied the paper, then signed his name under the judge's. "You wrote this down in connection with the Manitoba Joe case. What link does it have?"

"I'm not sure it has any, but I have to attach the court request with a case that is current, pending, or in review. There could be a remote association. The only time the bank uses their split back door is when the girls do their banking. Manitoba Joe swears it was open the day he robbed Sam Tjader. I thought perhaps I could find out which girls had been there that day."

"The bank back door is split? I never knew that! And I patrolled ever' square inch of this town."

The judge retrieved his hat, then paused at the doorway. "Banking is a complicated business, Sheriff. Extremely complicated. Now, here's the other thing I need you to do. Check with your pals at Fort Churchill. Levi Boyer told me once that Campos served there before he resigned and went into the banking business. Find out what position he was in and why he left the army."

"What does that have to do with this?"

"I don't know. I'm just searching for anything tangible — something besides a hunch."

Judith finished drying the breakfast dishes while David sat at the table behind her. A wooden pencil and several scattered tablets were spread in front of him. She picked up a page of notes and read aloud, "Home Evangelistic Revivals Eternal American Ministry to India? Isn't that rather long, dear?"

"I'll use the acronym, HERE-AM-I."

Judith turned to study David's eyes to see if he was teasing. His face was somber. "I suppose that comes from Isaiah's response, 'Here am I, send me'?"

"Exactly."

"Home Evangelistic Revivals?"

"That's the whole point. It will not be supported by denominations or churches, per se, but individual people. And our work in India will be home evangelism, one-on-one teaching of the gospel."

"It sounds so . . . risky."

"It boils down to money," David said. "I'm sure the Lord will supply. In fact, I already have $100 to deposit."

"That's wonderful. Where did it come from?"

"Barbara sold a painting and wanted to give the money to reach India."

"Which painting?"

"The landscape of deer foraging at Lake Tahoe in the winter."

"I don't believe I saw that one. Who bought it?"

"Jack's Saloon."

"Saloon money is sending you to evangelize India? That might be a little hard for the devil to swallow," Judith added.

"That's just what Barbara said." He plucked up one of the notebooks. "I think I'll go see Mr. Campos at the bank to open an account. We've already discussed it."

"You might stop by your father's office. I'm sure we will want to add to that account."

"I won't let you."

"But why?"

"Mother, I have a support goal I'd like to reach before venturing out on this mission. I'd like the Lord to touch hearts of people to give to this cause. It will help me find the Lord's will."

"You mean, the Lord isn't allowed to touch our hearts?"

"I want your support, and I'll be happy to take it after I reach my goal. But you and Daddy would give me support even if I was going off to Australia to dig for opals."

Judith smiled. "Opals are very pretty, dear."

After David left, Judith straightened his papers and carried them into the judge's home office. She stacked them on the corner of the big desk. She spied a two-inch-square, folded piece of white paper stuck under the corner of the brown ink blotter.

She pulled it out and opened it up: "Tell Turner . . . don't worry, all is forgiven."

She kept the slip of paper as she strolled back into the kitchen. *So, Judge Kingston, those words are still plaguing you too?*

Judith poured a fresh cup of green tea and sat at the breakfast table. Then she slowly opened the note and examined the words. Then she darted back into the judge's office, picked up a small blank scrap of paper and wrote: "I promised the Lord I wouldn't tell the father's name."

Returning to the kitchen, she laid it beside the other piece of paper. *If Turner is the father, then these last words meant Fidora's gracious forgiveness for the fact that he acted the rascal and the renegade. But if Turner is the father, why did she say she promised the Lord she would not tell?*

In the pain and fright of her dying moment, she must have changed her mind.

Or . . .

Judith chewed her tongue, brushed her bangs back, and continued to study the notes.

If Turner is not the father, the first phrase holds true, but the second has no meaning. Tell Turner . . . "don't worry, all is forgiven"?

What do you forgive?

You forgive sins.

You forgive cruel and harsh words that were spoken. I never heard Turner mention Fidora, but I don't suppose he would, even if he knew her.

You forgive rash and insensitive deeds. You forgive the omission of kind acts.

Forgive us our debts, as we forgive our debtors.

You forgive debts . . .

Judith lifted her head and stared across the counter at Roberta's childhood brass piggy bank, now filled with assorted buttons.

"Money!" she blurted out. "You forgive a debt of money. A loan. Could Turner have conceivably borrowed money from Fidora? But how would he know if Fidora had any money? She works the cribs; those girls usually don't have a penny saved up. However, she stayed in the St. Charles' fanciest suite . . ."

A knock at the side door brought Judith to her feet. She shoved both notes into the deep pocket of her navy blue and white cotton dress, then opened the door to find a gray-haired man in a suit, with hat in hand.

"Dr. Jacobs, have you been working all night?"

"Almost. I need a favor. Mrs. Campos

sent word that baby Daniel had the sniffles and wanted me to look at the child."

"Is he all right?"

"I think he's doing fine. I'd like him to be a little fatter by now, but she does have two babies to nurse, and that's not an easy situation. But here's the problem, Judith. Mrs. Campos wouldn't look me in the eye the whole time I was there and she has three bruise marks on her neck right under her right ear."

"Oh, no! Did you ask her about it?"

"She rambled something about stumbling on the stairs and hitting the handrail."

"Did it look like those bruises came from fingers?"

"Someone tried to choke her, Judith."

"Mr. Campos?"

"You would think if it were anyone else she would quickly report assault charges. But she wouldn't talk to me."

"I'll go see her," Judith said.

"I was hopin' you would."

"I'll say I wanted to see little Daniel, and attempt to give her a chance to open up." Judith sighed. "I do wish I knew her better. Ever since they moved here, they've kept to themselves. I thought it was because she was having such a difficult pregnancy."

"To suspect a husband of strangling his

wife is a loathsome accusation, if it isn't true," Dr. Jacobs said. "But if it is true, she's going to need a friend, that's for sure."

Flags bordered the streets of Virginia City in anticipation of Memorial Day, making a festive veneer as the judge hiked up Bonanza Street. He stopped to catch his breath, then weaved slightly back and forth, trying to gain steam for the sharp incline up the hill.

The Montanans had been loitering in front of the Bucket-of-Blood Saloon when the judge found them. He gave them their money and they immediately disappeared into the upstairs law office of Hiram S. LaSwain, Esq.

The judge contemplated the neatly painted, clapboard house on the steep Mount Davidson hillside. *This isn't the Virginia City of '63. No screaming. No gunshots. No drunks lying on the sidewalk.*

It is much more civilized.

But the old-timers describe a sense of something lost like a wild mustang that no longer bucks.

"Judge Kingston, what are you doing here?"

The woman who spoke was small, yet sturdy, with premature gray hair. She swept the front porch, which was eleven steps above the wooden sidewalk.

The judge pulled off his hat. "Mrs. Tjader, I came up on other business and stopped by to pay my respects. How are you doing?"

"Today is a good day, and your visit has made it so. Is Judith with you?"

"No, Roberta's been traveling East and is expected home today. Judith needed to be there for her."

"May I fix you some lemonade? It will be fairly tepid. I'm afraid our ice cave is empty. Come sit on the porch and I'll fix us both a glass."

They sat in white wicker chairs and gazed over the rooftops of downtown Virginia City, watching the flags drift in the slight breeze.

"Last year Sam and I came up here with the kids to see Mamma on Memorial Day. We went with a procession of old soldiers, firemen, and prancing girls to escort the Sarsfield Guard to the cemetery. We decorated my father's grave with flowers. This year, it's Sam's turn."

The judge cleared his throat. "There's been some fires in one of the mills, I hear."

"Yes, and some smallpox. Little Sammy was sick and feverish last week, but he's all right now. The doctor says it wasn't the pox." She sipped her lemonade. "I do miss my friends in Carson. But mother needed some help getting around, and Lord knows, I needed a different situation. I am so glad to hear that murderer Manitoba Joe Clark will be hung in a few days. Thank you for your assistance in that."

"The judge's role is to see that everything is done according to law, Mrs. Tjader. It's the jury that convicts."

"And I have gone down that road enough. Let's forget about that. I don't intend to become depressed. Now," she said, "why was Roberta in the East? Did she decide to go back to school?"

"Turner Bowman had to go to Chicago concerning the mill, so Marthellen and Roberta tagged along."

"I do hope those two will marry soon. I remember very well how excited he was about your Roberta. I believe that was the last time dear Samuel met with him."

"Did Sam and Turner meet often?"

"They were together every day for several weeks before Sam's murder. Poor Turner was hunting for that additional $25,000 to reconstruct the mill."

"You knew about that?" the judge asked.

"Sam was one of those men who stews

about his business at home. I knew most every dilemma he faced. But most of the time, Turner's business was discussed over our dinner table. He ate at our house every evening he wasn't with Roberta."

"I didn't realize that."

"I don't think he wanted you and Judith to know about this struggle. He wanted to prove to you both that he could rebuild that mill without the influence or finances of Judge and Judith Kingston."

The judge sighed. "I've heard that same tune many times before."

"Sam thought the world of Turner. Do you know he offered Turner the assistant bank manager's position? Turner was afraid the whole mill situation would collapse without that extra $25,000 in capital and Sam said if it did, he would hire him."

"What about Mr. Campos?"

"Sam was trying to figure a way to fire him."

"Why? I've never heard any complaints about Philip Campos before."

"That's the problem Sam faced. He didn't have any real incident to fire Philip Campos over, but he didn't have full confidence in him. Sam always said 'I wouldn't trust my own money to that man, so how can I ask other people to trust theirs with him?' "

"Did he tell that to the bank trustees?"

"No, you knew Sam. He hated to say anything negative about anyone, especially if he didn't have any facts to back it up. But he was determined to figure a way to fire Campos and hire Turner. Manitoba Joe ended that problem with a bullet in poor Sam's back."

"Mrs. Tjader, don't tell me anything you consider confidential business, but do you know if Turner ever got that loan from your husband?"

"No, and it nearly broke Sam's heart. He wanted to loan Turner the funds, but a sum that large needs the trustees' approval, and frankly, they had gotten word from Mr. Longbake in New York not to approve any loans on the mill."

"Wilton Longbake has that kind of influence?"

"Apparently so. I was so thrilled that your darling Roberta did not marry that man, yet it caused much trouble for Turner. However, the board of trustees consented to approve the loan if he had the proper cosigner. Judge Hollis A. Kingston's name was mentioned at that point. But Turner wouldn't think of it."

"Was Turner upset with the bank? Or with Sam?"

"Not with Sam. They were good friends." Mrs. Tjader set her lemonade glass on the wooden porch. "Do you know what my Sam offered to do? He said he would mortgage our house in Carson City and personally loan Turner the money if it would help. That's just the way Sam was with his friends."

"What did Turner say to that?" the judge pressed.

"He declined, of course. He said a friendship is strained by debt and broken by unresolved loans."

"But Turner did get the money someplace?"

"Oh, yes, that is quite a story in itself." Mrs. Tjader looked up and down the street as if watching for an eavesdropper. "There are some elements of banking in Nevada you might not be aware of," she whispered.

The judge leaned back in the chair and sipped on the lemonade. "You wouldn't be talking about the girls at the back door?"

A warm, easy smile spread across Mrs. Tjader's face. "I should have known you knew about that. Sam used to say there is nothing that goes on in Nevada that's unknown to Judith and the judge."

"I'm not sure that is true."

"Sam said very few of the soiled doves

saved money, but the ones who did would surprise you. Just because they sinned to earn it, didn't mean they couldn't save it."

"And Turner got a loan from one of the girls?"

"Yes, Sam was quite pleased to arrange it. Say, how is poor Fidora's baby doing?"

"I believe he's just fine. Mrs. Campos is nursing him until the matter is resolved."

"No!"

"Is something the matter with Mrs. Campos? She was the first nursing mother that came to Dr. Jacobs' mind when Fidora died."

"I don't think that is a good home. Mrs. Campos is a dear woman, but rather weak-willed and completely dominated by her husband."

"I suppose that could be said of many homes."

"But I got the impression that Mr. Campos has a mean streak. I was in the bank one day when an alley cat wandered in and he grabbed up the cat, opened the back door of the bank, and slammed the cat against the side of the ice house."

"I'm sure we've all met cats we'd like to do the same to."

"Thinking of something and actually having the temperament to act on it are two different things," Mrs. Tjader commented, then hurriedly amended. "But I'm sure he would not harm those babies."

"I appreciate your words of caution, Mrs. Tjader. I'll have Dr. Jacobs monitor the situation closely."

The judge stared out across Virginia City again. Clouds had stacked up and filled the gulch, but there was a tremendous clearing in his mind and heart. For a split second he felt like dancing across Mrs. Tjader's porch. *"Tell Turner, don't worry, all is forgiven . . ." It's the debt that was forgiven! The $25,000. No wonder he's so determined to set up a trust for Daniel. It's Fidora's money!*

Mrs. Tjader leaned closer to the judge and whispered, "This may be an inappropriate thing for me to ask, but did Fidora ever identify the father of her baby?"

"No, only the good Lord knows who that might be."

"Oh no, Judge Kingston. There's a man out there somewhere who also knows."

The chubby cheeks on the brown-haired sleeping infant revealed just a tint of blush from the cloud-diffused sunlight as Judith sat on the train platform and rocked him back and forth. The woman next to her wore black and also rocked a sleeping baby

293

girl, cradled in a portable bassinet.

"I can't believe I'm doing this. What will Philip say? What will he do?" Elisa Campos wailed.

"Your husband needs time to think through his deplorable problem with anger."

"But it's always my fault that he gets angry."

"He is totally responsible for his violence against you, Elisa. Any mother has trouble keeping her children quiet at times, even when her husband needs to sleep. However, no husband should deal with it by trying to strangle his wife."

Elisa Campos' head rocked back and forth but her body remained stationary. "He did stop, eventually."

"But will he stop next time? You said each spell gets worse than the previous one. That is something you and he must realize is a growing problem. He needs help in controlling himself."

"But I didn't even leave him a note."

"Dr. Jacobs and the judge will explain that you went to visit your parents in Stockton."

"He'll be furious."

"But he won't take it out on you."

Mrs. Campos glanced down at the baby in Judith's arms. "I will miss little Daniel so much."

"I know, but you are not allowed to take him out of the state until the judge rules on the matter. I will personally see that he gets good care."

"Does this mean I won't be able to adopt him?"

"I would suppose so. But you need to deal with one situation at a time. The Lord will provide for you in other ways."

"I'll write to you. You must write to me too," Mrs. Campos insisted, tears in her eyes. "I don't have any other friends right now."

"I certainly will write, and you will be in my prayers."

"Philip and I can work this out, I know we will. I just need to get away for a while."

Judith nodded. "It will give your husband an opportunity to know how serious this situation is."

"I wish you were going with me, Judith. I mean . . . I feel like after our long conversation this morning, we've just become acquainted, and now I'm leaving town."

Judith reached over and patted her hand. "The Lord will provide for you in that way also. Do you remember the name of my friend in Stockton?"

"Martina Hackett?"

"Yes. She will be a good one to talk to. She endured much distress early in her married life. You just tell her that you're a friend of Judith and Judge Kingston's. You can talk to her about anything you wanted to discuss with me." Judith watched passengers begin to load up on the westbound Virginia City and Truckee. "You better board now," she said.

Both ladies struggled to stand, carrying babies and bags.

"I can't look at Daniel or I'll break down and cry," Mrs. Campos said. She took a deep breath. "Good-bye, Judith. Keep praying for me."

"Whenever I see Daniel, I'll remember to pray for you," Judith promised.

After the train pulled out, Judith hiked to the street. She was immediately confronted by Chug Conly's hack and a grinning Daisie Belle Emory.

"And who do we have here?" Daisie Belle asked. "Is that Fidora's little Daniel?"

"Yes, it looks like I'll have a lot of baby-sitting to do."

"And baby nursing! I believe this calls for a quick trip to Mr. Cheney's." Daisie Belle turned to the driver. "Mr. Conly, could you help Judith and baby Daniel into the carriage, please?"

By the time they finally arrived back at the

Kingston residence, they had collected two more passengers: Willie Jane Farnsworth and Marcy Boyer. All four women burst into the Nevada Street door, with Chug Conly left to unload the packages.

Willie Jane carried the baby. "Isn't he the most beautiful little thing in the world? I think he has Fidora's eyes, don't you think so?"

Daisie Belle glanced at the blanket-clad baby. "His eyes are closed," she noted.

"Yes, but if his eyes were open, they would look just like Fidora's."

"I am so jealous," Marcy said. "I wish I didn't have to wait eight more months, twenty-six days, and twelve hours." She studied her waistline. "I just know my baby is going to be a girl, so I picked out some pink things today."

"You've bought baby clothes already?" Judith asked.

"Just a few things. And I ordered some others from the Montgomery and Ward Catalog."

"I can't believe I get to keep Daniel all day!" Willie Jane cooed. "I don't know how you talked Mr. Cheney into letting me off."

Daisie Belle spoke up. "She just said, 'John, dear, I'll need Willie Jane at my house all day today. You don't mind letting her have the day off, but paying her anyway, do you?' Then she blinked her eyes at him."

"I most certainly did not!" Judith snapped.

Marcy laughed. "I've never seen Judith do anything like that."

"I certainly have," Daisie Belle said, "but usually it's in the presence of a familiar, tall, good-looking gentleman."

For several moments the four women scurried around the back of the house, setting up Marthellen's room as a nursery, warming milk on the stove, and trying to read the instructions on the box containing "Dr. Bull's #6 Nursing Bottle."

The side door swung open and David strolled in, Barbara Day at his side. "Are you ladies having a party?"

"We have little Daniel," Judith announced.

Barbara meandered into the kitchen. "A Dr. Bull's #6? That's the exact kind I used with Douglas. My breasts are such that I couldn't nurse and I had to use one of these."

All four women stared at Barbara, then in unison craned their necks toward David. He disappeared into the judge's office.

"What did I say?"

Barbara proved to be a good instructor in the use of the nursing bottle. Soon all five ladies crammed into the kitchen and took turns feeding the baby.

"The judge will for sure rule in my favor now," Willie Jane said.

"I think your chances are quite excellent," Judith concurred.

"When do you expect the judge home?"

"Not until this evening. Why?"

"Since me and Tray already got the marriage license, I thought maybe we could get married today."

Daisie Belle gasped. "You mean, now? But what about all our plans?"

"I surely do appreciate them, and it has been the nicest thing anyone ever did for me. But seeing little Daniel . . . well, the important thing is gettin' him a home with a mamma and daddy. It seems to me that might be more eminent than a cavalcade of roses and all that."

Daisie Belle's face brightened. "A reception! We can have the wedding right away. Then, we'll have the reception at my place on Saturday as planned! How does that sound?"

"Does that mean me and Tray will have to wait until Saturday to live together?" Willie Jane asked.

"Oh, no, my dear. As soon as Judge Kingston or Reverend Kingston pronounces the words, you are married."

Willie Jane let out a deep breath. "OK. Marcy, you be in charge of baby Daniel while I go downtown."

Marcy gladly took the baby in her arms. "Where are you going?"

"To find that Tray Weston. He's going to marry me sooner than he thought. And don't let Reverend Kingston go anywhere!"

"Oh, this is thrilling!" Daisie Belle said with a giggle. "I love it!"

"I hope the sheriff will let Tray off for the afternoon," Willie Jane said.

Judith slipped her arm in Willie Jane's. "Go by and tell the judge what is happening, then have him ask the sheriff to let Tray have the afternoon off. The sheriff can never refuse Judge Hollis A. Kingston."

"Yes," Daisie Belle said, "and the judge won't even have to bat his eyelashes."

"Daisie Belle, I rolled my eyes just a little, that's all," Judith said.

A knock at the side door brought Judith and the other ladies out of the kitchen. Duffy Day clutched Lorna Clair's arm. "Sounds like you ladies are having a party in there," he exclaimed.

"We're planning a wedding," Daisie Belle announced.

"But we ain't set a date yet," Duffy protested. "We have to wait at least until

Barbara goes to India, I reckon, so we'll have room."

Judith Kingston held her breath.

"Duffy, I did not say I was going to India for sure," Barbara interjected. She looked in the direction of the judge's office. "Besides, I haven't been asked."

Judith breathed again.

"Anyway," Duffy continued, "me and Lorna's engaged. I don't reckon we need to be in a hurry now." He inspected the house. "I wanted to talk to David about his sermon on the fear of the Lord, but he isn't over at the parsonage."

"Barbara has told us such wonderful things about David's sermons. And Duffy had some questions I just couldn't answer," Lorna added.

Judith glanced at Barbara Day. Her face was placid, unreadable. *She does have good taste in sermons. Of course, she has good taste in men too.* "David's in the judge's office," Judith said, "I'll go get him."

"I believe I'll go in and talk to him," Duffy answered.

"You will?" Judith said. "Duffy, I don't believe you've ever come into my house before. Are you sure?"

"My sweet Lorna talked to me about that. She said it was because that mine shaft crashed in on me and put the fright in me. But she promised to go into ever' building with me and pull me out if they crashed down on my head. I reckon with help like that I don't have no reason to fear." Duffy marched into the house and toward the office.

Judith Kingston held out her hand to Lorna Clair. The younger woman stepped inside the house and Judith hugged her. "Thank you for taking such good care of our Duffy."

Lorna hugged her back. "A hug by Judith Kingston. Now I feel like I have been truly accepted into Carson City."

"You're right about that, honey," Daisie Belle said.

Marcy looked up from feeding little Daniel. "Judith Kingston has hugged everyone in town!"

"Not everyone . . ." Barbara mumbled.

Judith glanced over at Barbara Day who stared down at her clunky black shoes. *Oh, Lord, what have I done? Or not done? Sometimes I am so petty!* Judith slid over and took Barbara's hand.

"You don't have to do this," Barbara murmured.

"Honey," Judith whispered, "the day I saw your picture of my David, I knew our hearts were alike. I don't know what the Lord has in store for you and him, but I do want to do this." Judith slipped her arms around Barbara.

When they stepped back, all the women began to talk at once.

It was a strong voice from the living room door that finally silenced them.

"Mother? What in the world is going on?"

Judith stared across the room. "Roberta! Marthellen! You're home!"

Daisie Belle Emory swept across the room and grasped Roberta's arm. "We are busy planning weddings in here. I'm afraid you and Turner will have to wait in line!"

Chapter Nine

David volunteered to go downtown and corral the judge and the groom while the women and baby Daniel assembled in the Kingston living room. Roberta and Marthellen were recounting their wild trek from Sacramento to Cheyenne to Deadwood to Chicago and back home. Duffy stayed in the house, but preferred to squat on his haunches in the side entry, with the door partially open.

At times both Roberta and Marthellen chattered at the same time, forcing one of them to repeat an incident.

Finally, Judith managed to ask, "Did Turner come home with you?"

"Yes," Roberta said. "He rushed right over to the mill. The sale went through with Mr. Jacobson and he needs to send design papers to Chicago immediately. They're going to build the foundation in Arizona and have it ready, so he wants to notify the crew."

"How long will it take them to dismantle the mill?" Daisie Belle asked.

Roberta sat on the settee next to her mother. "He thinks about three months. Then they will all go down to Arizona and do the rebuilding. That will take another three or four months. Turner figures they will have enough work until Christmas or the first of the year. Mr. Jacobson said that any of the men who wanted could be hired in Arizona."

"Does that mean Turner will be moving to Arizona?" Willie Jane asked as she rocked Daniel.

"We don't know yet. But he's definitely coming home for the wedding." Roberta leaned over and kissed her mother on the cheek.

"Oh, yes!" Daisie Belle shouted. "But could you aim for February? That would be plenty of time. I've always wanted to do a Valentine's Day wedding."

"That will be a few days after my little girl is born," Marcy said. "Maybe she could be in the wedding. I'll have to carry her, of course!"

Roberta calmly laced her fingers and rested them on her knee. "The wedding is to be December 31st, at 11:30 p.m." Her tone was confident, well practiced.

"A midnight wedding?" Judith asked.

"It's perfect!" Daisie Belle said. "Why didn't I think of it? Just as you walk out of the church, the guns go off, fireworks light the sky and the entire town shouts 'Hurrah!' as they welcome in a New Year. I love it!"

"I hope Daddy won't mind staying up that late," Roberta commented.

Marthellen laughed. "For you? The judge would stop the sun and moon for his Roberta."

"December is a long way off," Judith said. "Meanwhile, we have a wedding today." She looked at Marthellen as if to say, "How do you feel about Willie Jane, Tray, the baby and everything?"

Marthellen saw her look and gave her a smiling nod.

"I think the bride needs a laurel of flowers to wear," Barbara Day announced. "Judith, do you mind if I use some of your gladiolus to weave one?"

"That would be great. The ones on the south side of the house might be in the best shape; the ones on the west were recently trampled by a rogue Bengal tiger named Timothy."

Before Barbara had a chance to move, the front door flung open and Philip Campos barged in.

The baby whimpered and Judith leaped to her feet.

Campos' suit was banker neat, but his eyes were wild. He waved a snub-barreled .45 revolver around the room, then pointed it at Judith. Roberta tried to pull her mother back, but Judith pushed her away and stepped toward Campos.

"Where's my wife and babies?" he shouted, his head jerking around the room.

Judith tried to stop her lower lip from quivering. *Lord, deliver us from evil and the evil one!* "Mr. Campos, your presence in my house is not wanted. Your behavior is inexcusable. I demand that you —"

"I want my wife and children!" he yelled, cocking the hammer of the revolver.

"Your poor wife and baby girl went to visit her parents in California," Judith informed him, her voice quiet but audible. "She needed to be away from you for a while, Mr. Campos."

"You had no business taking them away from me!"

Judith could feel her voice rising. "And you had no business trying to strangle your dear wife."

Philip Campos looked startled. "I didn't hurt her. I was just teaching her a lesson."

"And now, perhaps, she is teaching you a lesson."

His reckless brown eyes lit on Daniel. "That baby belongs to me. I'm taking him with me."

Willie Jane held the baby close to her breast. "This is Fidora's baby," she said, her face white.

"He's mine. The doctor and the judge said so."

"That was only a temporary arrangement," Judith said. "But your actions here prove you are unfit to raise that child."

"Unfit? I'm unfit? You're the one who is unfit, Judith Kingston. You live in a fairy tale world where you arbitrarily decide what every last person in this town can and cannot do. Well, I'm telling you, I'm taking that baby."

When he took a step toward Willie Jane, Judith jumped in front of him. "You are not taking Daniel," she said.

"Who's going to stop me? A bunch of women?" Campos grabbed Judith's shoulder and shoved her toward the hearth. Barbara Day caught her just before she hit the bricks.

"I reckon I'll have to stop you." Duffy Day ambled in from the back room.

Campos wheeled around and snickered

when he saw Duffy. "You? You couldn't stop a leaf from falling to the ground!"

"Be careful, Sugarlump," Lorna cautioned.

Duffy eased in front of Willie Jane. "You ain't goin' to take this baby," he insisted.

Campos shoved the barrel of the gun against Duffy's temple. "Move or you die, crazy man. Even a moron like you can figure that out."

Duffy didn't flinch. "I reckon there are worse things than goin' to visit Drake and my mamma."

"No!" Lorna screamed and rushed toward Campos.

Campos turned his head and the gun barrel followed. At that moment, an expensive, heavy glass squirrel sailed across the room from the hand of Daisie Belle Emory, striking Campos' ear. The gun discharged into the ceiling beam and Duffy fled out the side door.

When Marthellen's roundhouse swing with the fire tongs caught Campos just below the knees, the gun dropped and he staggered backward. Roberta emptied the umbrella stand and landed a blow to his right ear. Barbara clobbered him on the left.

Lorna's blow with a black iron duck was aimed at his midsection. But when Marcy crashed the china vase full of hard candy over his head, Campos staggered forward and the iron duck hit him somewhere below the belt.

Campos collapsed face-down at Willie Jane's feet, who had remained seated through the ordeal, trying to quiet the baby. Bruised, battered, and bleeding, Campos raised up, then groped for the revolver lying next to the chair. Willie Jane kicked it with her right foot. It slid toward Judith.

Judith plucked up the revolver by the barrel and marched over to the gasping Philip Campos. Then, as if driving a sixteen-penny nail, she hammered the butt of the grip against the man's head. He collapsed unconscious on the floor.

The women crowded closer to the fallen man and stared.

Finally, Daisie Belle brushed her hands, as if a speck of dirt had the audacity to stick there. She picked up the glass squirrel and rubbed it with her gloved hands. "As I always say, there is never a dull day at the Kingstons'. Now that we have this matter taken care of, let's get ready for Willie Jane's wedding."

By the time the judge, Sheriff Hill, David Kingston, and Tray Weston arrived, the ladies had arranged the furniture for the wedding.

Tables and sofas lined the walls.

The carpet was rolled up.

Only Philip Campos littered the floor.

A stern lecture from the judge and soft counsel from David Kingston persuaded Willie Jane and the ladies to wait until evening for the wedding.

Tray and the sheriff toted the unconscious banker out to the carriage, just as Timothy and Alicia burst through the door.

"Wow, Grandpa Judge," Timothy said, "did that man get attacked by the Bengal tiger?"

"That man wishes he had tangled with a tiger," the judge declared. "These ladies were responsible for the damage."

Alicia's eyes widened. "Did you cold-cock him, Grandpa Judge?"

"No, your grandmother did those honors."

"She did?" Timothy cast an admiring look at his grandma.

"I had plenty of help," Judith replied.

"How many times did you clobber him, Grandma Judith?"

"I just hit him once."

Timothy craned his neck toward the open door. "My Grandma Judith knocked him out with only one blow!" he shouted to the world.

"Your grandmother is a brave lady," Daisie Belle said as she knelt down and tried to hug the boy. He squirmed loose and rushed outside.

Alicia held on to Aunt Roberta. "And my Grandma Judith isn't afraid to walk out to the privy even when it's real dark and scary," she said.

"There you have it," Daisie Belle said, "the legend of Judith Kingston continues. Why, a hundred years from now when someone writes the chronicles of old Carson City, they will have to call the chapters about Judith Kingston fiction, because no one will believe they were true."

"Daisie Belle, you exaggerate everything," Judith replied.

"Of course I do. How do you think Timothy and I have so much fun in life?"

Timothy ran back inside and slid on the bare wooden floor. "Hey, are we going to have a party in here?"

"Later this evening, we're going to have a wedding," Judith announced.

"You mean Aunt Roberta won't be an old maid anymore?"

"An old maid!" Roberta howled. "We'll see who the old maid is. I'll race you to the church and back, Timothy Hollis Kingston. The loser is an old maid!"

"I get a head start," he insisted.

"No you don't."

"Yes, I do, I'm only a kid."

"Then, I'm the one who should have the head start. I'm already an old maid."

"One, two, three, go!" Timothy shouted.

Tray and the judge returned to the house just as the two sprinted across the street. The judge shook his head. "Does Turner Bowman have any idea what he's getting into?"

"He knows, Judge," Marcy said. "And he figures he's the luckiest man on earth."

"Well," Tray commented, "I reckon I'm even luckier than Turner 'cause I not only got me a beautiful woman, I got a ready-made baby."

"You don't have them until a few more hours," Marthellen reminded him.

"You're right, we need to get Campos down to the jail and figure out this mess. This whole thing is leavin' me confused. I surely hope you know what's goin' on, Judge."

"I don't have all the answers, but I have a lot more than I did yesterday."

"And I'm anxious to get this wedding over with," Tray admitted.

"Are you sure you don't have a ticket to Omaha in your back pocket?" Willie Jane teased.

He looked at her with wide eyes and said, "Do you?"

"Nope." Willie Jane looked down at the tiny sleeping baby in her arms. "I traded it in for a bassinet and some baby clothes."

Callie Truxell slumped in the leather side chair by the window that looked down on the alley behind the judge's office. The sun was barely above the Carson Range. She wore a yellow satin dress with full skirt and black lace. Her black velvet cape was tied with a ribbon around her neck, her blonde hair stacked neatly on top of her head.

"I'll need to go to work pretty soon, Judge."

"The sheriff should be bringing Campos up any minute."

"What do you want me to say?"

"Tell them what you told me. Just the truth."

"I ain't goin' to get in trouble doin' this, am I, Judge?"

"You'll only get in trouble if you lie, Callie."

Sheriff Hill lumbered through the door, leading a shackled Philip Campos. Tray

Weston and Doc Jacobs followed.

The judge motioned for them to be seated in the chairs at a large oak table in the northeast corner of his office. A tall, well-dressed man, with new beaver felt hat and black silk tie strolled in carrying a sheaf of papers. He nodded to all present.

"I believe you all know Mr. Spafford Gabbs, my former clerk," the judge announced, "now clerk for the Nevada Supreme Court? Mr. Gabbs has been gracious enough to come over and transcribe this discussion for possible use in court. He is very capable and, I guarantee, won't miss a word that's said."

"You can't have an arraignment in here," Campos protested.

"You're right. Think of this as an interrogation. It's much more pleasant here than in a jail cell."

"You've got it in for me," Campos whined.

"Because of your threat to the lives of my wife and daughter and other people in my home, I have decided I'm not an impartial juror and have set up your arraignment with Judge McCormack, 2nd District, on Friday. I act only as an attorney representing the interests of the deceased, Fidora. The purpose of this meeting is to interrogate you, Mr. Campos, so that we might clarify several matters to bring before Judge McCormack."

"I don't have anything to say," Campos retorted.

"Well, I have a lot to say. Let's begin with the scene in my home this afternoon."

"I didn't mean for that gun to go off. I was mad . . . and scared. My wife and child had been snatched away and I lost control, that's all. You don't know how frightful it is to have your wife and children stolen from you."

"Mr. Campos, do you have any idea how frightful it is for a wife to be strangled by her husband until she believes she will surely die?" the judge countered.

"I didn't hurt my wife."

"Dr. Jacobs, are you prepared to testify that on Friday, in your professional opinion, Mrs. Campos had been severely strangled?"

"Yep," Dr. Jacobs replied. "There's not a question about that."

"My wife won't ever testify against me," Campos said.

"Nor will we ask her to. But we do have witnesses to describe how your wife told them of your attempted strangulation. The only point of that, Mr. Campos, is to demonstrate why it was necessary, just, and kind for your wife to be removed from that environment. And we have nine witnesses who will testify that you broke into my home,

316

brandished a weapon, threatened to harm each one present, tried to kidnap a child who isn't yours, and endeavored to murder Duffy Day."

Campos pressed the top of his head with his right hand. "I told you that was all an accident."

"Campos," the sheriff roared. "We'll have eight ladies, led by Judith Kingston, plus Duffy Day, to testify otherwise. Even in your wildest imagination, do you reckon any jury in the state of Nevada would agree with you?"

Campos lowered his eyes to the floor and refused to reply.

"Here's the point in all this, Mr. Campos," the judge said. "There are things you were involved with that are much deeper than domestic conflict and attempted murder. Those charges will probably get you only two or three years in jail. But something much more sinister has also transpired. We are investigating the death of Sam Tjader, Atley Musterman, and the misappropriation of bank funds."

Campos's eyes narrowed. "What does that have to do with me? Tjader's murderer is in the state prison and scheduled to be hung on Friday."

"I reckon Manitoba Joe Clark will not be

hung this Friday for anybody's murder," the sheriff said.

"This is absurd," Campos ranted. "You're trying to blame me for everything!"

The judge got up from behind his desk and paced the room in front of Campos. "Here's what we know. You lied to me about Turner Bowman and Sam Tjader having a violent argument over a refused loan. The only violent argument was on the morning of the 10th of February between you and Sam Tjader."

"That's preposterous!"

"Callie, would you describe what you heard that day?" the judge said.

Callie Truxell cleared her throat and nervously glanced at Campos. "It was a Monday, so Sam was doin' the bankin' and I was standin' at the back door waitin' for him to let me in."

"Had you already given the secret knock?" the judge asked.

"No, like I said, usually only Sam is there and he thought the secret knock was pointless. Normally, there is no one else present, so I was surprised to hear voices."

"What were they talking about?" Dr. Jacobs asked.

Callie stared straight at Campos. "Sam was refusin' to give Campos a personal loan.

He said the house was already mortgaged to the maximum."

"How much was the loan for?" the judge probed.

She gently brushed her cheek rouge with her fingertips. "They were yelling about $25,000."

"What kind of testimony is this?" Campos blustered. "A crib girl on laudanum who thinks she hears something in the alley? She didn't see me at the bank because I wasn't there!"

"I don't work the cribs anymore, Mr. Campos. I have my own place, as you are very well aware. I have never taken laudanum, and you're right, I didn't see you. But I know your voice, 'cause you call through that back door ever' time before I do my banking. I know exactly how your voice sounds from behind a door." She turned back to the others. "Besides, I heard him say the house that was mortgaged was at 402 Minnesota Street. I heard that."

"That's your house, Campos," Tray Weston said.

"This is absurd and circumstantial. What if I did get turned down for a loan . . . what does that mean?"

The judge lowered his voice to keep it steady. "I suppose that was a very humbling thing for the assistant bank manager to be rejected for a loan in his own bank."

"I was used to it," Campos groused. "Tjader never liked me, and I knew it."

"Why did you need a quick $25,000?" the sheriff pressed.

"That isn't anyone's business but mine."

The judge grasped his elbow and rubbed his beard. "Let me suggest that you needed it to cover money you had stolen out of Fidora's account. When she informed you over the weekend that she wanted to advance $25,000 to Turner Bowman and would withdraw the funds on Tuesday, you panicked. You tried to get a loan, but when that didn't work, you gave her other bank funds, hoping to rewrite the books before you were caught."

"That's ridiculous. I don't even go to the bank early on Tuesdays. The account register you took from me proves that no transactions took place with any of the crib girls on that day."

The judge picked up a black leather ledger from the clerk's desk. "Callie, is this the ledger that you and the others sign concerning your accounts?"

"Yes, sir, all except the page for the week of February 10th through the 14th."

"It looks like the others. How do you

know it's not the right page?" the judge probed.

"Look at my signature on Monday, Wednesday, and Friday. I always dot the 'i' in my name twice. I've done this ever' since I was ten years old. It's just a funny habit of mine. Most folks don't even notice it. See how it is on them other pages? Whoever tried to copy my name on this page and insert it, didn't put two dots on the i. This is a forged page."

"Now, why would you forge a page, Mr. Campos?" the sheriff asked.

Philip Campos glared at Callie. "I didn't forge anything."

"I might come up with a reason," the judge countered. "Sam Tjader surprised you that morning by coming to the bank fifteen minutes earlier than normal. Fidora had just left with her money, the top half of the back door was still open, and you were beside yourself to figure out how to explain the money that was missing. You hid in the back room, waiting for an opportunity to flee unnoticed."

"I don't have to listen to this," Campos said. He tried to stand up.

"You ain't goin' nowhere," the sheriff replied, shoving him back in the chair.

The judge continued speaking. "But then

you had a break. The hapless Manitoba Joe Clark picked that exact moment to rob the bank. You witnessed the whole matter, and in a fit of fury, which you have repeatedly demonstrated being capable of, shot Tjader in the back from the storeroom. It was simple enough to turn Sam's body around and make it look like his back was to the front door. Then, you slipped out into the alley because everyone was occupied with the commotion Joe made when he tried to steal the stagecoach horse and all that money blew down the street."

"That fabricated story doesn't have a shred of evidence," Campos said.

"We have a forged ledger and a dead bank manager."

"You can't prove I had anything to do with any of that."

The judge laid the ledger on the clerk's desk. "The bank trustees will have accountants examining the bank books tomorrow. They will especially be anxious to find out what has happened to Callie's and her friends' accounts. We will see what that turns up."

For a moment, Philip Campos looked like a trapped Bengal tiger.

"I'm wondering if you didn't pad the amount of money stolen because it was blown away and couldn't be accounted for," the judge said.

When Campos glanced toward the door, Tray Weston put a firm hand on his revolver.

"Did he hire that attorney for Manitoba Joe, Judge?" Tray asked.

"That seems a logical conclusion, but the story gets more interesting."

"Campos got nervous about the judge's interest in Manitoba Joe," the sheriff said. "So he sat out on the hillside and tried to plug him."

"This is getting more inconceivable!" Campos shouted.

The judge leaned against his desk, his arms folded. "Colonel Roberts told me you were an advanced marksman in the army, but you were discharged because you got upset with a band of Paiutes and started firing at their camp at a distance of five hundred yards."

"Did he hit any of 'em?" Tray asked.

"Unfortunately, yes," the sheriff reported.

"But he didn't stop with a wild shot at Manitoba Joe," the judge continued. "About that time, Atley Musterman had realized he could extort more money from Campos, because he bragged about a new retainer that would be a steady income."

"So he plugged Musterman, too?" Callie asked.

The sheriff shrugged. "Seems so. But what he didn't count on was Fidora having some influential friends . . . and anybody on earth believin' Manitoba Joe Clark."

"What he didn't count on," Doc Jacobs offered, "was Judith and the judge."

"I won't admit to anything," Campos declared. "And who's going to believe my word against a crib girl's?"

"That's your choice, Mr. Campos. If you are proven guilty by a jury, you will, of course, hang for those crimes," the judge said. "If you confess your involvement, you have a chance of getting life in prison. That's something you will have three long days to think about."

"Go to Hades, Judge!" Campos shouted.

"If that happens, Mr. Campos," Doc Jacobs replied, "there's not a man in Nevada with a ghost of a chance of gettin' into heaven."

The sun nearly blinded the judge as it balanced on the tops of the mountain peaks, spraying a haze over Eagle Valley. As it lowered, the brightness softened, the sunny mist spreading out like delicate beams.

The judge entered the large building made of rock. The row of cells at the Nevada State Prison, three miles outside of Carson

City, were made of three-foot-thick brown limestone. Manitoba Joe Clark's cell was at the extreme south end of the row, with no windows, because it was dug into the side of the mountain. Hearing the judge's leather-soled boots tap on the cold concrete floor, Manitoba Joe rushed to the iron bars and strained to see down the hallway.

When the judge came into view, he said, "Am I gonna hang Friday, Judge? Or are you bringing me good news?"

"Fairly good news, Joe." The judge strolled up to the iron bars and appraised the bushy-bearded, bald-headed man.

"You got the hangin' postponed for two weeks?"

"I just talked to Governor Kinkead. Looks like there won't be any hanging for you, Joe."

The prisoner looked blank. "Don't josh me, Judge," he said. "I ain't in the mood for it."

"I wouldn't do that to you, Joe."

Suddenly, the coarse and rugged bank robber broke down and cried. "There is a God in heaven," he sobbed. "I said to myself, if Judge Kingston can get me two more weeks to fight this thing, there is a God in heaven. But no hangin'? The angels must be lookin' after me, the worst of all sinners."

He rubbed his eyes hard and began to shake.

"If that's so, Joe, you'd better use your time wisely," the judge said. "At this point, Mr. Philip Campos is going to be arraigned for the theft of at least $25,000, and possibly for Sam Tjader's murder. I happen to believe he's the one who took the shot at you, too, but that's harder to prove. In the meantime, you have a decent attorney, Mr. Hiram S. LaSwain, to represent you."

"Where did he come from?" Joe asked, his voice husky.

"Two of your Montana friends came to town and hired him from Virginia City. He should be in to see you tomorrow."

"I owe you a favor, Judge. I still cain't believe you'd stick up for me."

"I stick up for justice, Joe. You ought to be punished in proportion to the crime committed, not according to the crime you didn't commit." The judge gazed back down the hallway. "It's getting dark outside. I've got to go. I'm supposed to help officiate at a wedding. There's some more tobacco for you out front. They wouldn't let me bring it to you. And I brought a spare Bible of mine. Thought you might want to do some reading."

"I don't read good, Judge."

"You've got nothing but time on your hands. This could be a good time to learn."

"I reckon I ought to accomplish somethin' while I'm in here. But jist because they ain't goin' to hang me don't mean you have to stop visitin'. You reckon you could check on me from time to time?"

"I reckon I could, Joe."

The light green leaves of the cottonwoods were fluttering in the Carson City breeze as the judge finally left the courthouse on Friday afternoon. He strolled across the street toward the capitol building. Levi Boyer hailed him before he entered the iron gate.

"Hey, Judge, what's the ruling on Campos?"

"He's going to stand trial for bank theft and two counts of murder."

"You think they'll convict him?"

"He can't get out of the bank theft. The records show that he took most of the crib girls' money and spent it on personal investments. The murder charges are tougher. However, the motive, and his pattern of violence, will be strong factors."

"What did he spend the crib girls' money on?" Tray asked.

"A land promoter convinced him a railroad would be coming down through the Las Vegas valley. He illegally purchased several sections of land in Las Vegas."

"Las Vegas?" Levi chewed on a wooden toothpick. "I was down there in March. There ain't nothin' there, Judge, but the ruins of the old Mormon mission and two Mexican families raisin' chickens and goats. How much did he pay?"

"Fifty thousand dollars for seven square miles."

"Campos is not only violent, but stupid. Will the bank pay the girls back?"

"Since the embezzlement was done by a bank employee, they're figuring some way to reimburse them. For sure, they'll get that Las Vegas land."

"That's worth about $50," Levi said.

"Maybe, if they keep it a few years, the price will go up."

"I seen it, Judge. You could keep that a hundred years and it wouldn't be worth more than $50. The man who sold Campos on that deal is the one who ought to hang."

"You have the day off, Levi?"

"Yep. Marcy is over at the Doc's and I'm takin' a walk."

"Is she ill?"

"Nope, she's insisting he check out the baby now."

"You know, Levi, there's a chance she's not . . . with child."

Levi shook his head. "I don't believe Marcy would permit that possibility. You headed to see the governor?"

"Yes. He wanted a report on the arraignment."

"I'd better go pick up my Marcy," Levi said. "She wanted to stop by the depot and see if her Montgomery Ward order was here yet."

When the judge completed his briefing for Governor John Kinkead, he hiked south on Carson Street to the Virginia City and Truckee Railroad depot. At the telegraph office he ran into Daisie Belle Emory, who stood in line.

"Well, Judge, where shall we go today?" she said.

He blushed. "We?"

"I was teasing, dear Judge. I'm cabling New York for those steamer tickets to Europe."

"Are you going on a trip?"

"Of course. This is the big one to Paris . . . with your daughter."

"Roberta's going to Paris?" he said blankly.

"Didn't Judith tell you? We'll be gone a month."

"But I didn't hear anything about this."

"Judith and I decided early this morning that it just would not do for Roberta to buy a wedding dress in San Francisco, so I'm taking her to Paris. We'll shop for one there."

"Who can afford to travel to Paris for a wedding gown?" he sputtered.

"That's exactly why we must do it. Nobody else will. It's my burden in life, I suppose. Now, don't worry, dear Judge. This trip and dress are my present for our Roberta."

"Daisie Belle, you can't do that. I won't allow you to spend that kind of money on Roberta."

Daisie Belle pulled the judge out of line and led him to a bench against the wall. As they sat down, she pulled out a hanky and dabbed her eyes. "As you know, Judge, I buried our four little daughters behind a one-room cabin just a few miles up Kings Canyon. They all died the same winter with cholera. They would be twenty-six, twenty-three, twenty-one and nineteen now, had they lived. Roberta is the closest thing to a daughter I'll ever know. You are quite wrong. I must spend this money on her. I really must. Please don't take this away from me."

The tears slid across Daisie Belle's rouge-blushed cheeks.

The judge said nothing. *But I'll miss having a clerk for a whole month. At least, I think I'll miss having a clerk. Meanwhile, while I try to rule my family with a fierce kind of stewardship, Daisie Belle's mission seems to be to bring them as much joy and comfort as she can.* He tried to give Daisie Belle a reassuring smile.

"Are you sending a telegram?" Daisie Belle asked.

"I'm buying steamer tickets too," he announced.

Daisie Belle grinned. "Are you going to Europe?"

"No, I'm going to the Hawaiian Islands."

"Alone?" There was a teasing lilt in Daisie Belle's voice.

"No, I'm taking that Kingston woman."

"Is she the darling petite woman with the curly bangs and the butterfly brooch on her lace collar?"

"Yes, that's her."

"When are you going?"

"In September," the judge said. "We'll be gone a month."

"I'm so glad you're going when I'll be gone, or I would die of jealousy."

The judge strolled south on Carson. Three familiar people stood in a weed-covered, empty lot between Cracker's Drug Store and the Nice-N-Friendly Café. They were staring at the ground.

"Did you lose something?" the judge called out.

Duffy Day ran to his side. "Hey, I've gone twenty-four miles on my pedometer since I saw you last." He patted the waistband of his pants. "And me, Barbara, and my sweet Lorna are thinkin' about leasin' that lot."

"That sounds ambitious. Are you going to build a house?"

"It's for Barbara. She wants to start a picture business. Lorna and I are tryin' to give her advice."

They sauntered over next to the women.

"Is this in a good location for a retail business?" Barbara asked.

"It's the best empty lot in town," the judge replied.

"She's going to move that old Virginia City and Railroad green caboose right in the middle of it and open herself a shop," Duffy announced.

"Douglas and I will live at one end, and the other will be an art gallery," Barbara explained. "I've decided to start selling my paintings." She studied the judge's face. "I have a reason now. I'm going to split the profits to send to David's mission in India."

"Ain't that great, Judge?" Duffy said with a beaming smile.

"It's wonderfully generous," the judge said. "But, does this mean you're not . . ."

Barbara shielded her eyes from the sun as she looked at him. "I'm not going to India with David, if that's what you mean."

"I was content to allow the Lord to lead you and my son."

"I know, Judge, but I'm happy this way. For the first time in my life I have a cause — to help David reach the lost in India. But I realize I could never compete with his Patricia. She's his guiding light still. He's a wonderful man that I will enjoy helping."

"Would you be interested now in selling a portrait of that young missionary?"

"I can never sell that. Besides, it will be the focal point of the gallery."

"My offer still stands. I'll pay you $100 more than the next bidder."

"I'll consider that an insurance policy, Judge," Barbara said. "Now, I have a question for you. What would you think if I built a thirty-foot tower on the back of this lot, behind the caboose?"

"A thirty-foot tower?"

"With a little lookout room on top. I want to sit there and paint the sunrises and sunsets of Carson City."

"I think it's very unusual, but it could be a great addition to the uniqueness of this town. And it's much safer than climbing up on the church roof."

"That's exactly what my sponsor said."

"Your sponsor?" the judge quizzed.

"The one who's financing all of this."

The judge felt his neck tighten, his forehead crease. He held his breath. *Surely not Judith.*

"It's Daisie Belle," Barbara said. "She thought the caboose and the tower were wonderful ideas. It might even become a tourist attraction."

The judge glanced around at the lot full of weeds. "It would certainly be an improvement."

Barbara tugged at one of her long braids. "Judith said she'd talk to the mayor about it."

The judge rubbed the back of his neck and strained to imagine a thirty-foot tower. *Judith will talk the judge into talking to the mayor, you mean.* "Duffy, if Barbara moves out of your house, you'll have room for Lorna at your place."

"What for, Judge? She's got a nice little place here in town."

The judge glanced at Lorna. She smiled back. "I meant after you two were married," the judge added.

"Me and my sweet Lorna like being engaged a whole bunch. We thought we'd jist try this out for a while."

"That's a wise attitude, Duffy."

"Ain't no one ever accused me of bein' wise before."

"I have a feeling with your sweet Lorna at your side, that will change. People will say, 'Look at that Duffy Day and that nice-looking lady of his; he surely is one smart man.' "

Duffy grinned. "I bet they will."

"Thank you, Judge Kingston," Lorna added. "That was a very kind thing to say."

The judge picked up a package at the gallery and continued his stroll home but was stopped by Doc Jacobs at the corner of Musser and Carson streets. The Doc's satchel was tossed in the back of his carriage.

"You leavin' town, Doc?"

"You bet I am. I need a vacation. The mayor and me are going up to the lake to fish for a few days. You want to come along?"

"Sorry, Doc, I can't get away." *But maybe when Turner Bowman takes over the clerk duties, I'll start relaxing more and have the time for outings like that again.* "But do I want to? I'd like to go to Lake Tahoe and fish for the next twenty years."

"Maybe we ought to forget this doctoring and judging and buy us a big boat and spend every day fishing," Doc Jacobs suggested. "We could build us a big old resort hotel up there and retire in luxury."

The judge laughed. "Get behind me, Satan."

"Yeah, I couldn't do it either. But I can catch me some lunkers for the next few days. I'll bring you some on Monday, Judge. Hey, did you hear? Marcy Boyer was right. She's carrying a baby alright."

The judge watched the carriage roll down toward Carson Street and headed the same way. *Our house is two blocks away. There is no way I can possibly beat that gossipy news home.*

As soon as he loosened his tie and plopped down on the big brown leather chair in the living room, Alicia climbed up his lap.

"How was school today, young lady?"

"It was awful, Grandpa Judge."

"What happened?"

"It's that Marjorie Walters. Her parents got her a horse and she spent the whole day bragging about how her horse was the fastest one in town."

"What did you do?"

"I told her just wait and see, that my horse is going be a lot faster than hers."

Timothy lay upside down in the green velvet settee beside his father, his feet sticking straight up, the top of his head on the hardwood floor. "You don't have a horse," he chided.

"Grandpa Judge is going to buy me one," she replied, then leaned her head on the judge's chest. "Grandpa, would you please buy me a horse?"

Roberta sat down at the base of the stairway. "Remember when you bought me Porky?"

"Was he a fast horse?" Alicia asked.

"Oh, yes," the judge said with a laugh. "He was so fast we could very seldom catch him to put a halter on him."

"He bit, too," Roberta added. "He bit the fence and he bit the other horses. Once he bit Grandpa on the shoulder."

Judith stepped into the living room, wiping a crystal glass on her apron. "Remember that time Roberta bent over to pick up the oat bucket and Porky bit her on the —"

"Mother!" Roberta squealed.

Alicia put an arm around the judge's neck, her nose only inches from his. "I want a paint horse that is very, very fast and won't bite me on the fanny."

"I think we should start looking for a couple horses," the judge said, with a wink at Judith, "one for you and one for Timothy. Grandma and Grandpa can ride them while you're in India. We'll take care of them until you get home again."

Timothy spinned and bounced in the settee. "I want a huge horse I can take to India to lead a brigade into the Himalayas and defeat the Mongol horde."

"David got his first contribution for his mission work," Judith announced.

"So soon?" the judge said, turning to look at his son.

"It came in from San Francisco," Judith replied. "The newspaper must have printed that notice I sent them."

"But there is a small problem," David admitted. "The envelope contained $20 and was addressed to the Home Evangelistic Revivals Eternal American Ministry to Indians. I wonder if I should send it back."

"Technically, that's an accurate statement. But you might want to send a clarification in the thank-you," the judge suggested.

The judge pulled out a package wrapped in string from behind the sofa. "We have a present for you all," he announced. "It's really for Christmas, but what with Roberta's wedding and David's leaving for India at any time, Judith and I thought we'd give them to you now." He pulled out a half dozen cabinet-size photographs.

David took Timothy and Alicia home after a slow, relaxed supper. Judith and Roberta helped Marthellen clear the dining room table, while Turner Bowman and the judge adjourned to his office to study the plans to dismantle the Consolidated Reduction Mill.

All five met later in the living room.

"Is it too warm for a fire?" the judge asked.

"Motion sustained, your honor," Roberta said.

"No courtside humor," the judge said. "I'm worn out from being judge."

Turner and Roberta sat in the green velvet love seat, Judith on the brown leather sofa. The judge stood by the hearth.

"Come sit down and rest, Marthellen," the judge said, motioning to her.

"I have some extra scrubbing to do," Marthellen replied.

Judith stood up. "I'll help you."

"How can I put this delicately?" Marthellen said. "This kitchen has not been properly cleaned in weeks. I need to do it my way. In addition, I have to stir up some bearclaw batter to let set overnight. I must have had a dozen requests since I've gotten home."

Marthellen glided back into the kitchen.

The judge studied the hole in the ceiling beam. "I wonder if the day will come when I don't burn with resentment at that bullet hole. When I think of what Philip Campos did in my living room, I'm infuriated."

Turner reached over for Roberta's hand. "I know what you mean, Judge. Christian charity seems impossible when I think how terrifying it must have been for the women."

"And Duffy," Roberta added.

"I think it was so unexpected and so threatening, we didn't assimilate the fear," Judith admitted. "It seems more scary four days later than I felt at the time. I don't think any of us acted very clear-headed, but the Lord was gracious."

"Mr. Campos always seemed to me a meek, calm man," Roberta said. "But I only saw him in his position at the bank."

"His anger seemed to break out like a seizure," Turner said.

"I think it's demonic," Judith added. "Satan comes to kill, steal, and destroy."

"You could very well be right," the judge said. "Sometimes the criminal mind seems devoid of humanness."

"I think I had more than a taste of that," Turner confessed. "There were times in the past weeks when I recognized the potential in myself."

"Enough of this," Judith declared. "There must be other more pleasant subjects to talk about."

"Judge, that was a very nice wedding for Tray and Willie Jane the other night. You and David make a good team," Turner said.

"Well, Roberta informed me we will have to dress much more handsomely on December 31st."

"December isn't that far away in wedding planning time," Judith said, "but I dearly look forward to a long, slow summer."

Turner shook his head. "It's been a bizarre May. Besides everything else going on, I kept worrying what you and the judge were thinking. I just knew you were sitting around calling me a miscreant or a knave."

Judith raised her eyebrows. "A miscreant?"

Roberta pulled his hand to her lips and kissed it. "I tried to tell him you wouldn't think that of him in a million years!"

"When did you first learn about my loan from Fidora?" Turner asked.

Judith glanced at the judge. "It all started

with Fidora's dying words, 'Tell Turner everything is forgiven.' "

"She might have forgiven the debt, but I haven't. That money is hers and it goes to her boy."

"That's one of the delights of having Willie Jane and Tray raise little Daniel," Judith added. "Willie Jane will tell him all about his mother . . . at least, the good parts. Elisa Campos, even in different circumstances, may never have done that."

"Poor Mrs. Campos . . . she lost one of the twins and now her husband is in jail," Roberta said.

"I pray the Lord will comfort her and give her a new direction for life," Judith added.

"Speaking of new direction . . . Daddy, we haven't talked through yet about my retiring as your clerk. I know I mentioned in the letter about Turner being interested in that position, and Mamma said you were really looking forward to having Turner, but —"

Turner got animated as he finished her sentence. "What Roberta's trying to say is, I've decided I want to work for Mr. Jacobson at the Arizona reduction mill. I'll get a chance to run the mill after all. It will be a new venture, with a solid financial base, and I'll build me and Roberta a fine home. I promise I will take care of her in the manner to which she is accustomed."

The judge stoked the fire. *Son, you don't need to make promises to me. Just keep the promises you make to my daughter.* "I can see that the Arizona opportunity holds much more excitement for you and Roberta than a simple desk job."

"Don't get me wrong, Judge . . . your confidence and support of me is an inspiration. I figure, if Judith and the judge think I'm good enough for their Roberta, why I can do anything on earth!"

Suddenly the judge felt weary all over.

"Daddy, don't worry. I have someone already in mind to take on that job," Roberta said, her voice bubbly with enthusiasm. "I was talking to Barbara Day the other morning and I was impressed with how intelligent she is. Really, she's smart. I know she's starting a new business, but she could come over a few hours every morning . . . then Duffy's Lorna has the afternoons off. And if you need weekend help, Levi Boyer would like to earn some extra money . . ."

Turner leaned forward, his face intense. "Listen, I talked to Mrs. Emory, and Daisie Belle said if you ever need some volunteer work, she would love to come give the judge a hand."

Judith and Roberta glared at him.

"Did I say something wrong?" he gulped.

"I'm sure it will all work out," the judge said. "Perhaps I'll retire and not need a clerk at all."

"Oh, Daddy, you can't ever retire! You've always been the judge!"

"Well, I can retire to bed. I'm tired," he announced abruptly.

"I'll join you," Judith said.

"Poor Daddy, didn't you get a good night's sleep?" Roberta asked.

"I'm not sure the judge has had a good night's sleep all month," Judith replied.

The judge took Judith's hand and pulled her to her feet. The two of them ambled up the stairway. He bent low and whispered in her ear, "I haven't had a good night's sleep since the day that girl was born."